Seeker's Revenge
Copyright © 2012
James Walter Orr

I0622338

Author of:
Reflections of Love
The Beckoning Hand
Third Book from the Sun
Seeker's Valley

Published by James Walter Orr
Mesquite Publishing Company
Mesquite, Texas

Library of Congress Control Number: 2013935070
ISBN 978-0972391139
First Printing

Notice:
This book is a work of fiction. Every place, person, incident, event, time line and/or episode is a product of the author's imagination. Any resemblance to any actual person, place, thing or event is purely coincidental and bears no historical significance or resemblance to actuality.

This book is dedicated
To May
To the characters that I have created
and come to know intimately;
To the places that I have created
and come to love dearly;
To the circumstances that I have created
and the suspense they have given me;
To the nature that surrounds me
and has given me such pleasure;
To the fantasies in which I live and have lived,
and experienced so much fullness;
To the dreams that I have dreamed
and the people, places and things that have populated them;
and to those I love and those who love me in return,
and those who wished and/or tried to love me.

Jeb was screaming and holding his hand. His brother slapped leather but before his pistol flashed clear of the holster, one eye disappeared in a cloud of spray from the .44 caliber bullet that exploded his head into eternity.

Jeb was grabbing cross-handed at his side-arm with his left hand as I turned toward him, but my action was unnecessary. Earlene had already beaten me to him. I hated to see her have to do it, for fear it would prey on her mind. She must not have had time to aim well, for the first slug had hit him square in the lower pelvis. He had only a couple of heart beats to bemoan the loss of his manhood, for the second shot, which for some reason lagged the first by several long seconds, hit him right square in his heart.

"Darn it all! Earlene exclaimed. "I just hate it when I am so clumsy! Now look what has happened!"

-=-   -=-   -=-   -=-   -=-   -=-   -=-   -=-   -=-   -=-

Pug grinned again. "It's going to be fun tearing your head off your shoulders."

I grinned back at him. "Tell you what, Pug. You get on back to your table and we'll play like none of this ever passed between us."

Pug took the stance of a professional fighter. "Get up before I take your head off while you're still sitting. Nothing on God's green earth is gonna save you from getting so crippled up that it'll take you a year to quit crying yourself to sleep. Get up!"

"Listen Pug. I'll ask you one more time to please go on back to your table."

"I've never had as much fun as when a man starts begging me to let him go, unless it's when I spit on his broken body and kick his ribs in." He started around the table at me.

I sighed and picked up the iron rod that Arnold had stood up against the table leg and rapped him on the side of his knee. The knee shattered and bent inward. I swung the rod again against the point of his left elbow and swung over the top against his right fist, which was nearly tucked under his chin. It shattered his fist and forearm, dislocated his elbow, and put him on his knees on the floor.

"Are you having fun yet?" I asked him. "Have you come to the part where you spit on my body and kick my ribs in?"

The tranquility and peace of Seeker's Valley and the Bend of the Rimrock are shattered in an unpredictable way. In far off London, England, the wastrel nephew of an English Lord falls deeply in debt to the owner of a finance company, from whom he has borrowed heavily to support his gambling addiction.

When he is unable to pay his gambling debts, the owner of the finance company suggests a way that he can not only pay his debts, but become rich in doing so. Murder and fraud seem small prices to pay for the glory that he envisions for himself. The scheme that he and his creditor came up with fit right in with the dreams of grandeur that he has. After all, he was born into the British Elite. He deserves to stay there. And then too, there is his beautiful cousin, assistant to his Uncle Edward.

How can a simple rancher stand up against a man with royal blood in his veins?

Sex and sensuality, bloodshed and gunfights: these are all woven into the tapestry of this unusual western, second book of the Seeker's Valley series.

Cast of Characters

1.   Easy Seeker

After traveling a long trail of vengeance alone, Easy has found love and a home in a valley that now bears his name. Others covet the empire he has become part of; once again he becomes entangled in a web of violence and intrigue, and must fight to survive.

2.   Earlene Rogers

The daughter of Brad Rogers and the partner in the &RR (&ours) ranch, she is Easy's wife, but still maintains her own identity.

3.   Brad Rogers

Owner of the &RR ranch, along with his daughter, Earlene Rogers, he becomes embroiled in a bitter battle for survival and finds that his prize is the beautiful Cynthia.

4.   Rodney Hampton

Rodney came to the American West and had to pay his dues to reach success. Now he has to once again join with his American friends to defend his niche in the Rimrock Land and Cattle Company.

5.   Sir Edward Hampton

Rodney's father and the largest shareholder of the RL&CC, with its banking division, the RB&T. He has to visit his holdings in The Bend of the Rimrock to help defend what he has helped create.

6.   Richard Hampton

A nephew of Sir Edward Hampton, he squandered his inheritance and will stop at nothing to recoup it

7.   Todd Russell

Sheriff of Vaca County

8.   Tex Lonigan

Chief Deputy

9.   Faron Stern

Second Deputy

10.   Mike Thomas

Young Deputy

11.   Judge Pickwick

A circuit judge for the Territory of Colorado who is more interested in feathering his nest than delivering justice

12.   Mr. Shystwell

The managing partner of Shystwell, Shystwell, Upton and Moncrief who personally handles the affairs of Richard Hampton, even when they involve fraud, theft and murder

13.   Mr. Fendoff

A partner in the firm of Fendoff, Pender, Baker and Allen, who was once a criminal attorney

14.   Dr. Henry Kincaid

A young doctor who wanted to begin a practice in Vacaville

15.   Rod Laser

A top hand with a gun or a rope, one of Easy's right hand men, and a close friend

Chapters

Chapter One - Page 8
Prologue - Setting the Stage

I awoke and lay there, savoring the feel of Earlene's body curled into the curve of my own. I tried to dis-entangle myself without waking her up, so I could light the fire and warm the house before she had to get up, but she rolled over and wrapped me in her arms. I was so glad that she awakened, for when we both jumped from bed a half hour later, we were glad to let the cool air of the late autumn morning dry the sweat from our bodies.

A few minutes later, we were dressed, the fire in the iron stove was blazing and coffee was percolating on the wood range. I was buttering bread to make toast and Earlene was frying eggs and bacon.

We had tried to keep very quiet, so we wouldn't wake Brad, but he opened the front door and came into the house. He had already gotten up early and milked the cow.

"Did you two lazy bones finally get up?" he quipped.

"We've been awake for an hour," I replied. "We had some business we needed to discuss, and we figured you would still be snoring in bed, as usual," I added, as I stuck the tray of buttered bread in the oven.

"Monkey business, no doubt." He shrugged out of his coat and blew on his hands, then held them out to the heat of the stove. "There is a heavy frost on the grass. Maybe it will be a nice cool day for the work we have to do, or have you forgotten what we have planned?"

"Not likely," I grinned. "This is the last step in completing a dream that Earlene and I have had since the west wind blew me back into the Bend of the Rimrock." I paused for a moment, and then added, "Of course, I am speaking only of our dream of re-uniting our oasis with the rest of Seeker's Valley."

A large part of our time was taken by our duties with the Rimrock Land and Cattle Company, better known as the RL&CC, and its subsidiary organization, the Rimrock Bank and Trust. The next few days were going to be spent tearing down the stone debris that separated the two valleys included in the EEZ ranch.

In an effort to mechanize the job; I had constructed a water-wheel. I had bought a spool of heavy rope which was long enough to reach from the water-wheel up through a block that was attached to the solid stone wall of the canyon, thirty feet above the jumble of rocks that separated these two valleys and back to another block that was located beyond the area we intended to place the stones as we removed them.

The heavy rope was threaded through another block that made it come straight in to the water-wheel. It was wrapped twice around an enlarged part of the axle through the water-wheel, which served as a cat-head.

The other end of the rope was attached in a similar manner through a block that also allowed it to feed straight into another cat-head, and was wrapped twice. There were two nets made of several layers of hog wire. One of the nets was attached to each end of the rope in such a manner that as one net arrived at the top of the wall to be loaded, the net on the other side of the block arrived back at the place where the stones were being dumped. When one pulled the slack out of the two wraps, the rope tightened and pulled the net, loaded with stones, down to be dumped in the designated place. When it was dumped, the rope was allowed to go slack so that the cat-head turned within the loops of rope without friction.

The other end of the rope then had the slack pulled out of the loops around the other cat-head, and pulled the net back up to the top of the wall, so it could be reloaded with stones. It took one man to run the cat-head, two men to dump the stones, and two men to load the net. Earlene manned the cat-head, Brad and a hired hand dumped the stones, and another hired hand and I loaded the nets. In the afternoon, Brad and his man traded places with me and my man. Earlene continued to man the cat-head all day.

The work was very hard, but it was exhilarating to see the wall come down. After two weeks, I looked over at the pond below us in the Oasis Valley. Then I walked over and looked at the pond from the seep on the Seeker's Valley side. It seemed to me that there was a difference in the height of the wall, judging from the distance down to the water on each side.

When we shut down for lunch, I took the lariat from my saddle and walked over and measured down to the water on each side. The Oasis side was about seven feet above the Valley side. I walked back, pondering what caused this difference. It appeared to me that the same cataclysmic event that had brought the walls down in the first place, must have caused a rift in the earth reaching from north to south. The land on the east side of that rift was about seven feet lower than the land on the west side.

It took us three weeks, working six days a week to tear the wall down. We only tore it down to the water level on the west side of the wall. A slow trickle of water began to flow over the remaining wall, which now served as a dam between the two segments of the joined valleys. Although the flow was slow, when it was added up over the total distance between the two canyon walls, it added up to a significant amount. It joined the river of water flowing southward to the Wandering River. Now, at last, my dream was fulfilled. The two valleys were now one.

I still had some work to do to make it easy to ride horses and drive livestock over the rocky dam remaining, and there was the pond to cross, also.

There was another nagging thought in the back of my mind, but I had no time for contemplation at this time. Saving the thought for another time, I called the workers together and told them that we were finished.

I wrote out checks to the two hands. They both lived in Vacaville, so it was easy for them to drop by the bank to cash the checks. After the men had left, Earlene looked at me curiously.

"Easy," she said, "I thought we were going to bring the flow of the entire stream through the eastern valley. What changed your mind? I know you well enough to see that you have something in the back of your mind. What is it?"

I had to laugh. There was no way I could hide anything from Earlene, even if I had of wanted to.

"Earlene, we have another little test to run, just to satisfy my curiosity, but I don't want to do it right now, for we need to check out the pasture that includes the South Cedar breaks, now that the workers have stripped the cedar posts off of it. However, I will let you in on what will remain our little secret.

"You remember how one tunnel of the old mine through which we diverted the water to the east valley ran right up to the underground river that forms our water fall? It was there that I first held you in my arms, and it was there that we conceived the plan to get the water that has made the Bend of the Rimrock flourish.

"Well, it stands to reason that the tunnel was there because the old miner was following a vein of gold. When he got so close to the water fall that he was afraid to continue, he went back and extended the tunnel that leads to the gold vein where we found his body in the cave-in.

"You know that the gold that is panned from nearly every stream where gold is, was washed from the formation where the lode is, by running water?"

A spark of excitement lighted Earlene's eyes. "What you are saying," she exclaimed, "is that we may find gold where the rapid water from the water fall slows as it widens out into the pond! Am I right?"

"As right as the proverbial rain, my Sweet Baby," I exclaimed. "We have a lot of work to do, but we deserve a little dessert. Moreover, it will give me a chance to get you naked if we cross over to the other side and look to see where we would most likely find the gold, if it is there. In any case, when we strip off and go into the water to see if we can find some gold in the spot where it appears most logical it would be, I can take advantage of something that is more precious to me than any amount of gold."

"Hmm," said Earlene. Maybe I should bring a blanket, just in case you are thinking of the same thing I am!"

I grabbed her and we kissed for a minute; then we pulled apart and grabbed a bedroll off of Earlene's saddle and scrambled up over the low dam.

Chapter Two - Page 12
Appraising the South Cedar Breaks

The four on-site members of the board of directors were meeting in the conference room at the bank. Rodney had his father's proxy in the case any matter came up that required a vote. Each of us was to give a report on the areas of our particular responsibility.

Rodney began by giving his report on the bank.

"The bank is showing promise of being the leading profit center of the RL&CC," he began. "One of the principal advantages is that it is bringing in outside capital. The Independent Ranchers Association decided that it would be good to have water wells dug at each house, with the well being encased in the back porches, much as exists at the &RR. This will provide new revenue streams to the bank, for they are asking for financing for experienced well diggers and for brick to line the wells. Several are going to wall-in their present back porches to place the wells inside the houses and to build new porches. I have made arrangements with the Bank of Denver to keep the principal part of our funds there. It doesn't take long to transfer funds between our bank and that bank, and they have far more safe-guards against bank robbers than we do. Those are the principal things that have happened and that are presently happening in my department."

"Earlene, why don't you bring us up to date on the latest transactions of the RL&CC?" I asked.

"I've been looking through catalogs, finding the best prices on heavy hog wire fencing and factoring in the shipping costs, pending the results of our evaluation of the South Cedar Breaks, now that all of the usable posts have been harvested and stored at the headquarters. Isn't today the day you and I are going to ride over that entire block of land?'

"Yeah, just soon as this meeting is over. We have to take a look at the land in light of the information that we received that was put together by the Interior Department. We need to take another look at the situation, now while the new information is fresh in our minds and make a quick decision on what we're going to do with that land. Our decision will have a big effect on the type of fencing we'll use. We'll have a lot more information when we get together next week.

"Brad, do you have anything to add?" I inquired.

"No. Since we decided to use barbed wire on the entire cross fencing, now that we have bank financing, I have a fencing crew working on the land we will put into corn this spring. We need to get that land laid by so it will be in shape to plant. Now that we can get cattle through from your eastern valley to the oasis pastures, I want to get the west end fenced off so no cattle can get out into the desert, as if they would even if they could.

"Next in line will be some holding pens for the cattle we will be working at branding time. I'd rather we use squeeze chutes for branding than having to rope and throw all the calves. It's a lot less stress on the cattle, and it's quicker, too.

"I also have ordered a couple of Burdizzos. I don't know that it's all that much faster than a knife, but it sure is more sanitary for the calves and eliminates both infection and screw worms.

"I'm also doing a study on where it would be best for us to put in a mill for grinding corn. Ground corn is a lot more efficient for the beeves to convert to meat than whole grain. Since we don't plan on confining the beeves we feed out, it wouldn't be practical to have hogs follow the steers. Our operations will be too big for that."

I said, "Since the ride just around the perimeter of the South Cedar Breaks pasture and the return back home will be about ninety miles, plus riding out some cross sections, we will stay overnight in either the old Didrikson place or maybe the Heinzer place for the next two nights. Then we will possibly get home late the day after tomorrow evening. It is more likely that we will wait until the next day, depending on what all we end up looking at. Let's get the show on the road, then."

Brad, Earlene and I stood up. We told Rodney we'd see him later and walked to the stable. After saying good morning to Arnold, the blacksmith and stable proprietor, the three of us mounted up. Brad rode north toward the &RR while Earlene and I stopped off at the cafe for a couple of days' worth of food. Then we cut across southwest toward the west side of Promontory Point.

I leaned over and kissed Earlene. The kiss changed from a peck on the lips to a full blown kiss and we stopped the horses for a minute, since it's sort of hard to hold a kiss from the backs of two trotting mounts.

"Hmm," I said. "I know of several spots where we'll have to stop and, hmm, analyze the soil."

"Well!" said Earlene, drawing a deep breath. "I hope the first one won't be far!"

It wasn't. We had come to the line of trees that grew along the old wash that ran from the river back up to the west base of Promontory Point. We found a nice shady spot and did a little quick 'analyzing' and continued on toward the southwest to reach the west end of the Cedar Breaks pasture at a point near where the desert started.

It was unbelievable how different the land looked now that the cedar posts had been harvested and the scrub brush had been cut and stacked into piles. We were giving it some time to dry before burning. The sparse growth of grass was not enough to support a grass fire.

Earlene said, "You know, this is the first time that I have ever been any further south of the river than Vacaville. What do you have in mind for this pasture?"

"The information that I received from the Department of the Interior says that this land will make marginal cattle land but great sheep land. They also say that with all the second growth brush that will come back, that it would support a lot of goats along with the sheep," I replied.

"I can see quite a few places where a lot of greenery is growing. I would assume that is where the creeks are," Earlene stated.

"You would be right," I answered. There are a surprising number of creeks that head here. Most of them flow eastward toward the East Fork, but there is one just west of where we now are that flows into the Wandering River, about twenty miles west of the East Fork. There is very little grass grows along it. It runs from midway up that mountain," I said as I pointed out the nearest of the three peaks that were on the south side of the river. "The desert sand and rocks extend to a point about even with the middle of the Bend of the Rimrock. The land changes from sand to a heavier soil, there. I have doubts that the land west of where our cleared land ends will ever be used for agriculture. It is just too dry. The cleared land pretty much follows the junction of the tight and the sandy soils."

Earlene rubbed her pretty chin and said, "I would be surprised if these breaks were not created from sand blowing in from the desert over the past million years. It is going to take a good ground cover to keep it from blowing again, now that the brush is cut."

"Yep, I agree. The recommendations from Interior contain a mixture of plants, some grassy and some brushy. From what they say, I imagine it would wise for us to put a big flock of sheep back here, with some goats for brush control. The sheep would be the money crop. We might even run some cows on it, depending on how things look after we get it seeded. I think that sheep and goats both would get up on Promontory Point. There is good grass and a lot of Mesquite there. All of the land west of the Point for five miles is nearly solid Mesquite. With goats to control the Mesquite, it will probably make good cattle grazing; for sure it would make good sheep country."

Time sure flies a lot faster when you have a sweet woman to talk to while looking things over. We were only a few months into our marriage, and the honeymoon was still as sweet as ever.

We were approaching one of the many creeks that cut across the breaks.

"Why don't we stop here and eat lunch?" Earlene asked.

"You'll get no argument from me. I know what I want for dessert."

"Get your mind back onto sheep, goats, fences and grass," Earlene said, coloring slightly. "I can do enough thinking about dessert for both of us," she added. "For sure we need to stop now, since you've got my mind running parallel to yours. I can't very well lecture you about sheep, goats and fences, now since I can't get my mind on them either!"

A big cottonwood tree spread its leafy branches out across the clear little creek. The breeze felt good as we ate our sandwiches. It sure felt even better, after we finished.

When we started up again, riding in a rather crisscross pattern from north to south, as we traveled eastward, I called Earlene's attention to some horse tracks.

"Hmm, this seems to be a long way away from any trail that leads anywhere," she mused.

"We need to keep our eyes open. Anyone out here must be up to something that's a little on the shady side. Let's be sure we don't blunder into something that we can't blunder back out of," I said. "If someone has seen us, they could very easily let us ride right up on them without realizing it."

I changed our direction from southeast to straight south for a mile, then straight east. The land that we were inspecting was about fifteen miles square. Two hundred and twenty five square miles is a lot of land to cover and we were just getting a general idea of what we had, now that we could sort of see across it. The broken nature of the land made it to where we could see only a short distance, except when we were on top of the hills. I wanted to be sure that no one surprised us. We would make it impossible for someone to lie in wait for us. There were some hunted men that would go to a lot of trouble to way-lay us, especially if they had noted that one of us was a woman, and especially a woman like Earlene. I pulled my Winchester and rested it across my thigh. I noted that Earlene had already beaten me to the punch on that precaution.

We rode on, listening to the meadow larks singing and noting the new green shoots of grass emerging from the earth. As the sun dropped lower in the sky, we saw both a badger and a fox scurry from our path.

Earlene said, "Easy, maybe we ought to pretend that we are going to camp out, rather than let someone know that we are headed for the old Heinzer place. It makes me nervous to know that someone is prowling around out here where they have no business being."

"I've been thinking along those same lines," I concurred. "We have a problem in that if we stop in one of the low places, they can get above us and we would have no place to go. If we get on the high ground, especially if we light a fire, we will be outlined against the sky or the fire and it would be easy for them to bushwhack me, try to capture you and play some pretty bad games with you if they did."

"So what do you suggest?" she asked.

"I think we will stop and build a fire, as though we are preparing our meal. You can put some coffee on and I will lean back against one of the shade trees that weren't cut. I will keep a close look out in front and on both sides of us. You can work facing opposite to where I am sitting. You keep a lookout in that direction. If you see anything, warn me without looking toward me."

We put that plan into effect and it worked like a charm. The two men rode up on the side where Earlene was working. It was the side I was facing away from.

I stood up and stretched and walked around the tree so that I was facing them. Neither of them looked as though they had shaved in the past week. They were both blond and dirty, but their clothing was of good quality and they rode good horses, tacked with embossed and silver inlaid saddles and bridles.

"We just saw the smoke from your fire, and thought you might have a cup of coffee you could spare us," said one, who appeared to be slightly shorter than the other, whom he strongly resembled.

"I think we might spare a cup. I hate to be rude, but what are you fellows doing so far off the beaten path?"

The taller responded, "It ain't none a yer business; we ain't no more further offen the beaten path than you'uns, no how." His sharp, piercing blue eyes belied his lackadaisical actions.

As he spoke, he insolently dismounted and tossed his reins on the ground to hitch his horse and swaggered to the fire, all of the time leering at Earlene.

The shorter one spoke up, "Jeb, mind yer manners. Ain't no use'n being curt with these good people." He turned to me and said, "We got work at tha Vertical X's. Ya know tha brand?" Before I could answer, he said, "Hope y'all excuse muh brother. He's long on mean but short on manners."

"Nah," I'm not familiar with that brand."

"Yer gonna be, thet's fer shore. It's down there where that there East Fork joins tha big river."

He didn't wait for an answer, but turned to Earlene and said, "Honey, ya gotta cup er sumpin fer us ta drink out of?

"No," Earlene said. "I just have the two tin cups for us. In a minute I'll have an empty bean can you can share."

"That's awright, Honey. We'll just use these uns." He picked up the two cups and handed one to Jeb. "Here Jeb. Por ya a cuppa java." He turned back to me, and said, "If'n we's gonna share yer woman, might's well share yer cups."

Jeb took the cup and held it out toward Earlene. "Ya kin por it, Honey, n stur it with yur finger. I like sweet stuff," he leered.

He turned to me. "Ya allus travel with sech a purty woman?" he asked.

"No," I said. "Only when I have the chance."

"Wal, this here is tha fust time I evah had tha chance, 'n ah'll make tha most uv it this time."

He turned back to Earlene, who had picked up the pot of boiling coffee. She was holding it with a folded up neckerchief. The shorter brother was standing, smiling. Earlene stumbled and poured the pan of boiling coffee all over Jeb's right hand. He wore his gun on the right side, butt backward.

Jeb began jumping and swearing, alternately blowing on his hand and looking wildly around for a canteen. His hand was a mass of blisters and red, scalded flesh.

"This is gonna cost ya," he screamed.

I was watching the shorter brother, who had straightened up and had his hand on his pistol.

"Ya dirty lil bitch, ahm gonna teach ya a lesson," Jeb shouted.

"Oh, I'm so sorry! Just a second, I have something that will help it. She ran to her horse and got a tin of salve out, along with her leather gloves. She took off the lid of the tin and put on her gloves; then she ran back to Jeb, who was calling her every foul name he could think of.

She reached out and said, "Here, let me have your hand. The quicker we doctor it, the less it will hurt." She took his hand in her gloved hands, gripped it tightly and twisted one hand to the left and the other to the right. Half his hide came off in her rough glove.

"Is that better?" she asked.

Jeb was screaming and holding his hand. His brother slapped leather but before his pistol flashed clear of the holster, one squinted eye served as the doorway for the .44 caliber bullet that exploded his head into eternity.

Jeb was grabbing at his .44 with his left hand as I turned toward him, but my action was unnecessary. Earlene had already beaten me to him. I hated to see her have to do it, for fear it would prey on her mind. She must not have had time to aim well, for the first slug had hit him square in the lower pelvis. He had only a couple of heart beats to bemoan the loss of his manhood, for the second shot, which for some reason lagged the first by several long seconds, hit him right square in his heart.

"Darn it all! Earlene exclaimed. "I just hate it when I'm so clumsy! Now look what has happened!"

"Yeah, I see," I replied. "This is a time that we can be like a doctor and bury our 'mistakes'." I started for my horse to grab my little shovel. "On second thought, let's throw some of this brush over them and tell the sheriff what happened. I'll ride back with him the day after tomorrow so he can take a look at them. I have a feeling he'll have posters on them."

I knelt down and looked through their pockets. They each had a little bag with twenty five twenty dollar gold coins in them. "Hmm, it looks like they've been paid in advance for something. Sheriff Russell's gonna be interested in this.

"Honey, I have just had a change of mind. Let's bundle these guys up and start back. We'll aim for the east side of Promontory Point. I've never been along there before, but it will put us about fifteen miles from Vacaville. I've got a hunch the sheriff is gonna want to know about this as soon as possible. We can stay in Vacaville overnight."

Earlene had thrown the loose dirt over the fire and already had packed up the gear. "I have a premonition that something really bad has happened. It looks to me like they have just been paid for something, and you can bet it won't be anything good." Earlene had a look of concentration on her pretty face.

I threw the bodies across the saddles of their horses and tied them down and we struck out on a long trot for Vacaville. When we came to nice, firm little glades that had had no brush to be cleared, we would lope our horses across to where the ground was again scarred up by the wagon wheels of the post haulers when their loaded wagons crossed the soft terrain.

In a couple of hours, we reached Vacaville. We entered Main Street from the south end and stopped at the sheriff's office. A dim light was burning and I knocked on the door. The younger deputy was on duty and had been playing checkers, through the bars, with one of the prisoners whom had been picked up for disturbing the peace.

"Hey Deputy, I have a couple of bodies outside and I need to talk to the sheriff. These men have some gold coin in their pockets and we think they may have just been paid off for a job."

The Deputy had listened impatiently, as though he had something he needed to say to me. When I had finished, he said, "Easy, I hate to have to tell you and Earlene, but Rodney was shot in an attempted bank robbery this morning, soon after you, Earlene and her dad left your meeting this morning."

We were stepping down the stair to where the horses were tied, in the darkness of the night. The deputy walked around my horse and when he saw the dead men's horses, he exclaimed, "Hell's Bells! Those are the horses of the men who tried to rob the bank! I've got to get the sheriff and the other deputies up here, muy pronto!"

Earlene had mounted her horse. "You guys get those dead men off the horses while I get the sheriff." She put spurs to her pony and pulled up in a cloud of dust in front of the sheriff's house. She hit the ground running and leaped up the stairs, crossed the porch in a bound and banged her fist on the door.

"Sheriff! Sheriff Russell! You've gotta get down to the jail!"

Sheriff Russell came to the door, tucking his shirt into his pants.

"What in the world has happened, Earlene?" he said.

"Easy and I had a run-in with a couple of would-be-rapists out in the South Cedar Breaks. We brought them in across their horses and your deputy says they are the men who tried to rob the bank and shot Rodney."

"I'll be right there!" The sheriff started for the shed behind his house where he stabled his horse.

Earlene galloped her horse back to the jail and swung down. The deputy and I had stretched the dead men out on the jail porch.

A minute later the sheriff arrived. "Give me a breakdown on what happened while we go through their pockets and see if we can identify these men," he said, as he knelt beside the one called Jeb. He went through his pants and shirt pocket, but found nothing except a pocket knife, a half used plug of chewing tobacco and a sack of Bull Durham smoking tobacco. I handed him the two sacks of gold coins and told the sheriff that one had come from each man's pockets.

"Did you hear their names?" he said, glancing at me and Earlene, in turn.

"The short one called the tall one Jeb," answered Earlene. She looked over at me. "I didn't hear Jeb call the short one by name, did you, Easy?"

"No, I don't believe I did. I'd bet two bits that Todd has posters on both of them, though." I looked over at Sheriff Russell. "Do they ring a bell in your mind, Todd? I have a feeling that they haven't done an honest day's work in their lives."

The sheriff got up, brushing off the knees of his pants. "There is something looks familiar about them. They very well may have come in from out of state. Did they say anything that might give a clue as to what they were doing here?"

"Yeah, as a matter of fact they did. The shorter one asked me if I knew the brand, The Vertical X's. I told him that I didn't and he said that I soon would. He told me it was at the junction of the East Fork and the Wandering River. I'd bet another two bits that it's that big, new ranch house right across the river. It's the one some of the small ranchers said was hostile to them. I heard they trade at Post, up on the Rimrock twenty miles or so east of their headquarters."

"They weren't trying to keep any secrets." I told him about the coffee cups and what they had said about sharing my woman.

"There is no doubt they planned on killing you. You're lucky they didn't do it when they first rode in," the sheriff guessed.

"Well, Earlene and I had figured they were up to no-good. There is no way they would have taken us by surprise. I'm sure it would have been us killing them, just like it happened. I have zero doubt that they planned on killing me. They made some remark about traveling on with Earlene. If they had realized how cranky she can be, they would have forgotten that idea. I'm sure you saw how Earlene did his hand, and that was while she was in a good mood."

I went on to tell him of how Earlene ruined the one's gun-hand and how when he tried to draw left handed, she killed him before I could do it myself after killing the short one.

Earlene said, "Here we stand joking while we haven't asked about Rodney. I personally have been afraid of the answer."

The sheriff's face turned grave. "It's touch and go as to whether or not he will live, and the odds are that he won't. There is one curious thing about the robbery. Nancy O'Reilly was in the bank making a deposit when the robbery attempt took place. She said the shorter of the two men held a pistol on everyone in front while the taller one went into Rodney's office. The door was left open and she could see what happened inside. The man went straight into the office, shot Rodney, and they both ran out, jumped on their horses and left. It was nearly like they had come to kill Rodney instead of robbing the bank."

"I suppose that it's useless to look in on Rodney at this time of night," I said.

"I think that he's still in a coma. Anyway, he was sleeping and the new doctor felt that he would probably be a couple of days, at least, before he awoke."

"Well, I think that Earlene and I will stay in her office here in the RL&CC so we can check on him first thing in the morning. Unless there's something we can do now, we'll see you in the morning, Todd."

"Okay, I'm going to hit the sack myself." He turned to his deputy. "Mike, maybe we should drag them back into the jail for the night. We don't want some dog chewing on them. We'll turn them over to Tony in the morning. There's no use waking him up now."

I said, "Todd, I assume the doctor has Rodney there in his office where we were before they finished the Bank Building."

"Yeah, and you wouldn't believe how well he has fixed it up. He lives upstairs from his office, now that he has opened for business."

We said our good byes and Earlene and I rode up to the livery barn to stable our horses for the night. We then walked back to the Bank Building where we each had an office. Earlene's sofa pulled out into a bed and we were soon settled down for the night. We were both feeling pretty somber about Rodney having been shot.

We talked briefly of what could have easily happened if we had not been able to kill the two outlaws. My heart was full of tenderness as I held Earlene. "I just don't think I could live if something were to happen to you. I don't think I would even want to try."

Our love making was very gentle and we fell asleep right after.

The next morning we got up early and walked down to the cafe for breakfast. The day was crisp, fresh and cloudless. Stars shone brightly and the moon was hanging low in the sky. In the east, the sky was lightening. The birds that had not yet gone south sat on the boughs of the trees and the eaves of the buildings, their feathers ruffled against the chill and their heads tucked beneath their wings.

We walked into the cafe and were greeted by Ellie Green. She and her husband, Harlan owned and operated Green's Cafe. Ellie ran the dining room and kept it spotless. Her husband had once been a noted trail cook, and now his cooking skills kept the cafe crowded. At this time of morning, however, no one else was in the cafe, nor had we seen anyone on the street.

Ellie told us to pick a table and walked back into the kitchen. She returned a moment later, tying an apron behind her back. She had a pad, but before she could take our order, Harlan Green came into the dining room.

"I sure am sorry about what happened to Rodney," he said, looking at both Earlene and me. "I sure hope the men who did it are captured and brought to justice."

"Well, you got half of your wish fulfilled," I said.

"What do you mean by that?" he asked.

His wife lowered her pad and looked at us to try to see what we meant.

"The two men who tried to rob the bank and shot Rodney in the process are down in the jail, stretched out dead on the floor. They were brought to justice, but weren't captured, unless you count draping them over their horses and bringing them to the sheriff as capturing them. Earlene and I were out appraising the South Cedar Breaks pasture of the RL&CC when they rode into our camp and promptly informed us they were going to rape Earlene after they drank our coffee. It turns out that they neither drank our coffee nor had their way with Earlene," I informed him."

"Did I understand you to say the *two* men?" Harlan inquired. He exchanged glances with his wife. "Honey, weren't there three of them?"

"There sure were, Harlan. You remember the two unshaven toughs and the English dandy," she replied. "You remember how out of place he looked. He was wearing western clothes that still had the creases in them."

She turned from her husband back to us. "What are you having this morning?" she asked Earlene.

Earlene glanced at me rapidly and ordered eggs over easy with a slice of ham and a cup of coffee.

I told Ellie that I'd have the same, only to scramble the eggs. She rushed off to fill our orders, and I looked over at Earlene, and said, in a low voice, "You know, Earlene, something about this is beginning to smell."

"You can say that again. Do I remember right? Didn't the sheriff say that Nancy said that it looked more like they came in to kill Rodney than to rob the bank?"

"That's sure what he said," I replied. I think it's still a little too early to go by the doctor's office to check on Rodney. Why don't we stroll by the sheriff's office and see if he is up. I'd like to know if he has the information about the English appearing guy being with the two men we shot."

We finished off our breakfast and stood up, left money on the table and left the cafe. A nearly endless flock of birds passed over, headed south. I looked toward the jail and saw Todd's horse tied out front. We both started walking that way.

Sheriff Todd Russell and deputies Tex and Faron came out the door as we approached the porch.

"We're headed to Green's cafe for some breakfast," Todd told us. "Do you two want to join us?"

"We need to have a few words with you, either here or there," I said. "We have found out something interesting."

"We can usually have privacy at the back table in the cafe," Todd said. "Ellie sort of saves that for us, as we eat about this time each morning."

"I imagine that Mike is sleeping now," I said. "I'd like for you and all three of the deputies to give this some thought."

The sheriff said, "He's been up all night. I'll pass the word along to him when he wakes up." We walked in and Ellie looked at Earlene and me and said, "Is my mind deceiving me, or didn't I already feed you a few minutes ago?"

"You sure did," Earlene replied, "but it tasted so good we thought we would go out and round you up some more business."

Ellie grinned and took the lawmen's orders. She looked at me and Earlene and said, "Can you hold another cup of coffee?"

We nodded our heads and she hurried off to the kitchen.

The sheriff asked, "What is it that has you two out and around so early in the morning?

"You may already have this information, but it sort of opens up some new avenues of thought. We were talking with Ellie and Harlan. They said they hoped the bank robbers would be captured and brought to justice. We told her they had both been brought to justice, although as to whether you could say they were captured was problematical, but that they were both lying dead on the floor of the jail.

"Ellie said, "Two? There were three of them when they were in here eating, early in the morning when they had the place to themselves." Harlan was listening from the kitchen and he came out and the two of them described the third man. They said he was dressed in brand new western clothes, but talked with a strong English accent."

"Hmm," said the sheriff. "That is interesting."

"That's what we thought," I answered, "and especially in view of the fact that Nancy O'Reilly told you that it appeared to her as though they came in to kill Rodney, more than to rob the bank."

Todd asked us, "Have you mentioned this to anyone else?"

We both told him that we hadn't and Todd said, "I think we ought to keep this between the five of us, plus Mike when he gets up. Do the Greens know that you have a big interest in the English man?"

"No," I answered, "but I think it would be a good idea to ask them not to mention it to anyone, and find out if they have already told anyone else. Earlene and I are going to drop by and check on Rodney. I don't want to talk to him about the robbers, other than to ask him if he noted anything unusual. This is banking on the hope that he is conscious and the doctor says he can talk. Earlene and I will spend only a couple of minutes there. Then we're headed out to the ranch to talk to Brad."

Ellie returned with the orders and Earlene and I each took a quick couple of sips and left the cafe and headed for the doctor's office. A light was on and we saw someone's shadow cross the pulled blinds, so we walked quietly up the stairs and knocked lightly on the door. We didn't want to wake up Rodney if he were sleeping, instead of being in a coma. A moment later, a young man with tired, bloodshot eyes and a tousled head opened the door.

"Come on in, Earlene." He looked at me and held out his hand. "I'm Doctor Kincaid."

I shook hands with him and introduced myself. "I've heard of you," he informed me. "Rodney is still in a coma. I think we have taken enough precautions to keep him from developing an infection. It is touch and go as to whether he will pull through. The only good news is that apparently he has no internal bleeding, now that we have stopped the initial bleeding. No big arteries were severed, no organs were hit, and there is a good chance there is no leakage from the intestines into the abdomen.

"That doesn't mean that he isn't severely wounded. It just means that if he does regain consciousness, he has a fighting chance to survive."

"If he does come to, tell him we were by to check on him and that the man who shot him is dead."

Before I could continue, the doctor cut in, "The hell you say! What luck to catch them so soon!"

"Earlene answered him, "Yeah, it was good luck alright. The good luck wasn't theirs, though."

"If they hadn't started something with us," I added, "we wouldn't have had any idea they were wanted in Vacaville. We were out looking at the South Cedar Breaks pasture when we ran across their tracks. It seemed they were sure trying to keep out of sight, so we figured they were on the owl hoot trail, what with being so far off the beaten path. We set up camp so that we had a good field of vision, and sure enough, they rode into camp. They asked to join us and have a cup of coffee.

"Earlene was making supper and we agreed they could have a cup. They were over-confident, for they informed me they were not only going to share our coffee, but that they were going to help themselves to Earlene. Earlene incapacitated one of them, and when the other went for his gun, I killed him and turned to get the one Earlene had crippled. She shot him while he was trying to make a left handed draw while he was wearing a right handed rig.

"We hauled their bodies to the sheriff and had no idea who they were until Mike, the young deputy, identified their horses," I ended.

"It serves them right. They won't be robbing any more banks or shooting the bankers. They got their just deserts." The doctor seemed rather shocked at what had happened.

"We're heading out to the ranch. If you need someone to set with Rodney, we'll probably be back this evening," Earlene said.

"Glad to have met you. You take good care of Rodney." I tossed the words over my shoulder at the doctor as we left the office.

"Nice to have met you," the tired doctor said. "You can bank on Rodney getting the best of care."

The sun came up as we were crossing the river. It turned the waters golden as they gurgled away to the east. Our shadows lay on the water to the west, distorted and having an infinite height that was lost in the ripples of the river and endless distance that lay west of the earth.

The frost on the grass reflected the sun's rays in a cool glare, punctuated by a myriad of tiny rainbows, encapsulated in the tiny crystals of ice. Earlene and I rode so closely together that our legs sometimes touched, but both of us were deep in contemplation of the odd circumstances of the attempted bank robbery and what was the attempted murder of Rodney, at least for now,.

With our minds occupied with this puzzle, the miles passed swiftly. Out of the habits of the past, we each scanned the countryside as we rode, frequently changing directions. We had replaced the pole gate with one of barbed wire. I leaned over, opened the gate and carried the wire back enough to let Earlene pass. Then my horse edged back up enough to allow me to lean over again, from the other side, and fasten the gate shut.

We galloped past the house to the corral, unsaddled and gave the horses a handful of corn. Brad was milking the cow and Earlene quickly gathered the eggs while I rubbed the horses down.

By mutual unspoken consent, we waited until we got to the house and the coffee was poured before we brought Brad up to date. He had heard nothing of the attempted robbery, Rodney's critical condition, or of the killing of the outlaws by Earlene and me.

After listening to the story, Brad remarked, "The two of you were lucky to come out of that with a whole skin. What do you think we should do now?"

"It is my opinion that we should talk to the doctor about Rodney. If he thinks it is possible, I think we should bring Rodney out here where we can keep a guard mounted over him. If it should happen that he dies, we can bury him out here. If he recovers, I think we should pretend to bury him out here.

"It appears to me that someone is trying to take Rodney out of the picture, as far as being involved in the RL&CC is concerned. Since the Greens told us that an Englishman was with the two outlaws who later thought they had killed Rodney came into the picture, I think it calls for us to pretend they succeeded and see what their next step will be.

"Before we make any further plans, I believe we should check with the doctor about Rodney. Why don't we eat and then ride back into town. If it looks like Rodney will recover, we don't want the town to know it. We will talk to the doctor and get his cooperation to keep it a secret. That way, we might be able to set a trap for whoever wants Rodney out of the way." We sat in silent contemplation for a few minutes. I broke the silence by saying; this is a condensation of the situation:

"Sir Hampton's share of the holdings composed of the RL&CC, including the RB&T, are more than substantial. Those two entities are going to be worth a fortune very soon, and they aren't to be sneezed at even now. Are we agreed on that point?"

Both Earlene and Brad nodded their heads, listening attentively.

I continued, "If a person were to take a very cynical view of what happened, and based on that cynicism were to set up a hypothetical set of circumstances, those circumstances might appear like this:

1. "It would not be unreasonable to state that Sir Hampton, Rodney's father, has quite a large estate here in America. He nearly undoubtedly has much more in England.

2. "There is the distinct possibility that in England there is a definite line of inheritance.

3. "If we granted that this is true, it would be interesting to know who would inherit Sir Hampton's estate if something were to happen to him, especially if Rodney were dead.

4. "Just for the sake of argument, why don't we say that Rodney dies?

Both Earlene and Brad started to object but I raised my hand. "Hear me out. I have a point I am trying to make.

5. "Given that Rodney did die, if there were any validity to the circumstances we set up for the purposes of this discussion, the next thing that could happen would be the death of Sir Hampton.

6. "If such a preposterous thing were to happen, and if one suspected it ahead of time, one would want to ask himself how to flush such a plot out into the open.

7. "Again, just for the sake of our discussion, if we believed such a thing to be a possibility, what would happen if we brought Rodney out here to either recover or to die?

8. "Let's say that one of us went to England and talked with Sir Hampton and brought him into our plot.

9. "If Sir Hampton were to come over to look at his holdings and to see his son, or to attend his son's funeral, and let's just say that he was so grief stricken that he had a heart attack and we buried him next to his son, it would be reasonable to expect the heir next in line to Rodney to immediately make a move to take over his holdings.

10. "If a will happened to turn up that named him as the beneficiary, the resurrection of Rodney, hopefully, along with Sir Hampton might be enough to flush out the person behind the attempted robbery, the shooting of Rodney and whatever else might develop.

The reason someone would have to go to England would be so that Sir Hampton and Rodney's mother would know that Rodney was actually alive."

"It would seem to me," said Earlene, "that we should grab a quick sandwich and ride straight back now. If Rodney comes out of his coma, we don't want the word to get around."

We were all agreed on that point and we wolfed down a quick meal and started back to town.

-=-

We rode into town and stopped by the doctor's office. When we entered, the doctor was at his desk going through some medical reports.

"Hello Earlene, - Brad, - Easy. I have some good news for you. Rodney stirred around for a few minutes in his sleep and then opened his eyes and tried to sit up. I have him strapped down, for fear he'll pull some stitches loose. He was coherent and asked what had happened and where he was."

"How long ago was this, Doctor?" We were all listening for his answer.

"I'd say about fifteen minutes ago. I was just making a note of it in his medical records," was the reply.

"Who all have you told about this? Was anyone else here?" I felt like crossing my fingers for luck.

"No, but either Ellie or Harlan was going to bring me a meal. I haven't had a chance to eat yet, and I'm afraid to leave Rodney here."

The doctor yawned and stretched. He didn't look as tired as he had when we saw him this morning, but it was easy to see that he had had little sleep.

I said, "Listen Henry. This is very important. I don't want you to let anyone in to see him. We have reason to believe that the bank robbery was staged only to give the outlaws an opportunity to kill Rodney. Is it possible that we could move him out to the ranch where we can put a guard on him? Would it be safe for him? Could you call on him out there?

"We know there was a probable accomplice. We are going to set a trap and no one will know except you, us three, and the sheriff. The Greens will have to know at least part of it. We can't say the least word that will give *anyone* a clue."

"He would be better off here, medically speaking. I think he could be safely moved, however." The doctor ran his fingers through his yellow hair and yawned again.

"What's the chance of us seeing him right now? I don't want to wake him up if he's sleeping, but I would like to at least take a look at him." Both Earlene and Brad nodded their agreement. I looked expectantly at Henry and received his nod.

I opened the door and walked quietly to Rodney's bedside. In a very low voice, I said, "We're all pulling for you, Kid. We're going to make sure whoever the king-pin is behind this pays."

I started to turn toward the door and saw Rodney move his hand slightly, as if to stop me. I paused and saw his eyelids flutter, then open.

"It's good to see you, Easy," he muttered. "Wait until I am up so I can help you."

"I'm thinking you'll have your shot at them, Rodney. Right now is the time to concentrate on getting well. I know that it must hurt like blazes," I said.

"Only when I'm laughing." He winced as he tried to laugh. "Easy, you have to make allowances for me. I can't think of any fresh jokes, so I have to tell old ones."

"We'll give you credit for the old ones, then. We have to run an errand. We'll be back shortly. Earlene and Brad are going to stick their head in and wave at you."

I stepped back out of the way so that Brad and Earlene could wish him well. Then we stepped out of the room and I turned to the doctor.

"Okay Henry, we have to see the sheriff and the Greens. We'll check back by. If anyone asks you, let them think that it is nearly certain that Rodney will die. I want to talk to the sheriff before we decide for sure what we are going to do, but it is pretty certain that we will move Rodney to the ranch in any event."

We stepped outside and started up the street to the cafe. I stopped for a moment and said, "Why don't the two of you go on into the cafe. If you get a chance, tell Ellie that as soon as I get back from talking with Arnold, we would like to talk privately with her and Harlan. I'll be back over in a couple of minutes."

I turned across the road to the blacksmith shop, while they continued to the cafe.

-=-

Arnold was working on a buggy wheel when I entered. He stopped immediately and walked over and shook hands.

"I'm sure sorry to hear about Rodney," he said. It was a stroke of luck that the killers stumbled across you and Earlene."

"Yeah, good luck that could have been bad luck. Arnold, I have to go back over to the cafe in just a jiffy. I am going to try to take Rodney out to the ranch where we can keep our eye on him twenty four hours a day. It is going to be a real ordeal for him to be moved. I thought you might have an idea of how to make it as easy as possible. The bigger the wheels on the wagon, buggy or cart, the smoother the ride will be. Then we have to consider springs, etc."

"Several things come to mind," Arnold said. "Why don't you go on to your meeting, and let me see what I can come up with."

"I sure do appreciate it. After we leave the cafe, we have to see the sheriff. I wonder if Todd is in his office. I prefer to talk to him than one of the deputies."

"I saw him leaving the cafe about an hour or so ago. I think he is probably there now," Arnold mused. "Get on along so I can see what I can come up with."

I slapped him on the shoulder and walked across to the cafe. Earlene and Brad were sitting in the corner with Mrs. Green. There were no customers in the cafe at this hour, but Harlan was doing some cooking and baking, preparing for the evening rush. When he heard me come in, he took off his apron and walked back to join us at the table.

After greeting each other, Harlan and I sat down at the table with Ellie, Earlene and Brad.

"Let me get right to the point," I said. "It is crucial that we keep this information between just the ones at this table, the sheriff and the doctor. We have been thinking of the information that you, Ellie, gave us about the Englishman who was sitting with the two outlaws we killed. We think that it is a plot designed to kill Rodney, rather than rob the bank. If we are right, there will probably be another attempt. We are going to take Rodney out to the ranch so we can mount a guard. I want to again ask you to keep it a secret that anyone knows about the Englishman being with the two would be killers. At the same time, please take some extra precautions for yourselves. The Englishman, if he is in truth part of a plot to kill Rodney, might get to worrying about being seen here in the cafe with the two outlaws. Harlan, I advise you to keep a shotgun out of sight but easily reached. Ellie, stay alert for anything remotely suspicious. Try to keep from appearing to be on alert, but take all the care you can. You might even put a six-gun behind the counter and possibly another back out of sight behind the bread bin."

We said our goodbyes, after being assured that they would be on the alert. Harlan had been a pretty salty character when he was a puncher and also as a trail cook. A six-gun didn't feel alien to his hand.

We walked the short distance on down the street to the jail. The sheriff was in his office, just as Arnold had surmised. We walked into the office and greeted the sheriff and deputy Faron Stern. The night deputy was grabbing a little sleep, and Chief Deputy Tex Lonigan was looking into some suspected cattle rustling out south of the South Cedar Brakes near the small town of Moon Rising.

Earlene and Brad sat down and I started to, but stopped, snapped my fingers and said to the sheriff, "Todd, I plumb forgot to leave a message with Arnold. I wonder if you would walk along with me so we can talk without having to listen to Faron's jokes."

Faron grinned and said, "Talk about my jokes! Yours are so stale that we had to air the jail out the last time you were in here. We had a drunk in the back cell who was threatening to bring charges against us for cruel and unusual punishment."

I glanced over at Earlene and Brad and said, "I hate to leave you two to face Faron's humor by yourself, but I have to give a message to Arnold."

The sheriff and I walked outside together.

"What is it that is so all-fired important that you didn't want to let Faron in on?" he asked me, looking at me with his keen blue eyes that missed nothing.

"It isn't necessarily that I didn't want to say it in front of Faron. It is that I had rather you make the judgment of whom you want to know it. I had planned on telling Ellie and Harlan, down at the cafe about it, since they were the ones who made us aware of the strange Englishman. I decided not to while in the cafe.

"Here is what I have on my mind. The three of us, Brad, Earlene and I have reached the conclusion that the attempted robbery of the bank was staged to cover up the killing of Rodney. The doctor says that Rodney has come out of his coma and could stand the trip out to the ranch, if we are very careful. I have talked to Arnold. I trust him implicitly, but saw no use in mentioning that when we get Rodney to the ranch, we are going to let him heal there for a while.

"Then we are going to stage a burial out on the ranch to give the appearance that the murder attempt was successful. We figure that the combination of who would benefit from Rodney's death, along with the fleeting presence of the Englishman is a coincidence that can't be ignored. If someone were trying to horn into the RL&CC, the most likely prospect would come from England, since that is where the heirs would be.

"I also figure that Sir Hampton could be in danger, for there would be no heir without his death. I am afraid to inform him by mail, for fear the letter would fall into the wrong hands. Since we are going to pretend that Rodney is dead and have a mock funeral, I want one of us to go to England for a conference with Sir Hampton. I don't want him grieving unnecessarily for his son until this is all settled. The only ones who know that we are going to stage the death of Rodney are the three of us, plus you. The doctor knows that we are going to let the information leak that Rodney is not recovering. He'll probably end up knowing that it was unlikely for Rodney to die, if he sees him recovering when he comes out to check on him.

"It is up to you as to whether or not none, some or all of your deputies will know. They all seem solid and dedicated law officers. We both know that when one is talking of the resources of the RL&CC, plus the RB&T, there is a lot of money at stake. Sometimes money can warp the best of us."

"I have absolute confidence in my deputies. However, I'm not sure but that a need-to-know condition exists at this time. For the time being, let's not let anyone else in on what is going on."

We had reached the blacksmith shop and thought we might as well check to see what Arnold had come up with for transportation of Rodney back to the ranch. As usual, he had come through with a pretty ingenious method.

"What have you got going, Arnold? I asked him.

"Let me show you," he replied. You see this extra-long wagon? I have put the wheels off two old Mexican carts on this wagon. I have added two spring seats that both face the middle of the wagon. One is nearly against the front seat and the other at the back of this modified wagon. I've installed a pole in the middle of each seat. I have taken a hammock from Paddy O'Reilly's store and stiffened it with a light beam on each side of it. I have braces between the two sides to keep it from closing in on Rodney.

"I used a wagon tongue to make a beam from the pole on the seat at the front of the wagon to the seat at the rear of the wagon. I have hung the hammock to that beam. The spring seats will take a lot of the jolts out. When the wagon lurches from side to side, the hammock will swing to keep the lurch from affecting the hammock. That is about the best I can do on short notice."

"Arnold," I said, "you never cease to amaze me. That is great. I'm going to have a last minute confab with the doctor. If things look feasible, we'll go back to the ranch and get my team and come back to pick him up and move him during the night."

"I have a good team here, Easy. I have used them and they are steady and dependable. If you want to move him in the dark, I will wait until dark and we will harness up and move Rodney into the wagon on the doc's stretcher. I will drive the team while you, Brad and Earlene try to make it as easy as possible on Rodney. I think that Earlene could look after Rodney. I may be seeing ghosts where none exist, but I think that you and Brad should sort of ride point and swing out to make sure that we don't have any surprises. If we are going to try to be safe, let's go about it as though we knew we would be attacked."

"That sounds great to me, Arnold. What do you think of our plan, Todd?" I said to the sheriff.

"If you're going to take precautions, you might as well go whole hog," the sheriff replied.

"Why don't we go back to the jail and improvise a little conversation and then we can all go eat. It will be dark by then and we can get the show on the road. Get your deputies and this meal will be on me." I turned to Arnold, "Can you meet us at the cafe in a few minutes?"

"You bet!" Arnold turned back into his shop and the sheriff and I started back to the jail.

"I'll tell my deputies that we are going to move Rodney to the ranch. That will serve as the reason you drug me off down to blacksmith shop, so I could see the contraption that Arnold fixed up. That will satisfy their curiosity and not cause any hurt feelings. As far you picking up the tab, since the county picks up my tabs, count me out and you can pick up the tab for Arnold."

"Todd, why don't you send Faron on down to the doc's? I know he is half dead with fatigue, but I would hate to have anything happen to Rodney, here at the last minute."

"Done," Todd replied. "The doc might not have mentioned it, but I've had a man there every night, plus keeping a sharp eye out during the day."

Brad, Earlene and I turned back to the cafe, where Arnold was already waiting. We sat at the big table in the far rear corner and waited for the sheriff and his young deputy, Mike, to show up. Deputy Stern had gone on to the doctor's office.

We were soon served. Ellie lit the lamps while we were eating. Before we got well underway with the food, Tex Lonigan, the chief deputy arrived.

The rest of us listened while the sheriff brought him up to date on moving Rodney out to the ranch.

"It looks to me," Tex said, that we ought to stage a little ploy for the benefit of anyone who might be watching. It might save you," he glanced over at the three of us from the ranch, "having to worry so much about a possible attack on the way back to the &RR."

"Sheriff, what do you think of you and we three deputies all riding out of town in escort of the wagon carrying Rodney. As soon as we cross the river, the four of us could circle back on the north side of town and back to the jail. No one is liable to even think of doing anything, believing that we four lawmen, plus Easy, Brad and Earlene are with the wagon."

"That's a good idea, Tex! No one will know that we are transferring Rodney to the ranch in time to have already set up a bush-whack. When they see what is going on, they won't make the effort, thinking there will be a small army accompanying the wagon," the sheriff said.

"I think it's a good idea, but I don't think we ought to do it," I said. "That would immediately tell any possible watcher that we don't buy the bank robbing theory and let them know that we suspect something. I think we should act pretty nonchalant about the move. There is no way they will want to tip their hand. If they have gone to the trouble of setting up a bogus bank robbery to cover the attempt on Rodney's life, we can rest assured that we are safe for the time being. Right now, they think Rodney is at death's door. Let's keep it that way."

"On second thought, I think you were a step ahead of us in your thinking. The three of us will just mosey on back to the office. When you get Rodney loaded, tell Faron that I said just to come on back."

"Will do," I answered.

Brad, Earlene, Arnold and I walked back to the doctor's office. Arnold, the doctor and Faron got on one side of Rodney while Brad, Earlene and I got on the other side. We gently picked Rodney up by the sheet he was lying on and placed him on a stretcher, carried him out to the wagon and slid the stretcher onto the wagon bed. The wagon was too crowded for so many people, so Brad and I got on the far side of the improvised hammock, while Faron and Arnold picked the stretcher up and raised it up so that Brad and I could take one side of it while they kept the other side.

We gently laid the stretcher down in the hammock. The doctor informed us that we could use the stretcher to make it more comfortable on Rodney while being carried into the house. He asked us to return it the next day. Arnold informed him that he was going to go with us to bring back his team and the wagon, so would drop off the stretcher either tonight or the next morning.

Rodney had been biting his lip and flinching with every movement. His face was pale and the few words he uttered were weak and barely understandable. Earlene covered him and tucked in the cover so the breezes couldn't reach him. It was the time of year that had a bite in the wind. She patted his hand and placed it under the blanket, brushed her hand along his cheek and sat down next to me on the rear spring seat.

Brad sat down next to Arnold, who clucked the horses into motion and we moved slowly toward the river, our horses trailing along behind the wagon, secured by their reins.

The only sounds were the clinking of the trace chains, the clop of the horses' hooves, the wheels crushing the dry Curly Mesquite and Gramma and the sound of the wind. The horse's tails and manes blew out in the increasing breeze. The far off wails and yips of a pack of coyotes fell on our ears like the faint tinkling of wind chimes. As we crossed the river, the gurgle of the water, like the call of lost souls, gave an eerie quality to the night. An occasional low moan from Rodney added to our somber mood. I swore, for the one hundredth time, that someone would pay dearly for this travesty.

The two outlaws who had paid with their lives for their wayward manners gave little satisfaction. The person who had hatched the plot that was beginning to unfold was the one I would bring to justice, no matter where the trail led.

We soon arrived at the ranch. We had been both pleased and surprised by how well the wagon that Arnold had designed had taken the bumps out of the ride.

Arnold helped us get Rodney into bed. He turned down Earlene's invitation for a slice of pie and a cup of coffee, told us goodbye and headed back for Vacaville.

-=-

Bright and Early the next morning, before the chickens had gotten down from their roosts, I walked down to the barn and slipped up grabbed a fat old hen. Before she could raise a ruckus, I had wrung her neck and carried her back to the house.

Earlene had a tea kettle of boiling water. I laid the chicken in a large pan, scalded her with the boiling water and plucked the feathers. A few moments later, I had dressed out the chicken and Earlene dropped it into a deep covered pan to make broth for Rodney. I tiptoed over and looked at his face. It seemed to me that his color was a little better.

While the chicken was cooking, the three of us sat down at the kitchen table.

"What do you two think about someone going to England to inform Sir Hampton?" I inquired. It seems to me that it would be running a risk to send a message informing him of the hoax we are going to run to make Rodney appear dead. It could be someone quite close to him who is plotting against him. It would obviously have to be someone close to him to be his heir, and that heir could be right there in his manor or in the immediate vicinity."

"That seems pretty well a given," Earlene said. "It seems to me that the only thing to be settled is who goes."

"That's the way I look at it too," Brad put in. He poured himself another cup of coffee and stirred some cream into it. "I think that any of the three of us is tactful enough to spell out our plan to Sir Hampton. The guiding factor is to take into consideration which of us can most easily be spared at this time."

Earlene said, "I will have to handle most of the work that Rodney has been doing at the bank. I may even have to play banker for a while. Don't get me wrong! I would dearly love to visit London and get acquainted with Rodney's folks, but I just can't see it in the cards."

"I've been giving a lot of thought to the South Cedar Breaks pasture. I've about decided to have it fenced for sheep, with a few goats to keep the brush off. I want to go high enough with the fence to keep our sheep and goats in, and bear, coyotes and wolves out. I think the fence I have in mind will even discourage cougars. I also have a crew fencing off the west end of my place. I plan on digging a channel from the oasis pool across to the old river bed, making it flow along with the water that waters the small ranches.

"I know that Brad can do it all as well as I, but those are some of the things I have on my plate. What about you, Brad?"

"Easy, It appears to me that because of you establishing such a close relationship with Rodney, right at the start, that would give you a little more reason to handle such a mission with Sir Hampton. At the same time, you were the one whom Sir Hampton asked specifically to be the advisor on running the RL&CC, which includes the RB&T. I actually think that fact sort of outweighs the personal considerations of you being the one to bring Sir Hampton up to date on what's happened and what we expect to happen in the future.

"There is also the fact that you seem to have a better grasp on the strategy of fighting, if it comes to that, as it surely may. Should it happen that they wished a gunman to use some ruse to pick a gunfight, I believe you would be better prepared to handle it, looking at it objectively.

"That brings us to Earlene, Brad continued. I think that you, my daughter, could handle things very well in England. You have the quick mind, the diplomatic savvy and the feel for the right moves to make that Easy has.

"I think the negatives of you going include that you are a better doctor than either of us, and Rodney is a long way from being out of the woods. I think that because of your familiarity with the banking system and with the paperwork transactions that are underway with the RL&CC, they could be handled much easier by you than by either Easy or me. For example, you are more familiar with the Accounts Receivable and Payable than either of us, and you can hit the ground running in both those areas where either of us will have to dig the information out in a sort of laborious manner.

"Last, but not least, I think that it is more apt that someone might try to use you for leverage to obtain their ends with you than with either of us. I'm not saying that you would not be as capable of handling the situation, but that others might misjudge you and be tempted to try things that they wouldn't be tempted to try with one of us.

"That brings me to make the following suggestion. With all things considered, I reluctantly nominate myself as the best prospect for such a trip. I would like to hear everyone else's opinion on this."

"I personally have to agree with you, Dad. This is no time to be planning sightseeing trips. I think it should be you." Earlene looked questioningly at me.

"Then as far as I am concerned, the choice is made. I might add that you would have been the one I would have picked, given the circumstances," I said as I met Brad's eyes across the table. "There is one thing I would like to say, although I know it is unnecessary to say it. If you need to make a decision on anything while you are gone, you automatically have my proxy to vote with you." I glanced over at Earlene and saw her nod. "That goes for Earlene, too. Not by my say-so, but she just nodded her agreement."

"Then it's settled," Brad said. "The stage comes through tomorrow. I will be on it and will catch a steamship to England from the port with the quickest service to London."

"Okay," I said. "Now, if we can cover some of what is going to have to be done in the immediate future, I'm going to ask the sheriff to send Faron out here, on the pretense that he's going to take a couple of weeks off for vacation. I'm going to put every fencing crew we have available to work fencing the South Cedar Breaks." I paused to see if there were any comments, and continued.

"I'll have several crews start broadcasting improved grass seed. I think that I will decide exactly where we will want our cross fences for rotational grazing. That way, while we have a couple of fencing crews building each side of the perimeter fence, we can have another couple building the first of the rotational grazing pastures.

"I think that we will make all of the cross fences five strand barbed wire, but the perimeter fences will be two heights of hog wire, plus two strands of barbed wire at the top, and two at the bottom to discourage animals from trying to dig under. We will also re-enforce the joint where the two heights of hog wire join with a strand of barbed wire.

I think we will build a line shack centered in each pasture. That will put the home for each shepherd within little more than two and one half miles from the most distant corner of each pasture. I'd like to get a flock of sheep before winter sets in. We'll have to stock in feed for both sheep and cattle.

"I don't want to stock the entire place at once. We can move a herd of cattle in to graze along the creeks, if we feel it is merited.

We sat in silence for a minute and I said, "Brad, there is one other thing."

Brad looked up from his coffee. "What might that be?" he inquired.

"I think we should carry you down to the same place Rodney caught the stage when he went back to England. I don't think we should let the word get out that you're gone."

"You've got the right idea," he agreed. "Maybe you ought to find some work here and borrow one of Frank Harris' men to do it. He has some pretty salty hombres working for him. He ought to could pick out a good man who knows how to sling a six-gun to help out here for a while."

"My thoughts exactly," I answered him. "I think we ought to put on about four more permanent hands, anyway. I don't want to hire out-and-out gun-hawks, but I want some men who know how to look after our interests."

Earlene spoke up, "You know, Dad, we might be better off to wait a day or two for you to catch the stage. We ought to have someone here to help defend the house before you leave. Someone might have to ride along with you to bring back your horse. Although the horse would undoubtedly come back here if left to its own resources, if someone were to spot a saddled horse wandering around, it would be tempting to a thief at the worst and cause a lot of curiosity at the best."

"You know," I said, "I have to agree with Earlene. We are getting the cart before the horse. I know how important that it is to notify Sir Hampton, and we sure don't want to give him any false hopes, but we need to have Rodney's funeral before you leave. That will give us a couple of more days to see how well his recovery is going, so we can give Sir Hampton more accurate news on how he is recovering. That will also probably decrease the chance of an attack on the ranch in the immediate future. It will be believed that since he is already dead, there is no necessity to stage a second killing effort.

"That will delay your departure, Brad, for several days. That will be cutting it more closely in getting Sir Hampton ready for the trial, but I think it is a risk we should take."

After a few minutes of comment on that aspect, everyone agreed that it would be best to delay things for a week. We also decided to hold the funeral two days later, and spread the word tomorrow that Rodney died tonight.

There were still things that had to be done to keep the ranch work progressing.

-=-

Four hand-picked men from the RL&CC had been assigned to work on the &RR and the EEZ ranches and the funeral of Rodney Hampton had been announced. A viewing of the body had been held with only a few close friends invited. Earlene Rogers, Arnold Smith, Todd Russell and his three deputies, Ellie and Harlan Green, Pat Donahue, Doctor Kincaid and I made up those viewers.

The grave side ceremony had most of the population of Vacaville and the rest of the Bend of the Rimrock citizens. It was a closed casket affair and was a brief rite. The casket was lowered into the grave and several people dropped a handful of dirt on the casket, filed on by and headed for their buggies, wagons and horses.

Rodney was not only thought well of by all the citizens, but was one of the five people who had brought the new era to the Bend of the

Rimrock. He was also the man who had approved the loans that had allowed all of the ranchers that now lived on the north side of the river to have homes and ranches that far exceeded any dreams they had had when they had started out.

They would have had meager herds, at the best, until the formation of the RL&CC and the RB&T. He had been instrumental in the creation of the new school, the erection of the town hall, and the economic boom that the town of Vacaville was now enjoying.

It was a sad and somber group of townspeople who left the funeral, after giving their condolences to Rodney's closest friends and partners in the RL&CC.

There were only a very few of the townspeople who had seen the &RR valley. Despite the grief they all felt, they could scarcely believe their eyes when they saw the green grasses of the pastures with the stream of water bisecting its center, as far as the eyes could see as the green of the grass changed into the misty blue of distance.

None of them were aware that a war with a hidden enemy was raging between the present citizens of the Bend of the Rimrock in general, and particularly the RL&CC, their benefactor.

Chapter Three - Page 42
A Bar Room Tussle

I splashed across the river, stopping in the rapids to let Calliope drink. After sinking his muzzle in the water, he shook his head and snorted the water out of his nose and started on across without waiting for me urge him on.

I pulled up at the blacksmith shop to talk with Arnold for a few minutes while waiting for Frank Harris, the ranch superintendent, to show up for his Wednesday morning report. As usual, he was pounding on an iron strap, shaping it to fit some purpose or other.

He looked up and said, "You must have come straight here, because no one has reported their horses missing yet."

I laughed and replied, "I was too busy this morning to steal any horses. Why the concern? Are you running out of horses to sell?"

"No, if the truth be told, I was looking for some excuse to get out of work for a while, since I know you're going to invite me for a beer. You might be getting around pretty early this morning so you can keep cool, but it's sure hot here next to my forge."

I started to answer him, but he held up his hand, stopping me. "I've got something to tell you that won't bear waiting. There has been some guy who claims to be foreman of the Vertical X's just on the other side of the East Fork. He has a tough looking crew with him. I don't know how they find the time to hang out here, or why they're coming here when they've always been trading over in Post. Now here is something that I find interesting. Two of his crew are big men. They are cousins, and for some reason they have several times mentioned that if you come into town, they are going to stomp a mud-hole in your ass and then splash it dry. They are big enough to make me look like a boy. A piece of advice is to sort of keep out of their way, unless you're going to shoot them, 'cause they're just too big to fight bare-handed.

"The older of the two looks like he could shuck a six-gun pretty fast. The younger one looks like he doesn't have all of his marbles, but he doesn't carry a gun. If I were to venture a guess, I would say he is being egged on by the foreman to maim or kill you with his bare hands."

I stood there, rubbing my chin for a minute. "You know, Arnold, I have a strange feeling this has something to do with Rodney getting shot. I've been wondering what their next move would be. I figured it would be against me, here around Vacaville. I think that Sir Hampton is in danger too, there in England. You can bet that there is a movement that has a lot of money at stake."

Arnold nodded his agreement. "You've hit the nail on the head. What can I do to help handle those two big fellows over at Donovan's Saloon?"

"I'll tell you what," I mused. Why don't you wander over to the saloon and take a table where our back is protected. Why don't you take that piece of rod that you have leaning up against the post there. You might lean it up against the leg of the table on the side away from those men. It might save me having to kill somebody.

"You can order us a beer. Yeah, yeah, I know that ruins your hope of getting a free beer on me." I grinned at him and added, "I'll ride up in a minute and tie my horse at the rail and come in like I don't see you for a minute and then walk over to your table and sit down where I can reach the rod without being noticed, if I need to."

Arnold nodded, picked up the rod, along with a half shaped brand and walked off for the saloon. I waited about five minutes after he entered before riding up and tying my horse. I entered the saloon and walked to the bar. Before I could order a beer, Pat Donahue walked over and said, "Arnold has your beer already ordered. He's sitting right over there by the wall." He pointed to the table and I turned and walked over to the table, grinning at Arnold and saying, "So there you are, you scoundrel. I thought you were still home, sleeping off your drunk or something."

"Not me," he retorted. "I don't have a cushy job like you. I have to work for a living. Pull up a chair and sit yourself down."

He kicked a chair out from the table and I sat down across from him. The table where the four men from the Vertical X's were sitting was halfway across the room on my left and on Arnold's right. They were deep in a conversation, and from the looks they kept shooting at me, I was sure that I was the subject of their conversation. I didn't have to wonder for long, for the giant at the table got up and walked over to our table.

"I don't like yer looks, feller. I've half a mind to change em." He looked around at the table where he had been sitting, and received a nearly imperceptible nod from the foreman. "Whaddaya say to that?" he demanded.

"Listen Son, I don't want to get into a ruckus with you. I've never even seen you before. You don't need to convince me that you're tough. I imagine that some son of a bitch at your table is trying to get you to start trouble. They just keep you around so they can laugh at you send you out to get hurt or hurt someone else. I'll bet they don't even pay you a good wage, do they?"

The man seemed half bewildered. "Well, are ya gonna get up and fight?"

"No, I'm not. I'll tell you what I'm gonna do. I'm gonna offer you a decent job where everyone will respect you and you'll be paid the same as everyone else. No one will be laughing at you or sending you out to get hurt or get in trouble with the law for starting a ruckus. Here, pull out a chair and sit down. I'll buy you a beer."

The man stood indecisively for a minute. "Do ya mean it? he asked.

"Sure I mean it," I answered him. "Have a seat." I looked over at Pat. "Hey Pat, bring ..." I turned to the big man. "What's your name?"

"They call me Ox," he stammered.

"What do you want to be called?" I asked him.

"Mom always called me Clarence," he said.

I turned back to Pat. "Pat, bring Clarence a beer, please."

Donahue came out from behind the bar with a beer and glass in his hand and set it down in front of Clarence.

"Pat, I'd like you know Clarence. Clarence, do you have a last name?"

"Sure, and my last name is Murphy."

"Clarence Murphy, this is Pat Donahue. Pat, Clarence here is the newest member of the EEZ spread. As you know, I have been hunting for a long time to find just the right fella to help us out."

Pat smiled and clapped a hand on Clarence's shoulder. "You'll enjoy working at with Easy, Clarence. He only hires the best men available."

Clarence turned red and turned his face down toward his beer. Then he raised his glass, took a gulp and said, "Mr. Seeker, you won't be sorry you hired me."

"I know I won't, Clarence. This fella here across the table is Arnold Smith. He's the blacksmith. He and Pat here are two of my best friends." Every one shook hands and Pat headed back to the bar.

The other big guy from the Vertical X's stood up, walked over and said, "My, my, but aren't you a cozy little bunch. Seeker, I'm not as easily swayed as Ox here. I'm going to beat your sorry ass till you'll never walk upright again. Get on your feet."

"Mr. Seeker, do you mind if I take care of Pug Nelson for you? He has called me Ox for the last time."

Pug grinned like a wolf. Sorry Ox, I should have been calling you by your first name, Dumb. Your name is Dumb Ox, isn't it?"

Clarence started to get up but I put a hand on his shoulder.

"Pug, I hate to kill or seriously injury a man just because he's an idiot. Get on back to your table and I'll have Pat bring you a beer," I said.

Pug grinned again. "It's going to be fun tearing your head off your shoulders."

I grinned back at him. "Tell you what, Pug. You get on back to your table and we'll play like none of this ever passed between us."

Pug took the stance of a professional fighter. "Get up before I take your head off while you're still sitting. Nothing on God's green earth is gonna save you from getting so crippled up that it'll take you a year to quit crying yourself to sleep. Get up!"

"Listen Pug. I'll ask you one more time to please go on back to your table."

"I've never had as much fun as when a man starts begging me to let him go, unless it's when I spit on his broken body and kick his ribs in." He started around the table at me.

I sighed and picked up the iron rod that Arnold had stood up against the table leg and rapped him on the side of his knee. The knee shattered and bent inward. I swung the rod again against the point of his left elbow and swung over the top against his right fist, which was nearly tucked under his chin. It shattered his fist and forearm, dislocated his elbow, and put him on his knees on the floor.

"Are you having fun yet?" I asked him. "Have you come to the part where you spit on my body and kick my ribs in?"

I turned on my heel and walked over to the table he had come from. The foreman was sitting there with his mouth open. His gunman had both hands on the table, trying to stand up. I smashed the rod against both of his fore-arms and they folded. I brought the rod back into the foreman's open mouth and he began strangling on teeth and blood; then swung the rod down across his left shoulder and then his right and the bones on each side splintered. Grabbing him by one shattered shoulder and my other hand in his crotch, I flung him out onto the bar room floor. I grabbed his six gun and that of his gunman, walked over and took the gun from the broken body of Pug, and drug him over by the side of the other two men. "Pug," I said, "I'm going to leave you with one good leg, so you might be able to get to some school that can teach you to leave well enough alone." I turned my eyes on the other two.

"I want both of you to look me in the eyes while I explain something." The gunman turned his hate filled eyes onto mine. The foreman was trying to keep from strangling on blood, and didn't look at me. I cracked his jawbone with the rod. He was white with shock sitting in, but he turned his eyes up to me. If I ever see you again, it will make me lose my temper. When I get angry, I don't know when to stop. I won't tell you what I will do, for I like to surprise people.

"Get on out to your horses. We'll help you get on them, and if you decide you want some more fun, I'd advise you to get it at a picnic or church social." Arnold and I, followed by Clarence, walked out to the hitching rail and put the injured men on their horses. We put lead lines from the gunman and the fighter to the foreman's horse and sent them off toward the Vertical X's.

I walked over to the bar and asked Pat what I owed him for getting his floor all bloody. "Hell, Easy, you know you don't owe me anything. I don't believe I have ever seen a lesson in manners conducted in such an unforgettable way."

Walking back to our table, I told Arnold that I had to go over to the RL&CC office to meet with Frank Harris. I asked him if Clarence could hang out over at the blacksmith shop until I got through.

"You know it, Easy. I'll be glad to have him. I may put him to work while we're waiting."

I walked over to the office and asked Frank if he had anything he needed to discuss. He said that everything was coming along fine and that he had brought me the four men I had asked for. They were sitting on the dock down at Paddy O'Reilly's store.

I walked back to the blacksmith shop, leading Calliope. Clarence was carrying wood in from the wood lot and stacking it next to the forge.

"Do you have a horse big enough to carry Clarence?" I asked.

"As a matter of fact, I do. One of the ranchers brought in a horse that he used for working cattle and plowing the corn patch and garden. It ought to be just about right for him," he answered. He jerked his thumb at a big sorrel standing over by the water trough. I jumped on Calliope and galloped up to Donovan's saloon and led Clarence's horse back. It had the Vertical X's brand, so I had Clarence take his saddle, bridle and gear off of the horse and swatted it across the rump to start it back toward the Vertical X's.

Telling Arnold that I would see him later, I led the five hands back toward the EEZ. I had asked Frank which of the men I ought to make my segundo and he had called over one of the men and introduced us. I knew them all by sight, but not by name. The new man was named Rod Lasser, and his hands were callused and rope burned, but his six gun hung low on his thigh and looked like it belonged there.

"Rod," I told him, "I want you to ramrod the crew for a while until I see how I'm going to organize things. I'm just borrowing the four of you for now, but we'll see how things work out in the future. Since you already know the hands that came with you, I'll take you all over and introduce you to a new man I just hired. He may be a little slow and he was with a crew of hard cases, just on the verge of going bad. I think he will make you a good man. I hope you'll make allowances for him being a little on the slow side. I don't want to find out that any one allows their teasing to make him feel like he isn't on a par with everyone. I hired him under unusual conditions, and I want him to feel like he has found a home. If anyone gets too rough with their teasing, they may find themselves having to fist fight him. I don't think they would enjoy that at all."

Rod looked at me quizzically. "I suppose you would tell me what conditions you hired him under, if you wanted me to know," he stated.

"I don't consider it a secret. Why don't you ask him and see what he says when you are eating supper tonight. I'm going to put you boys up over at my new bunkhouse on the EEZ, but I'll want you to do some work over on the &RR. I'll want you to build a bunk house over on that place, and I want you to keep a sharp eye out all of the time. I have a feeling that we are in a war that hasn't come out into the open yet. I want to make sure that a sneak attack doesn't succeed."

"Do you know what kind of a cow hand Clarence is or will make? I don't remember seeing him but one time, and he was with a pretty salty looking crew then," Rod ventured.

"The only thing I know is that he was being sent on a fool's errand by the rest of his bunch. I offered him a way out and he took it. I tried to leave an impression on the rest of the crew he was with. It will be hard for them to forget it in the next few days. I'd actually like to know what he thinks about the whole situation. You might tell me what he says. It might let me know whether I made a mistake in hiring him." I urged Calliope into a short lope and the rest of the men followed.

I showed the men to the bunkhouse and told them to pick out bunks and leave their gear. We then immediately left for the &RR. Twenty minutes later, we pulled up at the site where we had logs stacked to start the bunkhouse. It was about fifty yards north of the house, adjacent to the corrals on the east side, and just around the corner from the barn, which was on the north side of the corrals. It was also a hundred yards closer to the east wall of the canyon. It did nothing to obstruct the great view from the back porch of the house down toward the end of the valley.

"This ranch, in case you don't already know it, is the &RR. We are operating it and EEZ as one ranch. Rod is my segundo. You will all be working on a bunkhouse. You will then build a cook shack. It is immaterial to me whether it is on one end of the bunkhouse or is just near it. One of the partners who owns this ranch is off on business right now. The other partner is tied up with some important matters back at the house. Her name is Earlene and she's my wife. She also is the joint manager of the ranch, along with her father. I don't have any idea as to whether she may fix up a meal or not. You men may have to do your own cooking for now, back at the EEZ. I am sure that Earlene will have something for the two of you who take the night shift to eat. She may have a specific way she wants the cook shack built.

"As Rod will undoubtedly tell you in a minute, we can't afford to be caught unarmed at any time. At least two of you will be here at every minute of every day.

"Rod, I'll see you men later today or tomorrow. I'm sure Earlene will drop by to meet you all in a little while."

I rode back to the house, hitched Calliope, and walked inside.

Chapter Four - Page 49
A Trip to Post

Earlene and I were sitting at the table talking about the day's work. I had brought her up to date about the new men. "Earlene, normally I would suggest that we go out and get you introduced to the crew. I am thinking that maybe you and I ought to ride over to Post and see if we can see or hear anything that might give us an insight into who may be behind the suspected plot to take over the RL&CC. I think that instead I will ask Rod to come up and introduce him. I'm assuming that you will want to side me on the ride to Post, since you have never been there."

"Normally that would be a good assumption, Easy. However, under the circumstances, I think it would be best for you to take one of the best hands and go by yourselves. Rodney is feeling a lot better, but I want to be sure that he has the proper care. Why don't you go ahead and get Rod while I clear off the table. I'll pack up a lunch you can eat on the way. You and Rod can wait on the porch for me to finish. Have you said anything to them about Faron being on 'vacation' out here?"

"No," I replied. "However, he did bring some fishing gear along. He can do some fishing down close to where the creek flows out through the canyon mouth. That will let him see anyone who comes or goes. He can also see what is going on with the bunk house building. He can stay in the room with Rodney for now. We won't have to make an explanation to any of the crew, for they aren't familiar with our routine." I stood up and stretched, kissed Earlene and walked out the door.

The men had finished eating and were laying out the bunk house dimensions from a drawing Earlene had made. One of the men had helped build several log houses and had sort of assumed the leading role for the work. Rod looked up and walked over as I arrived.

"We're getting things pretty well underway here. I've given instructions that everyone should keep an eye cocked on the Rimrock and the entrance to the ranch. I know all of these boys and they are good men," he said.

"I'd like you to come up to the house. I want you to meet Earlene. While we're walking up, I want to ask you a question that you may need to ponder. I have business in Post today. I think I'll take one of the hands and take a ride over. I have a feeling there might be some trouble when we get there. Out of the bunch of you men, who would be the best man to ride along in case there should be a little gun-play, and still have the minimum amount of slowdown in our little construction project?" I asked him.

"That's an easy question to answer. The answer might have been different if we weren't building the bunk house. See the fellow over there on the far side with the checked shirt? He has a lot of experience in building and I'm letting him sort of take the lead in getting the job done. We wouldn't lose time as long as he is here. As for having someone to side you, I have to say it would be me. I've handled a little trouble off and on and am pretty good at both talking my way out of trouble, and taking care of it satisfactorily if talking doesn't work."

"Okay, I'll tell you what I'd like for you to do. Go over and tell the men that I am going to show you around the place. Don't mention going to Post. Caution them to keep their eyes open for trouble here. I have to ask you if the man you are leaving in charge of the building is also capable of handling things in case trouble shows up here."

Rod didn't hesitate in answering. "Yes, he's a good all-around man, and is not one to get stampeded into anything foolish. His name is Waldo Simmons."

"One thing more. A friend from town is vacationing out here. He's been doing some fishing and loafing around. This place is like a park compared to most of the places around here. If trouble was to come and he is around, don't worry if he directs the action, 'cause he has a lot of experience, being as he happens to be the sheriff's chief deputy," I tossed out. "You might mention to Simmons that little fact, seeing as we have a professional around. I'll introduce you to him when we get to the house."

We continued to the house where I introduced Rod to both Earlene and Faron. I also explained that Rod was going to accompany me on the trip to Post.

Faron felt that he had to put in a word at this point, warning us, "From what I've heard of Post, it is a pretty lawless place, with most of the trouble, as well as the town's control, originating from the Vertical X's. You need to keep a pretty low profile."

"That's what people used to call me when I was about eighteen: 'Easy Low Profile'," I quipped.

The weather was one of those autumn days when the heat of

summer has vanished, but the sun still shines warmly, despite the cool breeze. We rode along, occasionally exchanging jokes or commenting on the countryside. Sometimes we would talk about by-gone days and experiences that we had had. Rod was a good riding companion, but I would have enjoyed the ride a lot more if Earlene had been my companion. When she and I rode together, sometimes when her leg would brush against mine, we would often stop for more intimate things. There were times when we were out riding alone, when our eyes would meet and I knew that she was also ready to stop for a short break in our task.

The miles passed swiftly and about an hour later, I pointed out to Rod the spot where I had killed the man who had been involved in the occurrence that led to my sister's trip away from Connecticut and subsequent death. Rod listened, but made no comment.

We rode mostly in silence, exchanging only an occasional remark. Rod had never been out of Texas except for cattle drives through Oklahoma and into Kansas. He had also, of course, crossed the corner of New Mexico when riding up into Colorado. I had never been this far east along the Rimrock and I was looking for the old buffalo trail that made the only way to get a horse up and down from the lower plains to the high plains for maybe a hundred miles.

When we stocked up the ranch, this was the most logical trail to bring cattle in unless one came in from the Texas Panhandle with a herd by following the Canadian River from the Texas Panhandle to where it nearly reached the Rio Grande. Then one would go up the Rio Grande to its junction with the Wandering River and follow it into the Wandering River Basin to the Vacaville area.

When we reached the old Rimrock crossing where thousands of buffalo over thousands of years had worn a wide trail down from the High Plains to the lower elevation of the basin, I was surprised to see how easy it would be for a loaded wagon to traverse the Rimrock going either up or down. We put our horses up the grade and the town of Post came into sight.

I said, "I believe the best place to try to get a lead on what is going on is one of the saloons. Rod nodded his agreement and we crossed over to the Cowboy's Lament. It appeared to be the largest saloon along the street. We dismounted and hitched the horses to the crowded rail. There was a rail on each side of the door, with a wide set of steps leading up to the walkway. The rail on both sides was full of horses.

We walked over to the bar and ordered a pitcher of beer and two mugs. The bartender looked us over carefully, but his only words were, "That'll be four bits." I laid a dollar on the bar, picked up my four bits and we walked to a table that was on the side away from the gambling games, but near a pool table.

One of the men who was watching the pool game looked up and saw us and nudged the fellow next to him with his elbow. Both men were dressed in range garb. The man who had done the nudging had a somewhat furtive air about him. The man who was nudged looked up at us for a long moment; then turned his attention back to the game.

I poured a mug of beer for each of us and we silently toasted one another, took a swallow and looked around the room. The establishment must have been pretty successful, but I couldn't understand so many men being in a bar at this time of the week.

Suddenly I noticed that the chatter had stopped and the patrons were all looking over at our table. I tuned my head back toward Rod and there was the man who had been nudged at the pool table.

"Where you fellows ride in from?" His voice was truculent and somewhat abrasive. His eyes were icy and mean.

"Out west of here a ways where people are too polite to ask such questions," answered Rod.

"Here in Post we ask whatever the hell we want to ask, and we expect a better answer than that," the man growled.

"I don't see a badge on your shirt, and since you don't have a pencil behind your ear or a pad of paper in your hand, I suspect that you're not with a newspaper, " Rod answered back. "However, maybe you're writing a book."

"Maybe I am," the man answered.

"Then stick it up your ass and call it a mystery," Rod drawled. The words dripped off of his tongue like cold water from a melting icicle.

The man backed up a step and dropped his hands to his sides, his fingers brushing his twin forty fours. "I'm the toughest son of a bitch in these parts. Is there anyone in this bar doubts that?" His eyes were locked on Rod's.

Before Rod could answer, I said, "Yeah, I guess I would have to say that I doubt it."

The man swung his eyes to me. "Get up on your hind legs then, and I will sure as hell show you."

"Hey, ease up a little. I didn't say you're not the toughest, and I sure didn't say that I was. What do the people who know you call you? I wouldn't be so impolite as to ask you, but since we're getting so well acquainted and are on the verge of becoming such good friends, I think it only fitting that I know your name."

"I'm Topeka Canton," he said, sticking his chest out as though he was claiming to be the king of England, "and you're not going to be around long enough for us to become friends."

"Well, hell, Topeka, you don't know how much it distresses me for us not to be friends, what with the sweet smile on your face and your jolly disposition. However, before we get off of the subject, for me to believe you're as tough as you think you are, I need to ask a favor of the rest of these fellows."

I stood up and faced the room. Hey men! Would you listen up for a minute? I'm new here in Post and the only son of a bitch I have met so far is this fellow, Topeka," I said, jerking my head toward the self-proclaimed tough. "I wonder if you men could help me find the answer to what this man's statement implies. He said he was the toughest son of a bitch in these parts. Now, I wonder if I could get all you sons of bitches to go over to the side of the room the door is on," I requested. "All of you regular men remain seated."

"What in the hell are you trying to do? Are you trying to be a wise ass? You'd be better off praying, instead of clowning," Topeka stated.

I ignored him and repeated to the men, who were all still seated, "You men remain seated while the sons of bitches go over to the wall by the door."

Not a soul moved. I looked back at the man who was accosting us. "It appears that you are the only son of a bitch in the place. No wonder you can claim you're the toughest one, since you're the only one. Seems to me that doesn't say much about how tough you really are!"

I could hear some of the men in the bar guffawing loudly. The tough guy's face was as red as his neckerchief. I had stood up when I was talking to the houseful of men. I had spread my legs, with one leg nearly against the gunman. I swung toward him, which placed me squarely against him.

He stepped back and I stepped forward in unison. He took another step back and I stepped forward along with him, keeping my body nearly against him. As I stepped, I slid his left gun from its holster and flung it behind me, toward my table. As I brought my arm back forward, I wrapped it around his waist and grabbed his right wrist as he drew his forty four and jerked his arm up behind his back and at the same time, put my left hand behind his neck and jerked down on his head. His gun dropped back into his holster.

The pressure against his arm, plus my hand on his neck bent him over and I jerked his head between my legs and applied all the pressure I could muster. At the same time, I jerked his right hand gun from his holster and pitched it behind me with the other. I was squeezing his neck so hard with my legs that I could feel it popping. It was about to break as I pulled his arm up to where it was about to pop out of the socket. I reached into my left pocket with my free left hand and got my pocket knife. Holding it between my teeth, I pulled out the blade; then sliced his gun belt in two and let it drop. It took several jerks on the knife to cut though the belt on his pants. I dropped my knife back into my pocket and slid my left hand between our bodies and jerked the belt out of his pants. His pants fell down around his ankles and left his bare ass exposed to the room.

I began beating his ass with the belt, while he was suffocating for air from the pressure of my legs. Big welts crisscrossed his ass with each blow. His shoulder was half out of the socket and he was screaming with pain. After a couple of dozen hard licks with the belt I shoved him backward and he sat on the floor, moaning and holding his dislocated arm.

I grabbed him by his hair and jerked his face up so he was looking at me. "I'm not particularly fond of tough sons of a bitch," I told him. I hope you remember that the next time my friend and I come to town."

The man only moaned and held his arm, sweat running down his face.

A man stood up at a back table. "One of you men get the doctor," he ordered. His British accent was even more clipped by his anger. I hadn't noticed him before.

"Might I trouble you for your name?" His gaze was cold and a light of fury gleamed in the back of them.

"I answered. "With no intention to be rude, who wants to know?"

"I'm Richard Hampton and I own the Vertical X's ranch," he spat out.

"We rode in from the west and will leave whichever way we choose to. We don't take kindly to any sons of bitches cross-questioning us. Since you didn't go over by the door a minute ago when I asked all of the sons of a bitch to do so, I have to assume that you aren't one of them, and that your curiosity is because you appear to be an Englishman and don't know any better. We just had a little floor show because of one son of a bitch's curiosity.

"Is that one of your men?" I asked, jerking my head toward the man who was writhing around on the floor.

"No, he certainly is not!" he exclaimed.

"Was he one of your men?" I asked. "He sure looked comfortable and at home as he sat at the table with you."

If glares had the impact of a bullet, I would have dropped dead on the floor. He wheeled toward the door without answering and half the men in the bar left behind him. A moment later a man returned to the room with a doctor in tow.

"Let's go," I said to Rod. We mounted our horses and I led the way on through Post, headed east. When we had disappeared in the darkness, I led us in a circle around to the north of the town and we rode several miles back west, parallel to the Rimrock but a couple of miles north of it. We stopped in a small bunch of mesquite trees by a spring and ate the lunch that Earlene had packed.

"We might as well wait until light to ride back," I said.

"I figured we might," Rod answered.

"I really appreciated the way you answered that so-called tough back in Post," I told him.

"You didn't give me the chance to pin his ears back. I truly can't believe a man can live to be grown with that kind of an attitude."

"Rod, I figured we might as well let them know that there were two of us that won't tolerate rudeness. I'd have hated for them to make the mistake of thinking there was only the one to contend with and try ganging up on us."

Rod grinned at me. "I sort of think they won't be getting that kind of an idea. All of that, and not a shot fired! If that isn't being peaceable, I don't know what it would take."

When I had circled around to the west from town, I had planned on us riding the horses down the hidden trail to the bottom of the EEZ. I decided to keep that secret for Earlene and me; we headed back to the old buffalo trail back down to the lower plains. When we neared the trail down, we split up, with me sending Rod to the west and I doubled back a ways toward the east. We each ground hitched our horses and crawled up to the edge of the Rimrock and took a close look to see if an ambush had been set up.

There hadn't, and after a few minutes, we both rode back to the trail down and in a few minutes we were on the lower plains headed back toward the &RR.

"If I read things right, you got a lot of the information you were looking for," Rod said.

"You are right about that," I answered. "I think everything is falling into place. I didn't make any more remarks in relation to the purpose of our ride to Post. We just rode along chatting about range matters. I felt that I was pretty lucky to have a man like Rod on the team.

It was several hours ride back to the ranch, but we had had an early start and arrived in the early afternoon. We both had a good appetite and rode up to the house.

"Sit down there in the shade," I said, indicating one of the rockers on the porch. "Let me see if I can't rake us up a sandwich and something to drink with it." I walked on into the house and Faron came out of Rodney's room.

"We've been sitting here playing checkers," he said. "I didn't know if you were bringing Rod in, and I didn't want to let Rodney be seen."

"Great," I answered him. "That's the way I wanted it played. I gather that Rodney must be feeling better."

"He's raring to go," said Faron. "Earlene just went to the barn to do a couple of chores. She should be back any minute."

"I've got to rustle up a couple of sandwiches. Rod and I haven't eaten anything since early morning." As I talked, I was looking around for sandwich material. I found enough cold steak to make a couple of sandwiches, along with some cold biscuits. I put them on a plate and took it out onto the porch. Sitting it on a little table, I spread a cloth over it to keep the flies off. "You got a choice between water and buttermilk to drink, unless you prefer water or buttermilk," I joked to Rod.

"In that case I'll take the buttermilk. It's not often that buttermilk finds its way to my table," Rod remarked. I went over to the well and pulled up the cooler with the buttermilk and poured us each a glass.

A few minutes later we finished. I shook hands with Rod and said, "Rod, in case I haven't already told you, I feel lucky to have a man like you with us."

As Rod shook hands, I could see that he was touched by my words. "Well Easy, I feel lucky to be working on a spread like this. They are few and far between. Besides that, where else can you find buttermilk?" he said.

"Well, I think I'll mosey on down and unsaddle and curry Calliope. I think he deserves a bait of corn." I was untying him as I spoke.

"I've about exhausted all of my excuses to keep sitting here. I'll walk along with you. I feel like we made a pretty worthwhile ride. You know, Easy, if nothing else, you took several men out of the fight, and I'll bet you've taken a little arrogance out of that Englishman. I have a funny feeling that we'll see more of that fellow and his crew than we've already seen."

Rod's statement sure didn't need to feel lonesome. I had that same feeling, which was actually more of a conviction. A man doesn't cause trouble without a reason, and it was obvious that Richard Hampton had some hidden agenda. It was likely a lot more than coincidence that Hampton shared his last name with Rodney.

It sure reinforced the conclusions that we had come to in regard to the attack on Rodney, which could be construed as an attack on the RL&CC. It also seemed likely that although I had never seen Richard Hampton before, that he had seen me. Still, his man hadn't known whether to try to kill me or Rod. It was probable that he had seen the two of us together, and didn't know which of the two of us was me; he would have had no reason to focus on Rod, other than that when Rod spoke up, he figured that Rod had to be the one he was after.

Actually, when I thought about, he could have known which one of us was the one Richard wanted killed, but it would have been difficult for him to ignore Rod, considering what Rod had told him when he came to our table to start trouble. He might have been that he was so confident of his ability with a gun that he figured he could first kill Rod and then start trouble with me and kill me.

One thing is for sure. It was unlikely that he would ever kill another man by drawing against him. It was doubtful that he would still maintain his gun skills after the condition I had left him in. I imagine that his standing among other gunfighters would be pretty low, after I left him with a bleeding ass on the bar room floor. That would probably be a source of jokes for the rest of his life and give him more trouble than his dislocated gun arm.

We finished caring for our horses and walked back to the house. I went up the steps and entered the house while Rod continued on to the bunk house.

Chapter Five - Page 58
A Stitch in Time

Earlene and I were eating breakfast. It was three days since Rod and I had had our little adventure at Post.

"How do you think Rodney is coming along," I inquired. "I haven't had the chance to look in on him for two days now."

"He is making remarkable progress. He credits it to my chicken broth," she answered. "Of course the credit for that lies more with the chicken than with my broth. You do know," she added, I have some secret herbs and spices that I put in it. They were handed down from generation to generation by the witches in my family tree." She laughed and asked me to pass the butter.

"Well, you'd better remember that some of that special spice is for me only," I said, looking at her with what I imagined to be a lecherous look. After a moment I said, "Let's knock on the door and see if he's up to having a cup of coffee with us this morning. We both got up and walked to the door of his room. I rapped on the door, but before I could speak, the door swung open and there stood Rodney, fully dressed and looking a little pale and shaky. His face carried the broad grin that was just like the one he had worn before the shooting.

"Well look at you!" Earlene ran by me and threw her arms around him and gave him a big hug. "Would you look at this, Easy? I think he must have been putting on an act to get out of his share of the work!"

I stepped forward and gave him a big hug and shook his hand. "You sure gave us a scare. Come in here and sit down and drink a cup of coffee with us and let us bring you up to date." I walked along solicitously, but he appeared to need no help.

He sat down at the table and took a sip of the coffee that Earlene placed in front of him. "Well," he said, "Let's skip the small talk and get down to business. Let's talk about what happened, the reasons behind it, what we're going to do about it, and what has already been done!"

We all sat at the table and related to Rodney all of the things that we knew, followed by all of the things that we surmised. We told him of all the precautions that we had taken to protect him from another attempted assassination and about Brad going to England to protect Sir Hampton from believing that his only son was dead. The rest of the citizenry believed him to be dead.

"Rodney, you remember the strange big ranch that we saw at the confluence of the East Branch with the Wandering River? When Earlene and I were accosted by the men who shot you, while we were surveying the South Cedar Breaks pasture, they said that if we didn't know about the Vertical X's ranch, we soon would.

When Rod and I went to Post to see if we could glean any information about the plot to kill you, we stumbled into a hornets nest. We had no more than taken a pitcher of beer to our table and sat down when some gunfighter approached us and asked where we were from and where we were heading. Rod told him we had ridden in from a ways west of there where people were too polite to ask such questions. The man told Rod that his name was Topeka Canton and that in Post, he would ask any question he wanted to and that he expected a lot better answer than he had received from Rod.

"After an exchange of words between him and me, and he was lying on the floor with his bare ass bleeding from a good whipping with his own belt, it is note-worthy that a man stood up at a back table and told someone to go after a doctor. He spoke with a strong English accent. I asked the Englishman his name, and he told me it was Richard Hampton and that he owned the Vertical X's ranch.

"I asked him if the injured man worked for him. He told that he certainly didn't. I asked if the man had worked for him. He wheeled around and stormed out of the saloon and it looked like half the population of Post stormed out behind him."

Rodney was sitting in dumbfounded amazement. "You're telling me that the man said his name was Richard Hampton? Richard Hampton is my cousin and a black sheep of the family. He has been involved in a lot of different schemes to take money from others.

"That could explain a lot. He had as soon have someone killed as swat a fly. The blood of kinship has no meaning what-so-ever to him. We've got to get word to Dad and Brad. He may have already had Dad killed."

I broke in by saying, "Whoa, Kid. Slow down a little. When Brad left here, we were expecting someone to make an attempt on Sir Hampton's life. You can rest assured that Brad and your father will have explored all aspects of the situation. I should not be at all surprised if everyone in England believes your father is already dead. I have been expecting Brad to get back any day now. Don't be surprised if your father is with him."

"Do you really think so? That would be great! You know, if the Richard Hampton you talked to is truly Cousin Richard, he will be laying plans to try to get legal possession of our holdings here in America. I'll tell you one thing! If that is the Richard I know, he will go straight for the jugular."

I gave Rodney a mirthless grin. "I think his attempt on your life was certainly going for the jugular. That is why we are making so much of an effort to keep Richard in the dark about what we have planned as our counter measures. In the meantime, you need to make every effort to get your health back. We might need your marksmanship sooner than you realize."

Rodney smiled wanly. "I didn't know I was so weak. I have only sat here for an hour and I am as weak as a kitten. I wish I could set out in the sunshine and maybe get up and walk around a little."

I scratched my chin, knowing that I should have shaved this morning. "I have an idea. Let's see what you and Earlene think of it. What if we were to keep Rod's crew here working on the bunkhouse and new corrals? We could have Faron hanging around the house over at the EEZ, keeping his eye on the entrance. The three of us could go down to where the Oasis spread starts, for I am trying to figure out what I want to do about the water fall and the water that we are losing that is going back underground across from the water fall.

"Much of the work that Earlene and I would be doing would be sketching and doing some mathematical calculations. We could bring a rocking chair, a hammock and your sleeping bag along. You could loll around in the sun, rest when you wanted to, walk around and even help us with our planning if you wanted to. I think the fresh air and sunshine, plus the chance to do some physical exercise for a few days would do you a world of good.

"At the same time, you could be getting up to speed on what needs to be done. There are two forecasts that I want to make. One is that Brad and Sir Hampton will be here within the next three or four days. The other is that Richard will either try to take control in a court action as the next of kin, or else will try another sneak attack.

"We will be more or less in limbo until Sir Hampton and Brad are here. I have a plan for defending us in court, but I won't go into that until the five of us are able to sit down together and discuss it. I have a feeling that your dad will have some good suggestions in case Richard tries to take control in court."

Earlene had been sitting there listening, without any comments. She said, "I really need to get back into town and see how the bank is coming along. Under the circumstances, I think it best that I stay here until Sir Hampton is present. There is one thing that I think we ought to consider. If Richard were to go into court, the first thing he would do is try to get our assets in the RL&CC shut down to prevent us from using the money, plus freeze our account in the back-up bank in Denver.

"I wonder if we shouldn't consider a large cash withdrawal to hide here on the ranch somewhere, in case they try to bring our operations to a halt while the court action is going on. Whether he won or lost in the court action would be of little consequence if we couldn't pay our hands and were left defenseless against an all-out assault."

"That's a great idea," I said. "One immediate problem is that it would take me away from the ranch when the threat of an attack might be imminent. I would want to have several good men with me, but I would also want to have enough hands here to set up a good defense. I hate not to be here when Sir Hampton arrives, as I think he will. I feel sure Brad will bring him back to help mount a good legal defense."

We sat in silent contemplation for a few minutes. Earlene got up and started a fresh pot of coffee. Rodney looked pale and tired, but resisted my suggestion that he go back to his room and rest.

Earlene poured us fresh coffee and gave us each a slice of dried apple pie. It had been a long morning, but was still too early to eat dinner. When she had sat back down, I said, "I am going to choose half a dozen men from the fencing crew. From them and the crew that we have working at the &RR, I'll take six with me to the bank in Denver. I will use Rod to help me pick the men.

"I will talk to Sheriff Russell and ask him to deputize the remaining half a dozen men. I had rather have him planning the defense than anyone else, since I won't be here. I'll take Rod and the other six men with me to Denver and bring back enough cash to see our entire operation through until this matter is all settled.

"We need to think of a good reason to take so many men with us to Denver. We have to come up with something that won't arouse the suspicions of either the enemy or our own men. Since we can't use the bank, we will have to put the money in a safe, but easily accessed hiding place."

We sat there, mulling over the possibilities.

Earlene said, "Is there anything that we could bring in for Arnold? He is trustworthy to not let the cat out of the bag."

"You're a genius, Earlene! We won't use Arnold, but we can bring in a load of whiskey for Pat Donahue! A load of whiskey would merit a guard. I could go to Denver on business and bring the whiskey back as a favor to Pat."

"That sure might work," Rodney chimed in. "It might seem a little strange, but who has the right to question it? Who will even know it until well after the fact?"

"Well, one thing is for sure. I had better get on into town. Instead of taking Rodney over to the EEZ, we will postpone that until after Sir Hampton and Brad get back. I want to start for Denver early in the morning.

"I turned to Rodney, "Hey Kid, do you think you will be okay without your nurse for several days? It would look strange for me to go to Denver without Earlene coming along." I looked at Earlene and laughed. "Ha-ha, you thought you were going to have to mention that, didn't you? It won't be as much fun with the crowd we will be traveling with, but we still will have a day in Denver together!"

Earlene laughed back. "Yep, you saved me from having to exert my feminine wiles to come along. Of course, the bank officers in Denver probably know me better than they know you. They are going to think it is pretty strange for us to pull out so much money. Maybe we can talk with Mr. DeLan. He is the president of the bank. We could ask him to sort of make it hard for anyone to know we pulled the cash out."

"That sounds good on the surface, but we don't want it to look like we conspired to take money out because of knowing the account might be frozen. The last thing we want is to get in legal trouble, no matter how well intended," I commented.

I stood up abruptly. "I am headed for town. I will stop by and get Rod for company to help pick out the best men. I also want to tell Faron that he is in charge of any actions involving fighting. Earlene, get that sketch you made of where the outbuildings and corrals are going to be. That might be good for Faron to have. He can tell the men where to build next, and pick out the places that would put us in the best defensive posture. Oh, by the way, why don't you put on your glad rags and come along with me?"

Earlene stood up and whirled around in a circle, holding an imaginary skirt as she twirled and made a mock curtsy. "This frock is what I'm going to wear," she said, rubbing her hands down her blue-jean clad hips and thighs.

Two hours later, the team of horses shook the river water from their glistening hair. Rod's horse was tied on behind. "Rod," I said, "Will you check to see if the ranch manager is here in town? If they are, we will wait for you to pick out the men and take them back out to the ranch. If not, I'll appreciate it if you'll go on out to the X-Pan-D and pick them out and bring them back out to the &RR. You might drop by and tell us if you are going on out to the X-Pan-D, for we will get on back to the ranch. We have some business to take care of over on the EEZ."

"Where will I find you if I have to go on out to the X-Pan-D?" asked Rod.

"I'll be at the sheriff's office," I said.

Rod swung his horse toward the RL&CC office in the bank building.

Earlene said to me, "I'll go by the store and tell them I want provisions for eight or ten men for a week. I'll leave the wagon there and walk back to my office. I have some things I need to check, while you're at the sheriff's office." She leaned over and gave me a kiss, and as I jumped from the wagon added "We all ought to eat at the cafe, whether we ride straight back to the ranch or Rod goes on to the X-Pan-D."

"I think I will be through in half an hour. I'll drop by the office when I'm through and we can go to the cafe from there." I said. I headed across the street toward the sheriff's office.

I walked in and found Todd poring over a new batch of wanted posters that had come in on the stage the day before.

Chapter Six - Page 64
Our Ace in the Hole

Todd looked up and waved me toward a chair. "What sorta problem are you fixing to saddle me with this time?" he said, grinning."

"Aw, I just came in here because it was the only place where I knew I could get away from the working world. I wanted to soak up a little peace and quiet," I answered. "Since it isn't noon yet, I figured you'd still be home in bed. What got you up so early? Did Doc Kincaid make you go with him to deliver a baby or something?"

"Did you come in to try to talk me into buying you a drink, or are you just trying to interfere with the hard-working law officers as they apply themselves to their duties?" the sheriff drawled.

"Well, since I realize the utter impossibility of talking you into buying the drink, I guess I might as well get down to business." I proceeded to outline my plan, and how I hoped that he and his office could help out.

Todd had some good ideas and when I left a little later, we had what seemed to me to be a good plan of action.

I walked along leading my horse, headed for my office in the bank building where I was planning on meeting Earlene. I was a little surprised to see that Rod was already waiting for me in Earlene's office.

"Did you get us a crew put together?" I asked him.

"Not only did I get a crew together, but I had them ride upriver a ways before they crossed over and headed toward the &RR. No one will see them headed there. I left my horse tied to the wagon down at Paddy's store," he answered.

The three of us headed for the cafe. Half an hour later, the wagon was headed back toward the &RR ranch.

I gave the men the rest of the day off to check their gear and prepare for the long ride to Denver. I had to admire Rod's ability to pick out a good crew, for they were all capable looking men. Their weapons were clean and well oiled; they hung in a business-like way on the men who wore them.

Rod had added one man whom he used as a cook. The man was still fully able to do other tasks, but an old injury made it painful for him to spend the day in the saddle. The supplies were transferred from my wagon into an old trail wagon with a tailgate that could be used by the cook.

We started off bright and early while the dew blanketed the grass and the stars were still twinkling in a brilliant display in the clear early morning air. There was the faintest lightening in the eastern sky, and the men had their collars pulled snugly around their throats in the chill air.

We rode east and had not met a single person when the sun pushed its way over the horizon, just as we climbed the old buffalo trail to the high plains and struck off across the grassy plain, following the faint trail to Denver. We stopped and ate breakfast when the sun was two hours high at a clear stream that ran from the mountains that arose on our west and where a minor trail from the main trail over Raton Pass had cut west.

That night, we made camp by a stream that might have been the same one that we had breakfasted by that morning. We set a watch around the remuda and to guard the camp from Indians and renegade whites.

The cook got up as the last watch went out and prepared breakfast. We ate at nearly the same time as we saddled up and hitched the supply wagon. We were fifteen miles further down the trail as the sun came up. It wasn't long after that when the men begin to peel off their jackets.

Rod and I rode out ahead of the wagon, with him angling off to the right and me to the left. Then we each circled back toward the trail. We stopped and chatted for a few minutes and then repeated our pattern as the wagon approached. I looked far ahead and saw a small group of people approaching us. There were three men riding behind a buggy. Two more horses were tied on behind the buggy, which was pulled by a team. Two men were riding in the buggy. While they were two or three miles ahead of us, they must have seen us. Apparently they weren't interested in socializing, for they swung wide to our left. A few minutes later, they disappeared into a slight draw in the prairie and were out of sight.

Rod had seen them too, and as soon as they disappeared from sight, galloped toward me. I put my horse into the direction that would intercept the group, short loping my horse so Rod would catch me as I waved him on to join me. We dismounted and led our horses as we approached the crest of the hill, and walked forward until we saw the tops of the men's heads as their horses trotted along the slope of the draw.

I pulled out my binoculars and focused in on the group, as we cautiously approached, hats in hand to make us less apt to be highlighted against the sun. We were close enough to allow me to see the features of two of the men. They were strangers to me. I swung my glasses ahead to the buggy. It was occupied by two strangers also, although one of them appeared to be a girl and the other a man old enough to be her father.

Suddenly I swung my glasses back to the third man. My hunch was right. It was Brad!

"Let's mount up," I said to Rod. "Let's ride in with our hands on our saddle horn. I am quite sure that I know who those people are.

"That must be Brad. You may have met him before. He was in Denver on business and said that he might bring guests with him when he came back. I don't know any of them except Brad."

We rode over the crest of the swell in the land and started down the slope. We were spotted immediately, and I saw the sun glint on Brad's binoculars. I raised my hat above my head and swung it slowly from side to side. I knew it would be hard for Brad to recognize me as he was looking nearly into the sun. I turned Calliope sideways so he would have a chance to recognize the horse. He turned toward the rest of the group and apparently said something to them; then he galloped toward us.

We walked our horses toward him, still keeping our hands on the saddle horns, in case he was still unsure as to whom we were. A minute later, he pulled up in front of us with a broad smile on his face.

"Howdy, Pilgrim," I greeted him. "Brad, this man is the acting foreman of the &RR and EEZ. This is Rod Lasser. Rod, this is Brad Rogers. He and Earlene own the &RR. He is my father-in-law and is on the board of directors of the RL&CC.

The two men shook hands and I turned to Rod. "Rod, would you mind going back and getting our group under way again. I imagine they stopped when they saw us gallop together out of sight. They're probably all set for a fight. I'll bring you up to date when I finish talking to Brad. I'll catch up with you in a few minutes. I want to meet the guests."

"You bet," Rod replied. I'll continue to ride ahead and keep my eye on things."

"I appreciate it, Rod." I turned back to Brad and we walked our horses back toward the buggy.

"Brad, what if anything do those men you have, know about the situation?"

"Easy, they don't know anything except that they were hired as guards. The man and girl in the buggy are Sir Hampton and his secretary, Cynthia. Cynthia is his niece, and she doesn't know anything either."

"That is the main reason I sent Rod back to the wagon. He doesn't know anything, although he is a truly good man and is nobody's fool. He can add two and two as well as anyone I know.

"Here is what we have so far. We are headed for Denver to draw a substantial amount of money from the bank. This is in case our bank accounts are frozen by a court action. I have some selected men from our hands along for a guard. However, they have no idea that we are going after something of value. They do know that we are on a high alert, with another selected group working on corrals and a bunk house at the &RR.

"We will have a pow-wow as soon as we get back. I want us to move Rodney to the EEZ as soon as I return. He needs the chance to get out in the fresh air and recover from his wounds. I want him and his father to be able to talk and visit and they have a better chance over on the EEZ.

"There is a whole lot of information you need to have, but I'll save that for when we get back from Denver. It will take a while to go over it all and I want all of us owners of the RL&CC to sit in on it. I imagine that you will want to tell Sir Hampton what we are doing by going to Denver and the reason the money will have to be hidden and guarded on one of our ranches."

"You bet," Brad assured me. "Let me introduce you and then we can both be on our way," Brad continued as we pulled up at the buggy.

Brad introduced me to Sir Hampton and Cynthia. When our visit was cut so short, I saw the knowledge in Sir Hampton's eyes that something was afoot. I shook hands with Sir Hampton, tipped my hat to Cynthia, and turned and galloped back to the wagon.

When I arrived at the wagon, I got a drink of water. I actually had come back to the wagon to invite Earlene to ride out with me. She rode around the side of the wagon and I leaned over and kissed her. Without words, we both rode off in my normal swing out to the left and then forward. Rod was covering the right hand side.

I told Earlene of the arrival of Sir Hampton and his secretary, and of our decision to wait until we had returned from Denver with the money to have a meeting to formulate our next moves.

We arrived in Denver and went to our meeting with the banker. We requested that he keep our transaction absolutely secret, for we didn't want any leaks that would let anyone know we had fifty thousand dollars in the RB&T in Vacaville. We told him of the attempted robbery of the bank and the killing of Rodney Hampton. He assured us that no one but him would know of the large withdrawal.

We pulled our wagon up to the Mercantile to buy some supplies that were not readily available in Vacaville. The supplies included twenty cases of canned goods, along with eighty cases of assorted whiskey for Pat Donahue. Divided between eight of the cases of canned goods, we had eight bags of gold. Each weighed just over twenty pounds. That was near the weight of the other cases. We placed them with the cases of canned goods, evenly distributed in the bed of the wagon. This gave an even floor for the other supplies to rest on, including two new easy chairs and a rocker. We placed a canvas over the load and Rod went by the saloon, rousted out the rest of the men and we started back toward Vacaville.

We passed an uneventful night after stopping well after dark and started off early in the morning. We ate a quick breakfast of crackers and sardines, and finished up with a can of peaches for each person.

We made camp within a long day's travel of home that night. We got up the next morning and saw a bank of dark clouds low in the northern sky. An unseasonably warm wind blew in from the south to meet the cold front. The cloud bank gained on us and the warm wind from the south gained force. A short time later, the bank of scudding gray clouds swept over us and abruptly the wind changed to the north with the bite of the arctic in its snarling teeth.

I reached back and untied my sheepskin coat from the back of my saddle. I tied a long scarf over the top of my hat and passed the ends under my chin to protect my ears and most of my neck, face and throat. I replaced my tight leather work gloves with wool gloves, covered by loose leather gloves and rode on in comfort.

Every two or three loops I rode around the right front quadrant of our line of travel, I would ride in to the wagon to check on things. Rod and I had changed our positions, with the one who had ridden on the left now on the right, and vice versa. This kept each of us on the side we were familiar with, with me being on the side toward the mountains and Rod on the side that consisted of the rolling plains.

I found Earlene all bundled up. She said, "I hope you don't think you and Rod are the only ones that get to ride off in the balmy sunshine, away from all the responsibilities of the wagon!"

"Sure, sure," I replied. "It is like a trip to a south sea island, with all of the beautiful flora and fauna. The bees droning lazily around the Sage and making their heavily laden way back to their hives. It's easy to see why you want to get in on the fun part of our trip."

"Have you seen any good picnic spots? I thought you and I might stop and have a little private picnic, but this tropical breeze might pose a problem if we started shedding all these layers of clothes so we could er, uh, sunbathe for a while." She gave her mischievous smile as she spoke.

"That sure is a temping little scenario you have set up, Sweet Baby, but I have a premonition that this isn't going to be as smooth a trip back as it was when we were coming." I broke off talking as I saw Rod come galloping in from the direction of a rather high hill back behind us and off to the east a mile.

"Hey, Easy. How are you, Earlene? He touched his hand to the brim of his tied down hat. "There is a group of about twenty men coming up behind us. It strikes me as odd that such a large group of men are out and about in this weather. I can't figure out where they would be heading, and I can't understand why they are in such a hurry. I don't know of any place around here where they could be going."

"You've got a good point. How far back are they?" I had a feeling that whatever had them out and coming hell for leather in this direction had to do with us.

"My guess is that they're about five miles back. It takes the telescope to see them. If they have us in mind, they have a mighty curious idea of battle tactics to choose today to carry it out, with the blizzard beginning. Either that, or they know something that they shouldn't." He gave me the ghost of a grin as he said that last sentence.

"Rod, I'm going to have to put you to predicting the weather or telling our fortunes, the way you can read the cards so well. You are right on the money. I think the cutoff toward Raton Pass is just on the other side of that double peaked hill. I believe we will turn off toward the pass and see if they do the same." The air was beginning to fill with small, stinging snow that was a cross between snow and sleet.

"We'll go about a mile and a half and swing back toward the old buffalo trail to the lower plains. Earlene, you and I will just stay here on top of that double peaked hill. Rod, you'll ride back and have the wagon speed up a mite. Swing the party off on the Raton Pass trail when you get to it. Swing our party down that trail and then loop them back toward the old Buffalo Trail.

"As soon as Earlene and I see which way they turn, we will cut across and intercept you. If they are following us, we will know for sure if they turn off and then swing back where you do. When we were on our way to Denver, I saw a good place to fort up out of the wind. If they double back after us, we will head for the place to fort up."

Rod thought for a moment. "As thick as the snow is getting, if they follow us off toward the pass, they won't be able to see where we swing back. It might be that we can make sure they don't see where we double back and they will go straight on. If they do that, we might can head on for the lower plains before we are snowed in and stranded. It might be a good idea to ride all night until we get back to the ranch."

"That's just what we will do," I replied. "Remind me to tell you how glad we are to have you on the team, Rod. If they do double back, we may just set half of them afoot in the snow. I think that might blunt their attack."

Rod grinned through the swirling snow. "Remind me to tell you how glad I am to be on the team, Easy." He touched his brim to Earlene and turned and galloped back toward the wagon.

There was no use in Earlene and me going up to the crest of the double peaked hill. We weren't going to be able to see anything better from there, the way the snow was falling. We rode west of the trail for fifty yards and into a small, but dense little copse of trees. It broke the force of the wind somewhat, and we could just barely make out the junction in the trails. Getting off our horses, we huddled together and waited for the wagon to pass.

A few minutes later, our wagon arrived and swung off to the left. In a surprisingly short time that I estimated to be half an hour, the group of men who were behind us arrived. They pulled up for a minute while two men got off their horses and examined the trail. It was obvious that they were trailing us, for they would have automatically known which way to go if they had a set destination in mind.

One of the men was sweeping the snow from the ground and apparently saw enough to know which way to go, for they charged off down the trail toward Raton Pass. The snow was falling so hard that I considered it highly unlikely that they would see where our wagon turned off. They would feel there was no reason to turn off before descending the pass. However, they appeared to be a determined bunch, so we would have to check to make sure.

"Okay, Earlene, this is our chance to ride through those balmy breezes you were talking about. We are going to have our own hands full finding the wagon in this storm. We can try following along behind the bunch until we feel like we have passed the point where the wagon turned off. We will be taking a chance that we can be seen, so we will have hang back to a point where we can just barely keep in contact."

"Yeah, I'm not as afraid of being seen as I am in being unable to find the trail to the lower plains. If we do find the trail, it will be hard to be sure whether we are ahead of our wagon or behind it." She brushed the snow from her nose and grinned. "At least, I get to share some of that tropical sunshine with you."

"Yeah, don't you though? Hold it! We're getting a little close to the bunch we're trailing. I feel confident that we have passed the place where the wagon turned off. Rod would be afraid to go much further, for fear the bunch that is trying to follow the wagon would catch them before they could turn off and allow the snow to cover their tracks."

While we had talked, the bunch ahead of us had disappeared into the snow. We reined our horses into a hundred and forty five degree turn to the right. That should take us back near the south side of the double peaked hill. We quartered across the wind, with its force half way behind us and half against our right cheeks, and put our horses into a slow lope.

I wanted to make sure that our angle of return was plenty acute, so we would be sure to hit the trail behind the wagon. I figured that Rod would take the wagon far enough down trail to be sure we came onto the trail behind him and then stop and wait for us to catch up. If we didn't catch up within an hour, I knew he would head on down trail to try to at least get to the lower plains where there would be shelter from the wind, behind the Rimrock.

I was right. I knew where the trail was by the double peaked hill, which jutted up just on the north side of where we had cut off on the

Raton Pass trail. Finding the old buffalo trail which led to the lower plains was easy. Following it was a horse of a different color. I remembered that the wind had been directly behind us when we were arriving at the cutoff to the pass. I put the wind directly behind us and started down trail.

Suddenly our horses stopped and pranced sideways, as though baffled. I was beginning to dismount to see what the problem was when I heard the muffled sound of shouting. A second later, a figure loomed out of the snowy darkness to our right. It was Rod. He had stopped the wagon just to the left of the trail and tied several lariats together. One end was tied to the wagon wheel. He had ridden his horse about sixty feet past the trail. He held the rope loosely in his hand, after passing it in a half loop around his saddle horn so as to let the horse take the strain of holding it taut. When our horse walked into it, the rope gave by sliding through his hands so as not to trip or injure a horse. It also let him know that we were passing, and gave him a chance to shout to us to keep us from riding on past.

They had been waiting about twenty minutes. The cook had made some coffee on a small kerosene stove and we all had a cup of hot coffee and a biscuit with cheese and bacon. Riding closely together to be sure no one would get lost; we started on through the blizzard. Most of us got off our horses and walked to keep our feet a little warmer.

It seemed as though we were motionless, for the small envelope of visibility moved along with us as we traveled. I estimated it to be about three in the morning as we started down the grade to the lower plains. The snow had begun to peter out and ended as we got to the lower level.

The visibility was still very low as we started along the Rimrock. About three miles along, we came to one of the little indentations into the Rimrock. Having the wagon wait for us, I walked in, leading Calliope, to see how things looked. Earlene saw me start off and quickly caught up with me. We walked along near the perimeter.

The opening was only about twenty five paces deep and half that in width. We found a place where a pile of dead Mesquite wood had washed down from the high plains. We were well sheltered from the wind. I jumped onto Calliope and galloped back to the wagons and had them follow me back.

Earlene had some wood in a pile and was ready to light it. The cook jumped down from the wagon and poured a little coal oil onto the wood and it immediately blazed up as Earlene touched a match to it.

She had built the fire under an overhang that nearly formed a cave. The fire was far enough out from the wall to allow us to all put our bedrolls down. The heat reflected back from the wall and made it quite comfortable for people who were used to roughing it.

"Okay, you waddies! Come and get it. We have plenty of hot coffee and cold sandwiches!" The men took their cups and sandwiches back to where they were sitting around the fire. I heard one man say, in a low voice, "If I could take her into my bedroll, I would stay here until roundup next spring." He nodded his head toward Earlene.

Rod said, "I want you to all pay attention to what I say. If I ever hear anyone make such a remark or do anything that is disrespectful of Earlene, I will either kill you or skin you alive. I don't care if you are joking; you'd better save that kind of joking for the saloon or a whore house. This is the first, last and only warning there will be on that account."

The young fellow who had made the remark started to respond, but a glance at Rod made him hold his tongue. Everyone was tired from the long walk and exhausted by the cold. They drank their coffee in silence. One man got up and started to spread out his bedroll when the young man spoke up again.

"Listen," he began, keeping his voice low. "I am talking to all of you, but especially to you, Rod. I am as sorry as it is possible to be about my previous remark. It was thoughtless and there is no excuse for it, but I can't un-say it. I wish that I could take it back, but all I can ask is that all of you forget it, for it will never happen again."

Rod nodded at him. "That's good enough for me, and I want it to be good enough for the rest of you. Now get some sleep. I'm going to keep my eye on the camp for a couple of hours and then I want to be relieved for an hour before we start on back to the ranch. Anyone want to volunteer?"

The cook told him, "Rod, I'll keep my eyes open while I fix coffee before we start on. I'll be getting up about five, anyway."

"No," said Rod, "I want someone to be putting their attention on watching, not cooking. I thank you for volunteering though."

One of the men stood up and told Rod, "Wake me up in an hour. You'll only have an hour to rest yourself before we're back in the saddle. I'll split the time with you."

"I appreciate it, Malo." Rod got up and walked to the entrance of the cul-de-sac to accustom his eyes to the darkness.

I was sitting on my bedroll on the other side of the wagon. Their voices had been reflected right into my ears from the rocky wall. I looked over at Earlene and said, "As much as I want to feel that warm body of yours, it somehow doesn't seem right for me to dangle candy in front of hungry men."

"Well, Easy, I'm not all that offended by the remark. The fellow that said it didn't know he was being heard by us, and he received a little education from Rod. If I'm gonna be a rancher more so than a housewife, I know that I will hear some rough language from time to time." She placed her other hand on top of the hand I had been holding. "Easy, when I said that I was a rancher, more so than a housewife, I sure didn't mean more so than a wife. If it were up to me, and we didn't have this audience, we would be warming up this cul-de-sac so much that the snow would be melted from here back to Denver!"

I grinned at her and replied, "I know that, Sweet Baby. I would say that we will make up for it when we get home, but I think that you'll agree, that once we miss one of our sweet sessions, it is gone and can't be made up for. Everything we do in the future we will be doing without worrying about making up for what we missed in the past. As far as that goes, I fervently miss every time that we missed from that day we met at our oasis until the day we first knew one another without reserve. We have missed very few times since then, and I promise you that I hope this is the last time that we ever do miss."

Earlene presented her warm lips, and then said a couple of minutes later, "I promise you that I will do my best to make your last statement realized. We had better lie down or whether you are dangling candy in front of the others or not, this will be one night that we don't miss."

-=-

We drank a hot cup of coffee and ate another biscuit and bacon sandwich, which we munched as we rode out of the cul-de-sac and started down the Rimrock toward home. I had the wagon move out onto the prairie a mile from the Rimrock. I figured there was a chance there would be snipers along the Rimrock, since they knew where we had to go to get home. I hoped they had followed the false lead we had given them all the way down Raton Pass.

The air was frigid, but the sun shone brightly from a cloudless sky.

With our warm clothing, we were plenty comfortable. The clouds of vapor rising from the horses' mouths were testament to the low temperature.

"As soon as we get back to the ranch, I want to make a rope ladder and secure it on top of the Rimrock, so it will be easy for us to keep a lookout posted up above until this problem blows over," I remarked to Earlene.

"I think that's a good idea, especially along the north wall of the EEZ. It would be a lot more trouble for someone to ride all the way around to the south wall of the &RR. It would be impossible for someone to cross over to the area between the &RR and the EEZ. Don't you agree? Earlene asked.

"That's the way I see it," I answered. "I think we ought to build a way up to the high plains somewhere along the north wall of the EEZ. We need to be able to ride to Denver and points north and east like Omaha without having to ride to Post to get up to the high plains. However we were to do it, it would be hard for us to defend ourselves against one or a whole gang of sharpshooters along the north wall. Even with a way up, we would be unable to use it if it were guarded. One man could hold it against an army. It would take hours to ride to the old buffalo trail to get to the top, and even that could be guarded. We would have to make a way to get up and down on the desert side, so we could use the way up at the end of the &RR and down into the Oasis pasture of the EEZ and ride out the opening into the desert and back up to the top of the Rimrock, by some created or newly discovered trail."

-=-

Brad and Sir Hampton had both been surprised by their encounter with Easy and his crew headed for Denver, as they, themselves, had been on their way from Denver back to the ranch. When Brad had a chance, he asked Sir Hampton if he wanted to take a little ride with him.

"Well, old chap, it's been a long time since I've straddled a horse," said Sir Hampton. "I quit riding the hounds some years back. Felt sorry for the poor foxes, doncha know? However, I would surely enjoy the opportunity to put my rear-end against something other than that buggy seat. Perhaps I should start accustoming myself to riding. After all, I am one of the principals in a ranch of no mean size. It is never too late to be a cowboy, don'cha know?" His engaging grin at Brad elicited this response.

"Well, Sir Hampton, if you like to ride, you will sure have plenty of space to do it in, until that rear-end you spoke of is as hard as the saddle it polishes. The RL&CC has nearly half a thousand square miles under fence and the potential to put a lot more remains, but the window of opportunity is closing."

"Brad, I sense that you asked me to come on the ride for more than a chance to give me a little exercise. What was the important message that Easy was carrying?"

"You are right about me having a message from Easy. Now I won't get bogged down in a long story unless you want to hear it. I'll just give you the grist from the mill."

Sir Hampton shifted in his saddle and said, "I think I want to hear the story from the start. It will help me to have a better grasp of the situation."

"Okay, here is what I know. There are a lot of things that have transpired since I left for London. You will probably find them out at the same time I do.

"Easy and one of his men rode over to Post the other day. Post is a town east of Vacaville. It is located just on top of the Rimrock on the only known trail to the high plains for at least one hundred miles. They went into a saloon to see if they could pick up any clues as to what had happened and to get an idea of what was going to happen in the future. Without a known reason, a gunfighter tried to pick a fight with him. Well, actually he didn't know which of the two men, Easy or the man with him was the man he wanted to kill. He was with the same man as when we met them on the trail, named Rod Lasser.

"The gunfighter tried to pick a fight. After Easy left him bleeding on the floor, a man who had been seated at the same table as the gunfighter stood up and sent a man after a doctor. Then the man, who spoke with a heavy English accent, asked Easy his name. Easy asked him who he was. He said his name was Richard Hampton and that he owned the Vertical X's ranch. He stormed out of the bar, with half the men following him." Brad stopped talking and stood up in his stirrups and took a look around.

"By Jove man, exclaimed Sir Hampton! "I've a nephew named Richard Hampton!"

"Well, I hate to be the one to break the news to you, but he seems to be on the wrong trail now. What do you make of all this?"

"I'm not one to get overly excited before all of the facts are in, but at first glance it appears you are correct." He started to say more, but the sound of a galloping horse cut off his speech. It was Cynthia, riding as if born to the saddle.

She pulled to a halt alongside of us and said, "Excuse me for interrupting your conversation, but the cook said if you don't come and eat, he's going to throw it all out. He's a rather testy individual, don't you think?"

Brad laughed and answered, "No, that's just the way of a trail cook. A good one can get by with some pretty cantankerous ways in cow country. The best hands won't go on a trail drive that has a bad cook. One thing they make sure of is that they don't get the cook upset with them, or they will be eating weevilly beans for as much as several months at a time."

"What on earth is a trail drive?" Cynthia looked at Brad.

Sir Hampton broke in. "Perhaps we'd better get back to the buggy and eat. We sure don't want an angry trail cook, do we now?" As he reined his horse back toward where the buggy had pulled up, Cynthia jumped her horse into a gallop.

"It would be hard to believe that girl would be mixed up in any kind of a swindle." Brad spoke softly, but Sir Hampton heard him.

"I am sure in my own mind that she has no complicity in what is going on. Never-the-less, I think we should stick with our need to know policy. I am convinced in my own mind that the Richard Hampton you mentioned is indeed my nephew. He has always had the feeling that he was shorted, since his father lost much of their money when a ship loaded with their cargo went down in the Indian Ocean. He has been pretty unscrupulous in his attempts to recoup the losses, especially since his father, who was my brother in law, was lost at sea on another separate voyage.

"He was trying to corner the market on some of the more popular spices and was pushing his luck to the limit. The ship that went down with a cargo of his spices and severely damaged his finances was overloaded. The same mistake contributed to his death on the second ship, for it was carrying far more cargo than it was designed to carry.

"Richard seemed to go through a transformation nearly over night. It is rumored that he has been mixed up in some pretty raw deals, some of which have had unseemly deaths attached to them. It is hard to believe that he would kill his own cousin for a shot at the possible riches to be gained. It goes without saying that for it to do him any good, I will also have to meet up with an untimely death.

"There has been talk before that some of the magistrates involved in court actions involving his schemes have been bribed. I think we need to make sure that the same doesn't happen in this case." Sir Hampton broke off talking as they arrived at the buggy and dismounted to eat.

After they had grabbed a quick sandwich, Cynthia approached them again. "Uncle Edward, do you think there is a chance that Brad can show me some more of the American west and explain how such a large assemblage of land is run?"

Sir Hampton smiled fondly at her and said, "There he is, Cynthia. Why don't you ask him?"

Cynthia turned toward Brad and flashed a bright and happy smile. "Okay, Cowboy! Will you show a poor London girl the ways of the west?"

Brad's heart did a little flip as the full warmth of Cynthia's smile hit him. However, he made sure to himself that he remembered that someone, and perhaps several someones had conspired to kill Rodney; perhaps those same someones were conspiring at this moment to kill Easy, Earlene, Sir Hampton and himself with the intent to gain possession of hundreds of square miles of land, already fenced and having improved grasses seeded as he was riding with this beautiful and talented girl.

"Sure! I seldom have such a pretty companion to ride with," he answered.

"Thank you, kind sir. That implies that you usually have company when you ride. Forgive me for being so bold, but are they Indian girls or girls from the small ranchers that I understand you were instrumental in helping?

"I forgive your boldness, but I never kiss and tell," Brad replied. He saw a blush sweep across her lovely face as she urged her horse into a canter. He also noted a little smile crease her lips.

-=-

Cynthia had never seen such expanses of land before. It rivaled the ocean itself. She had never experienced such a feeling of freedom. She stood up in her stirrups and turned her head as far as she could. To her left were the slight undulations of the prairie. That same prairie stretched as far as she could see before her and in a semi-circle around to as far as she could turn her head to the left. She turned her face back to the right. In the right front one could see the prairie stretching off toward the blue line of mountains. To the right rear, the same brown grass turned blue with distance and was again framed by the line of mountains.

Her greatest interest lay straight to her right. It was the capable man who rode the galloping horse as though he were a centaur. He was definitely different from any other man she had ever met, and was someone that her Uncle Edward seemed to respect and hold in high esteem. When he turned his head toward her and grinned, it was definitely more than the motion of the horse under her saddle that warmed her.

Never had she seen such a man before. She had read that the American West was a lawless land, with six-shooters part of the normal attire in the frontier towns and in the lands that lay far beyond the nearest town. However, the six-shooter strapped to Brad's lean waist seemed as natural as his boots, his blue denim pants and shirt, or the soft, faded bandana that framed his tanned and muscular throat.

In London he had been reminiscent of a regal lion in the cage of a zoo, out of its element but still a lion. Here, he was still the lion, but a lion turned free, master of all he surveyed. She involuntarily pictured him, his pride of lionesses ringing him as though he were the jewel, enclosed by their tawny bodies as though they were the setting of the ring where he strode.

She thought of herself as one of his harem and a heat spread through her body and she tightened her legs against the saddle she straddled, welcoming its warming friction against her body.

She sneaked a glance at him and surprised him looking her over. Her face flushed under her thoughts and the flush spread throughout her body in a wave of heat and desire. His look did nothing to cool the heat she felt inundating her body.

-=-

Richard Hampton felt a great elation. One of his men had just come back from Post with the mail. There, among all of the other letters, circulars and solicitations was a letter from London. It contained a single sentence, "I regret to inform you that your Uncle Edward was lost at sea as he traveled to India on business." The note was unsigned and there was no return address. This was of no importance to Richard. He knew who it was from and he knew that it was by far the most important element of his plans.

He had purchased the Vertical X's brand by mortgaging all that was left of his father's estate. He owed the money to a loan shark who would be very unhappy if he defaulted on the payments. Richard didn't want to contemplate the methods the loan shark utilized when someone defaulted on a loan to him. The only way he could cash in on this, the biggest gamble of his life, was to carry through on his plans. He would become rich again if he succeeded. He would be dead if he didn't.

He had just been saved the risk of killing his Uncle Edward in London. What a great stroke of providence! Now that he was in America, far from the people who might have heard the rumors about his activities in England, he would put the rest of his plan into action.

He rejoiced in his wisdom in culturing a friendship with the circuit judge who handled court cases in this region of the territory. These local hicks would be unable to compete with him in a court of law. He rubbed his hands together, and his broad smile nearly succeeded in hiding the savage cunning that he usually kept well masked.

Chapter Seven - Page 81
Lawyers and Marshals

Earlene, Brad, Rodney, Sir Hampton and I were seated around the table in the &RR ranch house. We were discussing our probable next moves in anticipation of the moves of our unknown enemy, although it seemed a certainty that it was Richard Hampton.

Sir Hampton started the conversation. "First, I think that since we are all equal members of the board of the RL&CC, and since our joint enterprise is here in America, we should start off by all getting on a first name basis. I am not hung up on all of the protocol that exists in England, so I propose that you all refer to me as Edward. In fact, I insist that you do. Each of us respects the other, and there is no use for any one of us to be addressed any differently than the others.

"With that said, I think that Brad and I should bring you all up to date on what steps that we have taken, since Brad arrived in England up to the time we all sat down at this table. Brad, would you like to begin?"

Brad studied for a moment. "No, since you are more familiar with the circumstances surrounding the time we had our conversation in London, prior to leaving, you should bring everyone up to date on things until we got off the river boat. I can take over from there."

Sir Edward nodded. "Before we get down to business, I would like to comment on one thing. We have agreed to keep everything on a need to know basis. However, we are pretty well isolated out here on the ranch, and I would like to propose that we let Cynthia set in on our meetings. Not only is it awkward for me to leave my right hand out of these meeting, but she has a very good knowledge of law, as well as being well educated in the accounting profession. Above all, she has an acute mind.

"I realize that since the theory you developed about the potential of someone wishing to take over the holdings we have here has pretty well been borne out by the appearance of Richard, my nephew, into the mix. That makes it even more necessary to proceed with caution. Since we know that some of my kin is involved with the attempted murder of Rodney here, we can exercise caution by making sure there is no opportunity for her to speak in private with anyone who can pass the plan that we will develop alone to an enemy.

"Taking all of that into consideration, I will still make the proposal that we call Cynthia into the conversation. However, if you should vote against it, I will accept that in good spirit."

Rodney cleared his throat so we would all know that he was going to speak. "The way I look at it, and I am the one who is supposedly dead from Richard's orders, I vote to let Cynthia into this council. I grew up around Cousin Cynthia. She is ten or twelve years older than I am, but she was always kind and would tell me fables accenting the importance of loyalty, social morality and kindness.

"She never was the kind of person to seek riches or a higher station in life. She would often talk of her belief that each person should stand on their own principles without being swayed by desires of one's own or by peer pressure."

"Earlene, what about you? I respect a woman's intuition and I beg of you all not to be swayed by my own opinion," said Edward.

"In a case like this, I believe we should exercise caution, but I know that we will all have dealings in the future. We will want to have good relations between all of us. I vote that she sit in on our discussions." Earlene started to add something, but then nodded toward her father."

Brad said, "I probably know Cynthia better than any of we three Americans. I know that the questions she would ask me showed not only an inquisitive mind, but an amazing grasp of the significance of the answer. She would ask me such questions as, "Well, why don't they do this or why do they do that? I have a lot of faith in her, based on the part of her that I have seen. I have to vote yes, and I am the one who first insisted that she be kept in the dark."

"Okay, Easy, it all comes down to you. What have you got to say?" Edward nodded toward me.

"I say that we should bring her in now. Edward, I think that you should walk outside where she is sitting on the front porch, and tell her that you had felt you had no right to bring her into a board meeting without the agreement of the board. Let her know that the decision was unanimous that she join us."

Edward showed no signs that it bothered him to have someone suggest that he do something. He walked out the front door onto the porch. We heard voices for a minute and then the two of them walked back in together. It was the first chance that we had all had to sit down together.

"Okay, I suggest we get down to business," I began. "Here is the way I see it. I expect any time from this minute on, we should be expecting to be notified that a legal hold has been made on both the ranch and the bank. It would not surprise me if Todd or one of his men is on the way out, even as I speak, with a court summons to appear in court and show cause why Richard should not take possession of both Edward's and Rodney's shares in our enterprise.

"From the thought that has gone into setting up the death of Rodney, and my conjecture that it is only the fact that Edward is presumed dead from his ship sinking that has prevented an attack on Sir Edward Hampton in London. I am sure the attempt would have been successful, for it is easy to walk up and killing an unsuspecting man.

"This is what I think we should do. This plan will have to be adjusted as we go along, for I have set up a hypothetical situation. It might be completely wrong. Let me go all of the way though it before we make comments. Earlene brought some pads from the office. We'll give each of you one so you can make notes or write questions as we go along."

The pads were already on the table, along with pencils. When they were passed around the table, I began again.

"First, I am proceeding on the assumption that our adversary is very smart and will have made a big effort to not only try to foresee everything that we might do, but to prepare ammunition that far exceeds what he feels he needs to take possession of the RL&CC. I want to enumerate these points so it will be easier for us to find the part that pertains to any questions you have asked or comments you wish to make."

I noted that Cynthia had taken a pad also.

I began to tick the points off, one at a time, by saying:

1. "I believe we will be summoned into court to show cause as to why Richard should not take over the RL&CC.

2. I think it is very likely that he doesn't know that we all have equal voting rights.

3. I expect him to have a forged will showing that he is next in line to inherit all of Edward's assets, right behind Rodney.

4. He believes he has killed Rodney and by now knows that Edward is supposedly lost at sea, so he would then believe himself to be the heir, through his false will.

5. It is possible that he will try to blame Rodney's murder on Brad, Earlene, and me to attempt to remove us from the picture.

6. I have a feeling that he will have attempted to bribe the judge

who will be trying the case.

"As I have already said, we will have to adapt ourselves to what actually happens."

Cynthia said, "Excuse me, but I have taken all of those points down. Would you like for me to read them back, one point at a time, so they could each be discussed?"

I looked at Cynthia in disbelief. "How in the world could you have taken all the points down that I just enumerated?"

Cynthia laughed and said, "I take shorthand. I can write it down about as fast as you can say it." She held up her pad for us to see, but it just looked like a bunch of squiggly lines to me.

Edward grinned, but made no comment. I could see that Earlene was impressed to see such a thing. For some strange reason, Brad had a look on his face that nearly looked like pride.

"Great," I said. "Does anyone want to say something before we get into the possible steps we will take to counter these possibilities?" I paused and looked around the table.

Cynthia started to say something, but then stopped.

"What was it you started to say, Cynthia? We want to have as broad a picture of things as possible. This is a critical time for us." I watched her a moment and said, "Come on, Cynthia. Speak up!"

"There are two reasons that make me reluctant to continue. One of them is that I am not a member of the board. The other is that what I have to say is of an accusatory nature, lodged against someone whom is not here to defend himself."

"First," I said, "You are an extension of your uncle, as his most trusted aide. Secondly, this can easily be a life or death situation. Despite that, any information derived from anyone in this room is only to guide us, not to be a trial of anyone mentioned. We are each and every one deliberate and unbiased until we see actual irrefutable facts that make us form an opinion about anyone."

Cynthia looked at each of and said, "I often have lunch with Richard in London. I thought that it was just someone talking. You know how it is when you are just using someone for a sounding board? Richard has several times said things to me, in what I thought to be a joking manner, "Hey Cynthia, you and I ought to get together and form our own company. It might sort of bruise our reputations, but I think I know how we could get us a company just like this one. You know how to run such a company, and I have the lack of scruples to do what is necessary to take over some company. What do you think?"

I always laughed at him and said something like, "I'm perfectly happy doing what I do now, working with Uncle Edward."

"He would say something like, "Cousin Cynthia, we might find more in common than just a business. You are a beautiful woman with connections. I have a lot of connections that are becoming a little tarnished. Some of my connections allow me to get things done that none of your connections would think of. Haven't you ever heard of kissing cousins?" He would always laugh when he said that, but I could see a little more than a joke in what he was saying. This past year, it seems there has been a sort of desperation in his jokes."

"Thanks a lot Cynthia. I can see why you were hesitant to speak up. I assure you that everything you have said will be erased from our memories, if we are wrong in our assessment of what is happening. It is even possible that this is not the same Richard Hampton."

I looked around the table and waited a second. No one said anything, and I continued, "Cynthia would you please read the first item?"

"You were mentioning that we might get hauled into court to explain why Richard shouldn't replace Rodney and Edward as board members of the RL&CC."

"Would I be right in assuming that Richard's attorney would probably start off by trying to lay out his case in such a way as to get the jury behind him before we even have a chance to tell our side of the story?" I looked at Edward, feeling he would have the most insight on something like that.

Edward, instead of answering me, looked at Cynthia and said, "I believe that is right, but what do you say, Cynthia?"

"That would probably be the way they would want to start out. We want to remember that if you are correct in point," she glanced quickly at her pad and continued, "six, and he has the judge behind him, they will do whatever the judge decides to do. He is pretty much the law, as I understand, out here where court procedures aren't as fixed as they usually are back where things are more settled."

"What is point two," I asked.

"Point two is your comment about him probably being unaware that all of the board members have equal voting power," she noted.

"Okay, if everyone is willing, let's skip that for now and go on to point three." I glanced around the table and no one objected.

"Let's look at the broad picture then, instead of going point by point and then we can discuss things. Let me lay out the scenario as I see it, just so we can have a starting point. They will have no case at all as soon as we call our witnesses, as that will dispel any charges he might have concocted about murder being committed by our side. If we go to the kernel of the matter, the only reason we are permitting it to go to court is so we can trap him and any of his cohorts. If he is guilty of trying to have Rodney killed, he needs to pay, one way or another.

"Our main worry is the power of the judge. I wish there were some way we could get a federal marshal into the courtroom. He would have the power to arrest the judge, if the judge is actually involved in a conspiracy. I have a feeling that Richard will have coppered his bet by having a crew of gun slicks present. If the trial is in Vaca County, Sheriff Russell and maybe half a dozen or maybe even a dozen of our men could be deputized to keep order.

"If we can somehow get a federal marshal to set in, without anyone knowing who he is until the climax of the situation, he could deputize the men, including even the sheriff and his men. That looks to me like the best bet. I'd like to hear your comments on that, and if anyone has any connections that could get us an honest and neutral federal lawman into the courtroom, now is the time we need to get started. All hell is fixing to break loose right away."

Cynthia said, "Uncle Edward, what is the name of that firm of Barristers you use for your shipping business? Smyth, Smyth and some other name. I'll think of it in a minute."

"Smyth, Smyth and Larney are the principal partners, but they have other partners in India, China and America. That's a good idea, Cynthia. They have offices in New York and San Francisco. San Francisco is a lot closer to here, but I think I may have copies of some legal papers that have the names of the partners in the various countries. Maybe a name will jump out at us. Cynthia, what is the name of the young man that used to have a crush on you before he finished college and joined that law firm? Trevor! That's it! Trevor Baker!"

"Yes, that's his name. He still writes me, from time to time," Cynthia replied. If you have any legal paper from Smyth, Smyth and Larney, I will look at it and see which office he is in."

"My briefcase is with my luggage there by the front door."

Before Edward had finished the sentence, Cynthia had grabbed the briefcase and placed it before him. He quickly opened it, glanced through a sheaf of papers and handed several to Cynthia. Moments later, she handed him back the sheaf and walked around the table, leaned over with one of the papers, and pointed to a name in a long list of names in the border of the paper.

"Here is his name and he is attached to the New York office. He would be in the one that is furthest away," she said.

"The furthest away, but the quickest and easiest to get to." Edward drummed his fingers on the table for a minute, and then said, "I definitely think Cynthia should be the one to make first contact with him. I think that either Brad or I should make the contact with the federal marshal's office. On second thought, I think I should be with her when she contacts him, and that I should arrange or help arrange to get a marshal here."

I spoke up, "I think that is a good idea, but I think that Brad and Rod should accompany you. While we don't believe anyone knows about you being here, Edward, we can't afford to have some unforeseen event catch us in a helpless position. When it comes right down to it, we still don't know who was in the bunch that we side-stepped in the snow storm. If someone knew we were carrying all of that cash, they might also know more than we think about what is going on here."

We made arrangements for sleeping, with Rodney sleeping in the little feather bed, while Edward took one room and Cynthia the other. Brad went to the new bunkhouse, and I had Rod accompany Earlene and me over to the EEZ. The night was dark and overcast, so the three of us were able to get back to our house with hardly a possibility that anyone could know we were there.

Early the next morning, while the frost was still making a silvery sheen across the grass, we three rode back to the &RR. The sky, which had cleared during the night, displayed the stars which looked twice as large as normal in the cold, clear air.

When we got to the house, Earlene went inside. Edward, Cynthia, and Brad were up and ready to go. She took a parcel of food, which she had asked the cook to have ready for her, and carried it down to the barn where I had just finished hitching up the covered buggy. We stopped back at the house for Edward and Cynthia to get into the buggy. We loaded the luggage into the buggy, tied three extra horses on behind as an extra precaution, just in case we had to abandon the buggy and take to rocky country. We had been less than fifteen minutes from the time we rode through the gate until the time we rode back out. We planned to eat while we rode. Everyone who had slept at the &RR had already eaten.

Earlene and I were fininishing eating our sandwiches as we rode past the entrance to the EEZ. Edward looked over at Earlene and said, "Earlene, forgive me for asking, but would you mind riding in the buggy with Cynthia and me, so she will have someone to talk to besides me?"

Earlene's eyes flashed over to glance into mine for one split second. "Why, not at all, Edward. I am happy you asked me. I have had a lot of questions that I have wanted to ask her about a big city like London, but as you know, things have been awfully hectic around here."

Cynthia turned her bright smile onto Earlene. "I wanted to ask you, but I didn't want to seem to interfere with the routine that you cattlemen seem to have down so pat. I am dying to know what your daily routine is when things are normal."

Earlene smiled back. "I don't know if such a thing as routine exists out here in the Bend of the Rimrock."

"I hate to interrupt your conversation, but I want everyone to listen to me for a moment, before we go on." As they all looked at me, I said, "Edward, I am going to put three Winchesters on this quilt. They are all loaded and ready to go. We may need all of the firepower we can get.

"I don't think anyone will know we've left, but we have to remember that we have to go up the old buffalo trail. It is the same trail that the Vertical X hands use to go to Post. That is where they get their supplies and a big ranch like they apparently have, takes a lot of provisions. Since that is the most apt place for us to run into trouble, I'm going make a detour.

"The detour will put me up on the Rimrock. I am going to pick a good place to snipe from. Keep the buggy horses in a slow trot. I am going to lope around and come up to the crossing from the top. Keep the buggy a mile out from the Rimrock until you see me waving. Earlene has her field glasses with her. You will be able to watch the rim and identify me before you come up the old buffalo trail. Any questions before I leave?"

I received negative responses. Earlene had tied her horse on behind the wagon. Brad took the reins and shook the horses into motion. Rod rode off ahead of the wagon. I turned my horse back toward the back of the EEZ. Thirty minutes later, I had climbed the narrow trail to the top and ridden back toward the old buffalo trail, staying far enough away from the rim to avoid being spotted from below. It also gave me room to maneuver in case I ran into enemies here on the upper plains.

I alternated Calliope between a lope and a trot to make sure that I would arrive at the crossing near the same time I expected the buggy to arrive. Calliope was feeling his oats in the cool morning hours and I had to restrain him from taking a good run. Ordinarily I would have allowed him to stretch out, but this morning, I had no idea what we might run into, and I wanted a fresh horse under me in case I needed one.

-=-

Brad pulled up the team and told everyone to get out and stretch their legs. After a five minute break, he said to the group at large. "I'm going to feel better about things from here on if one of you takes the reins. Edward, can you or Cynthia handle a team? I want Earlene to join me in checking out the crests of each of these swells in the land. They are getting too close together for Rod to check them all."

"We are both experienced in handling horses. I have a stable of horses back home. I don't have the time to look after them myself, and neither does Cynthia, but we're not exactly what you call *Tender Feet*, either." He started to take the reins, but Cynthia said, "Let me do that, Uncle Edward. If the need should arise, I think you handle a rifle a little better than I do."

Sir Hampton reached back and picked up a Winchester. He checked the magazine and chamber and placed it across his lap. Cynthia clucked the horses into motion and the buggy moved on toward the nearing crossing. Rod came back into sight from the south, where he had checked as far as he could see toward the Vertical X's. Earlene had pulled her horse up and was sweeping the Rimrock with her Binoculars. A minute later, she pulled off her bandana and waved it over her head.

She looked over toward Rod, a quarter of a mile ahead of them. He answered her wave and galloped his horse toward the steep slope of the old buffalo crossing and started up. Brad rode back toward the buggy and he and Earlene fell in on either side of the buggy as they started up the slope to the high plains. Five minutes later, they crested the top. They could see Easy sweeping the terrain with his field glasses from his point of vantage on the edge of the Rimrock.

A short distance off on the right, Post could be seen. Post had been built near a large spring that emerged from the ground in a draw between two hills. It formed a creek that flowed over the Rimrock in a pretty little waterfall; then flowed off toward the river.

-=-

I trotted Calliope up to the buggy as they crested the top of the bluff that had been worn into a deep and wide cut in the edge of the Rimrock by a million years of buffalo seeking the canyons of the low land that lay off to the southeast of the crossing. They wintered in those sheltered ravines, arroyos and canyons and when the spring came, they headed north in great herds that spread out across Kansas, Nebraska, The Dakotas, Colorado and Montana. Some of them ranged the eastern half of Utah, the northern half of Arizona and New Mexico.

"I see you made it," I said as a word of greeting.

"Yes, without seeing a single, solitary person," said Cynthia.

"I hope we can keep it that way until we get well north of Post," I answered.

Rod had waited a short ways east of the crossing, toward Post, but now he rode away from the rim of the trail, and with a wave toward the buggy, he continued ahead, ranging off toward the north east. I galloped after him and he pulled up and waited.

"Rod, it is my intention that as soon as we get out of sight of Post, we make as sure as we can that no one is in our sight. You remember that a few miles up the trail, there is a cliche rock outcropping? I want to turn off to the right and after we have followed the outcropping for two or three miles, let's strike a course that will let us head for the second stage station east of Denver."

"That sounds like a good plan to me. I had been mulling over the need to do something that would keep us from being seen en route or in Denver. Somebody had to have sent that group after us that we lost in the snow storm."

I swung Calliope to the left and soon passed in front of the buggy and ranged about half a mile to the side and a mile ahead of it. About an hour later I topped a slight hill and could see the whitish line of rock and clay leading off to the northeast. I closed in toward the buggy and as it arrived at the rocky outcropping, I had Brad swing the it right down the middle of the nearly plantless expanse.

About three miles down the cliche ridge, Rod asked, "Do you know what angle we should take, or do we just estimate and keep our eyes open?"

"I pointed to a distant landmark. That is my best estimate. We're aiming to hit the stage line from Denver to Kansas City about fifty miles east of Denver. That should bring us in to the trail somewhere near the second stage station from Denver. You all will take the stage straight through to Kansas City and catch a Missouri river boat to St. Louis. You'll probably have to change boats there to go on down the Mississippi to New Orleans. You'll catch a Steamer from there up to New York.

"I hope you can get something done quickly, because if Richard Hampton has the fix in with the circuit judge, they may try to have a court trial immediately to keep us from having time to prepare." I gave them a minute to let that sink in, and prepared to get back ahead of the buggy.

"It would be my guess that we can be back in ten days to two weeks," Edward said. "That will be if everything goes smoothly. If it doesn't . . . " His shrug spoke as plainly as words.

"If you can't take care of things quickly, it would be better to have you back, even without the U.S. Marshal. We have a back-up plan, but it might cause us future problems if we have to use it." I was riding along-side of Brad, but speaking loudly enough so that Edward and Cynthia could hear me.

"We'll have plenty of time to talk more before we get to the station." I raised my hand to them and rode off at an angle to the left of our line of travel that would place me both ahead and ranging well out from our path. We didn't see any sign of a human being for the rest of the day.

The next morning, just as we were looking around for a good place to stop for our lunch, we passed over the trail that led from Raton Pass to Denver. About an hour later we stopped by a small stream and ate a quick meal. It was the time of year where darkness came early and we decided to stop and spend the night. We would have been able to spot the stage road in the dark, but were afraid that we wouldn't know whether we had come into the trail on the east side or the west side of the stage station we were aiming at.

Edward said, "Cynthia, why don't you play us a couple of songs before we turn in?"

Cynthia turned to Brad. "Would you help me get that small trunk? Wouldn't you just know it! It's the one on the very bottom."

Brad got up from where he sat leaning against the front buggy wheel and stretched the kinks out of his back. He walked around to the back of the buggy and undid the straps holding the luggage. As Cynthia had said, the small trunk was right on the bottom, beside the one of Edward's and covered by the war bags of Brad and Rod, plus a box with some supplies and cooking utensils.

With shoulders brushing, Cynthia and Brad undid the straps and Brad set the other items aside as Cynthia opened her trunk and removed a small, stringed instrument from beneath some frilly garments that made Brad turn his face away to keep from embarrassing Cynthia. He turned back as she closed the trunk, a half hidden smile on her face.

I was a little surprised to find that the songs she began to play were some sad old Irish songs. She played for a minute and began to sing. Earlene joined in and a moment later so did Edward. Rod and I exchanged glances and tentatively joined in. We enjoyed an hour of singing. Our group seemed very close as we sat, encircled by darkness with the stars shining brightly down.

Earlene and I were sitting, so closely together that we shared each other's heat. The small fire crackled and spirals of sparks jumped skyward, to immediately disappear as the tiny embers burned out. Brad was seated on one side of Cynthia, close enough that her right arm brushed him as she strummed her instrument. Rod sat on the other side, the firelight casting red lights and dark shadows, by turn, on his somber face. Edward was singing under his breath and far off the wailing yips of a coyote sang a finale as Cynthia put the small instrument back into its case.

I had seen a side of Edward that I had not previously seen. I also could not help but notice how closely together Cynthia and Brad stood as they replaced the trunks, boxes and war bags, strapping them back into place as their shoulders brushed. Rod spread his bedroll by the fire and picked up his rifle. Shrugging into his sheepskin coat, he walked out beyond the light of the fire to take a turn around the camp.

The next morning, we grabbed a sandwich and a cup of coffee and started on, traveling about north by north east. In mid-morning we saw smoke rising a little to the east of our line of travel and swung over to head straight for the smoke. An hour later, we arrived at the station.

While the others made themselves appear busy, Rod and I walked inside to have a look around. No one was there except the hostler and his wife. The hostler was mending a piece of harness and his wife was fussing over a pot of stew and some bread she had baking. He looked like someone I had seen before.

"Are you going to catch the stage or did you just stop by for some of my wife's good cooking?" The hostler looked up from his work and grinned at us.

"I guess a little of both," I answered him. "We're going to need four tickets all the way through to Kansas City. How much time do we have before the stage gets in?"

"You got here with an hour or so to spare. Sometimes we have a pretty good load of passengers. Usually during the middle of the week, the stage is pretty lightly loaded, but we still have our small express shipments, plus the mail. You may want to take your dinner now, just in case the stage is loaded with passengers today."

He looked me over again. "Hey!" he exclaimed. "You're Easy Seeker from down Vacaville way. He stood up and shook my hand. My wife and I are going to take up one of those ranches you had fenced off a while back. I was running the stage station in Vacaville. We came out here to help the company out until they can find a permanent replacement for us."

"Yep, that's me," I said. "Listen, I have a favor to ask of you. Do you think you could put our buggy in the back of your barn, sort of out of sight? Our party will be coming back through here in a week or two. I had just as soon no one know about it. I'd like to leave the buggy horses here too."

"You bet! Any time there's anything that I can ever do for you Easy, I'll sure do it!" He grabbed my hand and pumped my arm again.

"I appreciate that. I'd also just as soon you not mention us passing through here to anyone." I clapped my hand against his shoulder and turned toward the door. Looking back at him over my left shoulder I added, "Give me a chance to get the rest of the party inside. They may want us to all eat together, before we start back to the ranch." I turned and started back outside, Rod following behind.

"I'm gonna check out around the barn and outbuildings. I'll be in in a couple of minutes," Rod said, starting toward the barn.

"Wait a minute Rod; I want to talk to you second. Let's unload the buggy and set the luggage by the front porch. I want to put the buggy in the back of the barn and turn the horses into the corral with the stage horses. I'd like first to get it done before the stage pulls in. I know that hostler and I'm going to have to trust him to keep the buggy hidden."

We pulled the buggy around by the porch and unloaded the luggage. Then we led the team into the barn, unhitched and turned the horses into the corral with the extra stage line horses; then we walked back up to the front of the stage station.

Edward, Earlene, and Cynthia were wandering around in the stage yard. Brad was standing out 50 yards from the station scanning the horizon.

I called out so all of them could hear me, "Let's go inside and grab a bite ahead of the stage. It'll be here in an hour or so. I hope they have room for all of you inside. The hostler said the stage usually is pretty empty on this run back east. Edward, I advise you to just say that you are looking the country over and that Rod and Brad are your guides. It should be clear sailing from here to New York."

"My thoughts precisely," Edward answered. "Come along, Cynthia. We can get the luggage after we eat." He broke off talking as they spotted the luggage sitting on the edge of the porch.

Edward and Cynthia entered the large log building. I explained to them the arrangements that we had made for the buggy and horses. A few minutes later Brad and Rod came in and we all sat down to a bowl of Mulligan Stew, followed by pie and coffee. We heard the sound of the stage arriving as we pushed back from the table.

Rod, Brad and I went out to see who were on the stage, as Edward bought the tickets. The stage was empty. I was glad, because a stage is not the most comfortable way to travel at best. When you are jammed into the seats like sardines in a can, it can be downright unpleasant.

We handed the luggage up to the hostler while the driver and shotgun guard went in to eat. Fifteen minutes later Sir Edward and Rod were seated, facing forward and Cynthia was seated across from Sir Edward, with Brad straight across from Rod. The stage pulled out to the crack of the driver's whip, the creak of harness and the rhythm of the horse's hooves.

I turned to Earlene and before I could speak, she said, "Easy, look around you! I had no idea how lonely this station looks with the sun beating down and the dust whipped up by the wind from the barren, stage worn ground."

"Yes," I agreed. "The only thing that keeps it from seeming similar to when I first left home is that I have the woman I love here with me. It still seems like so much of my family is now gone; gone on a long trip, a mission that I feel must be successful or we will have to fight tooth and nail to hang onto the places that we have worked so hard to start. This is the first time in so many years that I have had a family. Now I feel that it has come under the threat of some malignant ghost, for we can't see what is happening out of our sight."

Earlene wrapped her arms around me and turned her face up for a kiss. "I know that you will be able to do whatever it takes to keep us secure. I also want you to know that the days of your loneliness are forever behind you."

My lips sealed off the rest of her conversation.

We put our horses into a long ground eating trot now that Sir Edward was on his way back to New York. I had sudden sense of urgency about our defense back at the ranch. We rode quickly back toward the ranches, making sure that we did not over-tire the horses in case we needed their speed later on. As darkness began to gather, I looked for a good place to spend the night. A few minutes later I saw a copse of trees off to the right near a little spring. I decided we would spend the night there and get an early start the next morning.

We dismounted and gathered up some dried twigs and started a fire. A few minutes later we had a pot of coffee on the fire and bacon frying in the pan. I had brought some biscuits from the stage station. By the time we had drunk a couple of cups of coffee each, and eaten a biscuit with some hot sizzling bacon, the night had fallen around us like a dark blanket. We sat there together for a while watching the sky and counting shooting stars as they drew their fiery paths across the sky.

We got up the next morning with frost laying a silvery mantle across the Curly Mesquite grass. While Earlene heated up a little coffee and fried some bacon, I saddled the horses and put on their feed bags with a little oats. A few minutes later we were on our horses and riding out across the frosty grass. The grass crunched beneath our horses' hooves and clouds of white vapor came from the snorting horses' nostrils. The horses felt good in the cold air and wanted to run. We gave them their heads for a few minutes and allowed them to run rapidly across the crystal grass. We reined the horses back to a canter and looked at each other smiling, exhilarated by the cold air and the joy of living.

We spent that night in a small grove of trees just before we reached the trail coming up from Raton Pass. We were traveling back much faster than we had come up and in a couple of hours we came to the place where our trail forked off toward the old Buffalo Trail. When we were five miles from the edge of the Rimrock, we took an angle calculated to bring us to the point where our three ranches intersected.

"What have you got up your sleeve Easy? I've known you long enough to know you're up to something."

"Yeah, I know it's going to be awfully hard to ever put anything over on you. I guess I'll just have to make sure that I never try to keep a secret. I'm giving some thought to building a little block house on the Rimrock at the intersection of each one of our two canyons, and also one at the intersection of the three canyons. That will give us a good point of vantage to prevent sniping from the Rimrock and also to command the trails leading from the Rimrock down into the canyon."

"And I had something planned! You must seriously believe an attack is imminent. How much time do you believe we have?"

"I think it's highly unlikely that we will be attacked before we are engaged in a court trial. My biggest worry right now is that they will call the trial before Edward gets back with the United States Marshal. We can't afford to give up possession under any circumstances until we've had the marshal come down here to make sure that we have an opportunity to prove our case."

"It looks to me like that would be very easy to do once we have a chance to put both Rodney and his father in front of the jury. There is no way they can find the jury that could find against us once we show that both Rodney and Sir Edward are alive." Earlene took off her Stetson and let the cold air blow through her hair.

"We just have to make sure that we keep Sir Edward and Rodney safe and sound until this entire matter plays out," I answered.

We put our horses into a slow canter and rode the rest of the way to the confluence of the three canyons with scarcely any conversation. We were each lost in our own thoughts. I'm not sure what Earlene's thoughts were. My own were of the best way to build the block houses to guard our entrances.

It was dark when we arrived at the pathway down from the Rimrock to the floor of the EEZ. We each got off and led our horses down the darkened trail. Our horses made scarcely a sound as we rode through the lush grasses of the valley. Two hundred yards from the ranch house we ground hitched our horses and continued on foot.

It took us nearly half an hour to spot the guard. I was unable to determine who was on guard and I called out softly, "Don't shoot! Don't shoot! This is Easy and Earlene." Earlene and I will each be carrying our rifle. The guard whirled toward us, his rifle held across his chest. I repeated, "Don't shoot and don't aim your rifle toward us! Who are you? Hold your rifle by the barrel and come over here where I can see you are!"

A voice sounded from behind me, "Easy is that you and Earlene? It was Faron Stern.

"Yes it's me and Earlene."

"Oh? I see you but I don't see Earlene."

"Faron I'm right over here and my gun is aimed directly at your ear."

We all began to laugh at the precautions we had taken. The young man to whom I had first spoken said, "I don't know how you two sneaked up on me, because I've been checking out every blade of grass that moved in the breeze."

Faron said, "That's okay Holt, you've been doing a good job. This is Easy and Earlene. They're the people who are paying your salary. Faron turned to me and said, "Easy, I'd like you and Earlene to meet Holt Allen. He came across the desert riding the chuck line. One of the boys who have been helping us out needed to go home while his wife had her baby. He's been working for Marshal Philbrick in one of the mining towns over in Utah. He was carrying a letter of introduction to the sheriff of Potter County down in the Panhandle of Texas. He's highly recommended and since he was broke and needed a job for a few days, I took the liberty of hiring him."

"Looks to me like you got a good man, Faron." I shook hands with the young man and introduced him to Earlene, who had just walked up and joined us. She shook hands with him, and I asked Faron, "See any reason why we shouldn't go up to the house now?"

"No, I think everyone up at the house has been more or less expecting you to be in tonight. Why don't you go on up to the house but be sure to knock." Looking over at Holt he said, "Holt, go back to your station. I'm going to walk up to the house with Easy and Earlene. I'll be moseying around out here keeping my eye on things. Make sure you don't shoot me."

I could scarcely see Holt's grin in the dark, as he said "Do I have to promise?"

Earlene and I walked to the porch. While still some distance away I saw a dark figure sitting in a chair. It was not until several more steps that I noted the figure was holding a shotgun pointed directly at Earlene and me. I said, "Careful with the shotgun. I sure wouldn't want to it to go off. It might wipe the smile off of Earlene's face and I'm pretty fond of her smile."

I heard a voice which I recognized as Sheriff Todd Russell's say "Hey, is that you Easy?"

"Yeah Todd, it's me and Earlene. I'm surprised to find you awake."

"I was asleep until I heard you all stumbling around and falling all over yourselves. I thought someone had turned the cattle out and they were about the stampede over the house. Either that or a bunch of kids were playing kick the can out in the barnyard. You sure make it hard for someone to get their sleep."

"Todd, the only thing that keeps you from being funny is that shotgun you still have pointed at us. I figure you'd miss us, since we're all of ten feet away from you, but stranger things have happened." The three of us laughed as Earlene and I walked up the steps to the porch and shook hands with the sheriff. "How's the sheriffing business?"

"Oh, the law business would be pretty slow if it weren't for you desperadoes out here. I was expecting you all to come in about now. In fact, besides coming out here to see how everyone's getting along, I even have a summons for you to show up in court and show cause why you shouldn't give possession of the ranch up to Richard Hampton. When I say the ranch, I'm talking about the RL&CC. This service is being made to the several individuals composing the Rimrock Land and Cattle Company." As Todd said these words he handed a large envelope to me.

I reached out and took the envelope, saying "I've been expecting this but I had hoped it would come a little later. Let's go into the house where I have a little more light and have a look at these papers."

I opened the door and stood aside while Earlene and Todd entered. Rodney was standing over near the kitchen table and he walked over and shook hands with me and kissed Earlene's cheek.

"Did everything go all right on your little trip?" he asked. "I don't know why but I've been a little bit worried."

"We'll talk about that a little bit later if you don't mind. Right now I would like to know how you're feeling. You look like a million dollars compared with the last time I saw you."

"I feel like a million dollars compared to the last time you saw me.

I'm ready to tackle the world. You don't have any grizzly bears you need wrestled do you?"

"We might have something worse than a grizzly bear that were going to have to wrestle. Todd just got through handing me a summons to show cause why we shouldn't give up the ranch to your cousin Richard Hampton. When I say ranch I'm talking of the Rimrock Land and Cattle Company."

"So my dear cousin Richard is behind all our problems," Rodney said. "Since this shows we were right in that part of our deductions, it is reasonable to assume we are right in the rest of our conclusions."

"Well, to put things in the proper perspective, I think we should start out with having a look at this summons." I walked over to the lamp, took my pocket knife and slit open the envelope. I drew out a sheet of paper and read it slowly. I read it once again and then said, "Listen up folks. I want all of you to hear this.

"In the Circuit Court of the hundred and 14th Judicial Circuit, in and for Axel County, Colorado Territory, Case Number 1101CT61, Southwestern Division; Richard Hampton, Petitioner; The Estate of Sir Edward Hampton, et al:

"Summons: Personal And Collective Service On The Estate And Associated Individuals In Positions Of Both Ownership And Management.

"Important: An action has been filed against you. You have 20 calendar days after this summons is served on you to file a written response to the attached complaint/petition with the clerk of the circuit court, located at Number One, Courthouse Square, Town of Nugget Creek, County of Golden, Territory of Colorado.

"Your written response, including the case number given above and the names of the parties, must be filed if you want the Court to hear your side of the case. If you do not file your written response on time, you may lose the case, and your money, property and other assets may be taken thereafter without further warning from the Court. There are other legal requirements. You are advised to get an attorney right away."

I read the document aloud, and went back to the most salient points and reread them aloud. "Our time could begin to become crowded from now on. We have to hope that Sir Edward will return with the federal marshals and also hopefully with a good attorney. I don't really know how the court system works. If we file an answer too soon, we may have to disclose that Brad is not available. If we are right on our calculations, or perhaps I should say conclusions, we may be skating on thin ice. The judge may not be happy when he finds out that Rodney is alive, Sir Edward is alive, and that some documents that are forged might have been presented by Richard Hampton.

"I would not be at all surprised if the sheriff at Post is holding warrants for my arrest and possibly for some of the rest of you." I laughed and added, "They might even charge us with conspiracy to make fools of the court."

-=-

Sir Edward, Cynthia, Brad, and Rod had just arrived in New York City. The stagecoach ride had been dusty and tiresome but once they arrived on the steamboat, they found it very relaxing and enjoyable. This was the first time Rod had been on a steamboat. They had decided they should keep a low profile, so they spent most of their time in the parlor of Sir Edward's stateroom. While it would have been much more comfortable to have stayed in their own state rooms, they felt it would be much safer for Sir Edward and Cynthia if they all stayed together in the parlor.

After having exhausted the subject of obtaining a federal marshal and a good lawyer, plus matters relating to the perceived trial, they spent the rest of the time playing cards. Brad bought a box of matches at the commissary and they spent most of the time playing poker for matches. When that game begin to pall, Brad returned to the commissary and bought a set of dominoes. They began to play the game of 42 with Brad and Cynthia partners playing against Edward and Rod. All four players played skillfully and they all felt the most relaxed they had in ages. They drank coffee and tea until they felt like they could float the steamboat themselves, laughing and playing like children.

They took their food in the state room. If it had not been for the crisis they were facing, they would've hated to arrive in New York City. They knew, however, that time was of the greatest essence. Sir Edward procured a hotel suite. The luggage was brought up into the rooms and Brad went quickly down and hailed a hansom.

It was only a short distance to the office of Cynthia's friend and when he was told who his guests were, he saw them immediately. When they were shown into the office he instantly exchanged kisses on the cheek. Introductions were made all around.

"Uncle Edward, you remember Trevor Baker don't you? Trevor, I'm sure you remember Uncle Edward."

As the two men were shaking hands, Trevor said, "Oh, yes! How could I ever forget you, Mr. Hampton? Not only is your niece the prettiest girl in the United States, but your firm is one of our prized clients. How are you Sir? It is so good to see you!

Cynthia turned to Brad. "Brad Rogers, Trevor Baker. Brad, Trevor. Trevor, Brad. Brad is one of the principals in the Rimrock Land and Cattle Company. He and his daughter also own the *And Ours* ranch, a beautiful valley ranch that is separate from the Rimrock Land and Cattle Company.

"Rod, let me make you acquainted with Trevor Baker. Trevor Baker, Rod Lasser. Rod, Trevor -Trevor, Rod."

"Let's get right down to business," said Sir Edward. "Cynthia, what all have you told Trevor about our problem?"

"I have asked him to use his influence in getting the US marshal to accompany us back to Vacaville. I would like him to start with an introduction to the US marshal so we can explain the circumstances to him. Uncle Edward, I think it best for you to take over at this point in telling what you want done."

Sir Edward turned to Trevor and placed his hand on his shoulder. "My boy, all I would like for you to do at this time is to arrange a meeting between the US marshal, Cynthia and myself. This is on a very important matter and it requires immediate action. I cannot overstress the importance of acting now."

"In that case let's go out and hail a hansom. Please follow me down to the street." The five of them strode rapidly through the corridors to the street, where they soon found themselves in a hansom cab, rushing through the streets of New York. Three blocks down the street, they pulled up in front of a brownstone building. It was a three-story structure half a block off of Wall Street. The street was thronged with men in suits rushing from building to building as though their lives depended upon the speed of their arrivals.

Trevor handed a bill to the hansom driver as they dismounted from the cab. They entered a large open area with a booth that served as a combination information booth and reception area. Trevor said, "If the rest of you will be so kind as to have a seat here, I will try to get us an appointment. I hope this will only take a moment."

Brad noted that it took only a few moments for someone to come down the hall and escort Sir Edward and Trevor behind a large door with shiny brass fittings and colored glass windows. After about 30 minutes a lady came out through the doors and walked over to where Cynthia, Brad, and Rod were sitting.

"Are you the party who's accompanying Sir Edward?" she asked. When she was answered in the affirmative, she smiled at the group and said, "Will you please follow me?" The three stood up and followed her back through the large door.

The door had opened into a large room with four office doors opening along the back wall. The room was furnished with plush carpeting, a scattering of comfortable chairs with low tables loaded with magazines sitting in front of each one. Expensive paintings hung on the walls and marble and bronze statues were strategically placed along the walls.

There was little time to enjoy the office appointments for they were taken directly to one of the two center office doors. The first notable thing when one entered the room was a huge desk placed in front of the glass wall that fronted on the busy street. A husky gray-headed man whose face bore the marks of a hard outdoor life, which he had apparently lived in the past, arose from the desk and walked around to greet the group.

Sir Edward and Trevor also walked over and Trevor made the introductions. Brad said, "Somehow you don't look like the type of man to be seated behind the fancy desk in this office."

"You sure got that right," replied the man, whom had been introduced as Jules Hardy. "I served my apprenticeship for this job, serving as the sheriff and marshal of half the gold and silver boom towns in the West, not to mention half a dozen railhead cattle towns."

"I didn't think you looked like someone had spent their life behind the desk," said Brad,

"Far from it. When they opened the Marshal's Office for the territory of Colorado, they looked for someone with a broad array of experiences to head up the office. There is a reason that I might get involved in this personally, rather than sending one of my men. I have heard rumors that the presiding judge that would handle a court in your area is subject to taking a bribe to hand down a verdict favoring the person bribing him. This information is something that should not be repeated outside this room. I am relying on you to respect this confidence."

Sir Edward spoke up, "I imagine that you can see our need for immediate action. It is our own feelings that this matter will be rushed through before we have a chance to make adequate preparations. Once the verdict is handed down I would imagine that they will try to take immediate possession of the Rimrock Land and Cattle Company, including the Rimrock Bank and Trust. We have to be aware of the old adage, "possession is nine tenths of the law."

Brad said, "Marshal Hardy, I'm sure not trying to tell you your business but I have a feeling that the entire work force of the Vertical X's ranch may be deputized by the local sheriff. If everything we expect to happen does happen, I believe it would be prudent to expect that anything that can be accomplished by force will be attempted. Do you have any idea of how much force you can marshal to head off such a possibility?"

Marshal Hardy raised his hand and pulled at his nose for a moment with his head bent. Then he looked back up and said, "That's a point well taken. It would take quite a force to head off as many men as would be arrayed against us, given that everything turned out as you have suggested. I suppose you have an answer for that?"

"Yes, as a matter of fact we have discussed this with the sheriff of Vaca County. We have kept him abreast of everything that's happened since the very first day that things began to occur. He's a very good sheriff and has three top-notch men. We have men working for the Rimrock Land and Cattle Company that are as good as they come. Rod here is one of them and he has experience as a law man. I imagine we could furnish you all the men you need, for I doubt that they would be very likely to want to fight against a federal marshal.

"If you have a bad feeling about deputizing the sheriff and so many men from the Rimrock Land and Cattle Company, you could probably deputize quite a few men from the small ranches in the area. I have a feeling that it would be harder to keep the secret under wraps if we were to prepare to deputize the amount of people needed to give a strong enough show of force to prevent a fight from actually starting."

The old lawmen stood pondering the situation for a minute, brushing back his graying hair. "I've heard nothing but good things about Sheriff Todd Russell," he said. If we're going to organize in time to be of assistance, I imagine it will be necessary to take your advice. I think the next step on my part will be to get a warrant for the arrest of Judge Pickwick and a dozen John Doe warrants that we can execute on whomever we deem necessary."

He turned away as though ending the conversation, but immediately turned back. "It's going to take the rest of the day for me to prepare. I want to travel back to Vacaville in the same group with you. By the way, where is the young fella I've heard so much about down in the Bend of the Rimrock? The one with the funny name, let's see, I believe his name is Easy, Easy Seeker."

"He is back at the Rimrock Land and Cattle Company getting things organized. As soon as we get back to the EEZ, we'll have a preliminary meeting. As soon as we know all of any new developments that may have occurred while we were here to see you to make sure we're all on the same page, we'll bring in Sheriff Todd Russell and his deputies and formulate our strategy. By that time we may also know whether we're facing a tight schedule or still have a little leeway," said Brad.

"Okay," said Marshal Hardy. "I'll meet you at your hotel bright and early in the morning. It might not be a bad idea if you procure all your tickets this afternoon. I can always cut in at the head of the line in my position as marshal. I feel like that it would be prudent if we're not all seen together. When you get off the stage and pick up your buggy, I'll continue on to at least the next stage station and rent a horse there." He hesitated for a moment and then said, "On second thought I'm going all the way in into Denver and rent a horse and buggy. I'll also rent a good riding horse and lead him behind the buggy."

-=-

We had just finished building the second of two guard posts which were constructed in the manner of the block house of a fort. The block houses were two story structures. They were built in such a manner that the end toward the Rimrock projected out over the edge 3 feet. There was a strong trapdoor in the bottom of the second story floor. This was to permit a rope ladder to be used for emergency entrance or exit. The floor of this building was made of rough split wood of irregular widths and lengths. This made it easy to disguise the trapdoor, as the outline of the trapdoor appeared to be just more places where floorboards were fitted in. Another trap door similar to the one above was made in the bottom of the floor where it overhung the canyon. When it was opened, a defender could control the area of the canyon floor directly beneath the overhang of the building. Gun ports were also strategically located in both the upper and the lower floors. They allowed a defender to control the entire perimeter. Bars could be latched over all the gun ports on the bottom floor in such a way as to prevent someone from the outside from controlling the bottom floor in the event the defender was on the top floor. They were positioned so you could see the entrance to the canyon, the ranch house, and the entire canyon within rifle range.

Nugget Creek was a boom town that had started with the discovery of gold in a large creek that came boiling down out of the mountains. When several large veins of gold were discovered that led into the rocky mountain sides, placer mining gave way to hard rock mining. Each of the several mines employed half a hundred men. Each mine promised to furnish long time employment.

Unlike most mining boom towns, Nugget Creek began in an organized manner. A civic spirit was born and began to thrive in the breasts of the citizens. No shenanigans were allowed from the very start. A well-known and very capable sheriff was elected. The citizens were willing to furnish an adequate group of deputies.

All of the mine owners and the merchants of the town cooperated in forming a city charter. There were rules governing the saloons, both in their locations and in their manner of doing business. Any saloon that knowingly allowed cheating in their establishment was not given a second chance. They were kicked out of town with the admonition to not return.

The town was given an additional boost with the discovery of large silver bearing ores and formations. This caused a burst of civic pride that resulted in a large and imposing courthouse. This courthouse would've rivaled the courthouses of much larger cities in much more civilized parts of the United States.

The courthouse was built of native stone. It had broad marble steps leading up to the second floor where the court rooms, the offices of the tax appraiser, the assayer's office, and the sheriff's office were located. The building included a full basement, which had twelve foot ceilings. A row of windows, two feet in height and four feet in width encircled the building in the areas not used for the front or back steps to the first floor, where the offices of the town dignitaries were located.

Those windows could be opened outward to allow air circulation. Each window was barred with the highest grade of steel. About three quarters of the downstairs area was used for the jail offices and the jail, itself.

The jail was utilized as the territorial prison, in addition to its functions as the town and county jail. The cells were of ample size.

They appeared in rows of ten cells each. Each cell in each row was separated from the adjoining cell by a steel wall. Each steel wall projected beyond the bars at each end in a manner that made it impossible for a prisoner in one cell to make physical contact with the prisoner in the next cell.

There was a hall that encircled the cells, next to the walls and below the ventilating windows. A guard could patrol the perimeter and the areas between the rows of cells without coming in reach of any prisoner. The ventilating windows opened in a manner that, when one considered the height of the windows in relation to the height of the cells, made it impossible for anything to be thrown through a window into a cell.

It also made it impossible to shoot into a cell through one of the windows. A great deal of pains had been taken to design this jail. The charges levied against the county and the territory for housing their prisoners defrayed most of the town's expenses for having such a grand town hall. It also allowed them to hire plenty of law officers to keep peace in the town, which was rapidly growing to be a city. Nugget Creek was the county seat of Golden County.

-=-

On this day, the courtroom was crammed with people. The seats were arranged in two columns with each column consisting of 10 rows. They ran from near the back wall to the area in the front where the people involved in the hearing were seated, along with a desk on a raised stage in front for the judge. An aisle was left next to each wall, with a broad aisle down the middle of the room. A rope barricade reached from wall to wall in front of the area where the contestants were seated. The judge was to be seated behind the raised desk, facing the rear of the room. Fifteen feet in front of the judge's desk, two tables were setting. One table was located to the left and the other to the right. Several chairs were located behind each table, with one table being for the defendant and his attorney and the other table being for the plaintiff and his attorney.

The trial was scheduled to begin at nine a.m., and although it was only 7:40 a.m., the courtroom was already packed. Spectators stood along the walls. The courtroom was nearly in bedlam as the spectators discussed the upcoming case among themselves. The Rimrock Land and Cattle Company was widely known and hugely admired. The part its owners had played in the breakdown of the X-Pan-D and the formation of so many small ranches was still being discussed throughout the West. The Rimrock Bank and Trust was used by ranchers and homesteaders for 100 miles around.

Now, after the mysterious shooting and killing of one of the principals of the Rimrock Land and Cattle Co., the presumed loss at sea of the principal stockholder, along with the attempted takeover of the Rimrock Land and Cattle Company, together with the Rimrock Bank and Trust by another large rancher who just happened to be the nephew of the principal stockholder and the cousin of the murdered stockholder who was also president of the Rimrock Bank and Trust, the rumors were flying. To further cloud the issue, this nephew was also the cousin of the murdered man. Since this nephew was also next in the line of inheritance of Sir Edward Hampton, this case had all of the intrigue of a Sherlock Holmes mystery. It seemed that nearly everyone had their own theory as to what had happened. The theories were even more prevalent as to what would happen during this trial.

A man in a large gray Stetson was seated near the front in one of the choice seats. He had been sitting there for nearly an hour and a half. Nature called and he needed to go to the restroom. He asked his friend who sat next to him to hold his seat for him until he returned. When he did return, a heated argument was going on between a stranger and his friend. The stranger was loudly proclaiming that seats couldn't be saved. The man who had left to go to the restroom brushed by him and took his seat again. The stranger grabbed him by his shirt and jerked him back out of the seat and the fight started.

Before more than a few blows could be exchanged, a deputy sheriff rushed to the front of the room, broke up the fight, and sent the late comer to the back of the room to stand against the wall. Voices arose from the spectators throughout the room as different people begin to take sides with one or another of the two antagonists. Three deputies arose from the benches in the back of the room and walked down the center aisle. When they reached the front of the room, one turned to the left, one turned to the right, and one turned around facing the rear. When the two who had turned to the sides reached the side aisle, the three walked slowly toward the back. They looked directly into the face of each person who seemed to be involved in the argument.

Under the gaze of the deputies, a measure of quietness began to fall upon the room. In a few minutes the dull roar of the conversation continued as before. A crowd gathered in front of the courthouse clamoring to be let into the courtroom. Tempers begin to fray and burn thin as the crowd grew and was stopped from entering by deputies. Half an hour before court opened, the judge was escorted into the courthouse with one deputy walking ahead, one behind, and one on each side.

He was taken to the outer door of his chambers, where he rapped on the door, which was opened by his bailiff. When the distinct click of the inside locks were heard, the deputies walked back to the front door of the courtroom and entered, where they found seats on the benches which were reserved for law enforcement personnel.

At about the same time as the judge entered his chambers, the attorneys for both sides entered the courtroom, walked to the front, and unhooked the silken rope that served as a gate to the area that was separated off for the actual participants in the trial. The attorneys and their helpers begin to stack and arrange numerous papers, ledgers and the notebooks into neat little stacks on the tables.

The attorney for the plaintiff began to hold whispered conferences with his clerks. Each clerk spoken to by the attorney would immediately begin to sift through papers in file folders, rifle through stacks of neatly arranged papers, and/or turn rapidly through notebooks, marking pages by attaching paperclips as they went.

A few minutes later another person entered the area reserved for the participants and after a brief conference with the attorney for the plaintiff, took the chair immediately to the right of the attorney. He turned in his chair and looked out over the spectators and I saw him exchange nearly imperceptible nods with various toughs who were situated throughout the spectators. I immediately recognized him as the man who had identified himself as Richard Hampton in the encounter with the toughs in the saloon in Post.

I turned my attention to the subjects of the nearly imperceptible nods from Richard Hampton. I recognized several of those as men who had been with Richard Hampton in the saloon. I figured that I had identified at least twenty men who were probable associates of Hampton. As I attempted to catalog the probable antagonists, I was interrupted by the words of the court bailiff, "All stand for the Hon. Judge Pickwick, presiding judge of the fifth circuit court of the territory of Colorado. The case presently being heard is Richard Hampton versus the Rimrock Land and Cattle Company.

The judge picked up a sheaf of papers, rattled them briefly, cleared his throat and began to read. "In these papers it is alleged by the plaintiff, Richard Hampton that the defendant, Rimrock Land and Cattle Company et al, have conspired to seize control of the Rimrock Land and Cattle Company and all of its assets, which include the Rimrock Bank and Trust.

"Is the plaintiff ready to proceed?" The bailiff waited for a moment while the attorney for the plaintiff stood up and said, "The plaintiff's ready, Your Honor."

"Is the defense ready to proceed?" Again he waited while the attorney for the defendant stood up and said, "Yes, the defense is ready to proceed, Your Honor."

The bailiff turned to the judge and said, "Your Honor, the plaintiff and the defense have both indicated their readiness to begin."

The judge looked over his spectacles at the attorney for the plaintiff. "You may make your opening statement."

The attorney for the plaintiff stood up, walked slowly to the center of the open space between his table and the judges podium, looked at the judge and said, "Your Honor, there are several elements we intend to prove beyond the shadow of a doubt.

The first and foremost of these is to show that justice requires that the sole and total ownership of the Rimrock Land and Cattle Company rests with Richard Hampton. In order to show the legal justification of such a ruling we will have to show that the principals of the Rimrock Land and Cattle Company have engaged in, not only unethical behavior in relation to the manner they have managed said company in their capacity as employees of the company, but have committed nefarious, illegal, and downright criminal activities in their efforts to achieve total control of the Rimrock Land and Cattle Company."

At this point the attorney took his eyes off the judge, clasped his hands behind his back, strolled over in front of the jury and looked intently directly into the face of each jury member. He kept his eyes on each jury member until it jury member looked him straight in the eyes. Then he looked at the next jury member and repeated this action. Each time he looked at a new jury member without saying a word, the members of the jury seemed to become more nervous and began shifting in their seats. The spectators began to lean forward waiting for what the attorney would say next. After he had looked the last juror in the eye, he began to speak in a soft voice. "Gentlemen of the jury, you are all here to settle a matter of great trust and importance. Your actions are all that stands between justice and the perpetration of a crime that is so great it will shock the sensibilities of honest men such as yourself. You and I must say that such a crime cannot be committed with impunity, in this, the great territory of Colorado.

"You and I, gentlemen, as administrators of justice, fairness, and as the protectors of the citizens of the great territory of Colorado from the open commission of such a crime as will shock us all by the very audacity, arrogance and boldness, not to mention the utter disregard for the laws and social mores of a civilized society must do our duty." He turned his back upon the members of the jury for a moment and stared out across the spectators.

"This group of men have not only conspired to steal the great and growing ranch that we refer to as the Rimrock Land and Cattle Company from its rightful owners, but we're going to show, beyond the shadow of a doubt among all reasonable men that the despicable actions of these men extend far beyond the conspiracy for which we accuse them. We are also going to prove," at this point the attorney leaned forward in a conspiratorial manner and suddenly whirled around with his outstretched hand and jutting finger pointing straight at me, as his voice thundered out, "THAT MAN IS A MURDERER!"

For a moment the court room was in complete silence. The next moment it was absolute pandemonium. Everyone was on their feet and everyone was shouting. At the same time that some people were shouting, "That's a lie!" others were shouting, "Hang the dirty murderer!" There was absolute bedlam in the courtroom. Fistfights were breaking out between supporters of the defendants and the henchmen of the plaintiff. Judge Pickwick was slamming the table with his gavel. "Bailiff," he roared, "Restore order to the courtroom!"

The bailiff started forward and six hard-eyed deputies stood up from the benches that lined the back wall. A moment later all the spectators had reseated themselves and the courtroom regained some semblance of order.

When the courtroom had exploded into noisy displays of astonishment and disbelief, it had been an instantaneous reaction where the entire group of spectators had arisen as one. Richard Hampton had brought his entire crew from the Vertical X. They were all sitting on the right hand side of the aisle, whereas the citizens from Vacaville were congregated on the left. The judge ignored the people from the Vertical X, but turned a withering look on the citizens from Vacaville. "Another outburst like that and I will put you out of the courtroom! I will not tolerate such contemptible actions."

I noted that a near smile crossed the face of both the attorney for the plaintiff and the plaintiff himself. "Oh well," I thought, "He who laughs last, laughs longest."

"Your Honor," said the plaintiff's attorney, "The plaintiff has completed his opening statement."

The judge looked disdainfully at the defendant's counsel. "Are you now ready for your opening remarks?"

Our attorney rose to his feet and said, "Yes we are, Your Honor. I will try to be brief. I request that Your Honor dismiss all of these trumped up charges against the Rimrock Land And Cattle Company on the grounds that there is no merit to any of the things that the attorney for the plaintiff has stated. The charges are all totally groundless and to proceed further is merely wasting the time of the court, the good citizens who are here to watch and see that justice is done, and to the Rimrock Land and Cattle Company."

"Your request is denied. Proceed with your opening statement," said Judge Pickwick. "Please advise your client we'll put up with no further delaying actions or grandstanding. The court is busy and I assume that Mr. Hampton is likewise busy. I don't intend to allow this trial to drag on through any delaying tactics. Now please give your opening statement."

"Your Honor, gentlemen of the jury, and citizens of the territory of Colorado, I would like to thank you all for coming so far to set in on this trial and to be witness to what occurs. Rather than make a lengthy statement, I prefer to let the facts speak for themselves. I'm sure that all of you who have drawn the important duty of being members of the jury are far more interested in hearing the facts and seeing the proofs than you are to watching the posturing and hearing the oratory of a couple of lawyers. I will therefore skip my opening statement and challenge my learned opponent to show some of the proofs that he so blithely claims to have."

The titter of laughter that swept through the gallery of spectators earned a glare from the judge, a frown from the plaintiff's attorney and my own smile.

Judge Pickwick tapped his gavel and said, "The plaintiff may present his first witness."

Mr. Shystwell stood up and smiled at the jury. "I know how busy all of you fine gentlemen are. With that in mind I will attempt to keep this brief. To this end, without further ado, I will introduce indisputable evidence that not only is Richard Hampton next in line to inherit the Rimrock Land and Cattle Company, but that I also have a document in my possession showing that Sir Edward Hampton, principal owner of the Rimrock Land and Cattle Company, signed over his interest in that company to Richard Hampton two months before he was unfortunately lost at sea."

He walked back to the plaintiff's table, where one of his aides was holding out a sheaf of papers. He took the papers, shuffled through them importantly, and walked back in front of the judge's podium. "Judge, I would like to introduce these papers as exhibit A."

The judge took the papers, gave them a cursory glance, and handed them back to the attorney, who took them and strutted back to the jury box. He handed the papers to juror number one and said, "Will you please inspect these papers and hand them to the next juror."

Mr. Fendoff leaped to his feet shouting, "Objection Your Honor! I can't allow my worthy opponent to show papers to the jury that I haven't inspected. I demand that he gives me the papers for my immediate inspection!"

"So ordered," said the judge. "I'd like to admonish you, Mr. Fendoff, not to attempt to make mountains out of mole hills in my court. Take the papers and look at them immediately. We can't hold up this hearing indefinitely. We people here in Colorado have better things to do then dilly-dally around about inconsequential technicalities like you may do back in New York or Boston or wherever you're from."

Mr. Fendoff took the papers and sat there studying them for a few minutes. There were certain places in the documents that caused him to lean over and have a conversation with me. Neither Mr. Fendoff nor I were particularly concerned with the documents. After a quick but careful examination, Mr. Fendoff told the judge that he was satisfied with the documents. He then said, "Judge in the future I want to examine each piece of evidence prior to it being shown to the jury."

"Just try and remember what I told you about stalling and delaying this hearing," said the judge.

"Very well, Your Honor." Mr. Fendoff sat back down and watched as the documents were passed along from juror to juror. It took approximately ten minutes to examine the contract. When the last man passed the document back to Mr. Shystwell, who in turn handed it to his clerk where it was tagged and placed in a pile on the spacious table.

"I would now like to call my first witness," said Mr. Shystwell.

"Deputy, would you please bring in the first witness." The judge looked at one of the deputies sitting on a bench that was placed along the back wall. Immediately one of the deputies stood up and opened the courtroom door. Another deputy was standing just outside the door with a man in a tweed coat. Taking the man by his arm, he escorted him forward through the court room, unhooked the cord that served as a gate, and returned to the rear of the court room and went out the door.

The bailiff walked up to the witness and said, "Place your left hand on this Bible, raise your right hand and repeat after me, "I do solemnly swear that the testimony I'm going to give is the truth, the whole truth and nothing but the truth, so help me God."

The witness did as instructed and Mr. Shystwell directed him to be seated in the witness chair. "Please state your name for the court," he said.

The man in the tweed coat cleared his throat noisily. "My name is Barry Eagleton."

"And where are you from, Mr. Eagleton?" asked Mr. Shystwell.

"I'm from London, Sir."

"And what do you do in London," asked Mr. Shystwell?

"I work for a barrister Sir," he replied.

"And what do you do for the barrister?" asked Mr. Shystwell.

"Sir, I'm a messenger for his firm."

"And what do you do in your capacity as a messenger?" asked Mr. Shystwell.

"Mostly I deliver messages to businesses down in the dock area. I also pick up messages for our firm from some of its clients who are mostly also in the dock area. He also has other odd jobs that he wishes me to do."

"And what is the name of the barrister for whom you work most of the time?"

"Why, it's you Mr. Shystwell."

"Why so it is Barry. Why so it is. Do you remember the last time I was in London and you did a task for me?"

"Yes Sir, I sure do. You had me witness a signature for you."

Mr. Shystwell turned back toward his table, walked over and took a paper his clerk was holding out for him, and walked back in front of the witness chair. He held out the paper and said, "Barry, I want you to look at this paper carefully. Is that your signature on this paper?"

"Yes Sir, it sure is. This is the paper where Sir Hampton signed over his business interests in America to Mr. Richard Hampton. I'll never forget that because he gave me and Martin a sovereign each because of how late the hour was."

"And you're sure you're not mistaken. Is that right?"

Mr. Fendoff stood up and said, "Objection! Leading the witness."

"Objection overruled. Proceed with your questioning Mr. Shystwell. Let's not stand on ceremony." Judge Pickwick frowned at Mr. Fendoff and looked back at Mr. Shystwell. Move along Mr. Shystwell."

"Barry, I had just asked you if you were mistaken. Were you?"

"No Sir, Mr. Shystwell, there is no way I could've been mistaken." Barry coughed nervously and swallowed. His Adam's apple ran up and down his throat.

"I'm finished with my questioning. Your witness Mr. Fendoff." Mr. Shystwell walked back to his table and sat down.

Mr. Fendwell stood up and walked slowly to the witness chair and stopped in front of the witness. "Good morning Mr. Eagleton. We appreciate you taking the time to appear in court today."

Barry Eagleton squirmed in his seat, and again his Adam's apple ran up and down his throat as he swallowed nervously. "Th thanks. Uh, uh I was glad to come." He reached over and picked up his glass of water, then nearly spilled it. He drank half the glass of water and set it down noisily. He dragged his shirt sleeve across his mouth and repeated, "I'm glad to be of help."

Mr. Fendwell smiled at him in a friendly manner. "There is no need to be nervous Barry. We just have to be sure we understand what you're saying, or perhaps I should say we need to be sure we understand what you mean to say. You did tell us that you knew Sir Hampton, did you not?"

Barry mumbled something unintelligible and nodded his head yes.

"I'm sorry Barry, but you need to speak up so the jury can hear you. Please look straight at my eyes and repeat what you just said."

Barry raised his head and looked at Mr. Fendwell's face. "I said, yes sir, I knew Sir Hampton."

"Barry, tell me, when you say you knew Sir Hampton, did you mean you knew him personally or that you knew of him?"

Barry squirmed in his seat, cleared his throat, and looked down at his hands.

"No Barry, please look at my face," said Mr. Fendwell. "I mean did you know him personally. Had you ever spoken to him? Had you ever seen him in person, or did you just know who he was?"

"I just knew who he was," said Barry.

Shystwell leaped to his feet. "I object! I object on the grounds that Fendwell is badgering the witness. He is making him say what he wants him to say."

"That will be all Barry. You may step down from the witness chair," said Mr. Fendwell.

"Mr. Fendwell," said the judge, "I'll not have you badgering the witnesses. When they answer your question, don't attempt to make them change their mind as to what they're trying to say. Mr. Shystwell, you may call your next witness."

"I call as my next witness, Mr. Martin Wolverton." Shystwell walked back to his table, and accepted the papers being handed to him by his clerk.

A deputy had stood up from the bench next to the door at the back of the courtroom and opened the courtroom door. Another deputy entered holding a mousy looking man of indeterminate age by his left arm. He escorted him to the front of the room, undid the sash that served as the door to the area closed off from the spectators, where the bailiff took charge of the new witness.

The bailiff swore the witness in and had him take a seat in the witness chair. Shystwell approached the witness chair, where the witness sat with a false look of bravado. He smiled at the witness. "Please state your name to the court," he said. There was a somewhat sneering twist to his smile.

"My name is Martin Wolverine." He leaned forward with his elbows on the table.

"And where are you from Mr. Wolverine?" Shystwell leaned slightly forward, hands clasped behind his back. His eyes were fixed piercingly on those of Martin Wolverine."

"I'm from London, England, Sir."

"And do you have employment in London, England." Shystwell rubbed his hands together and shot a look at the jury."

"Yes Sir, I do. I'm employed for your firm, Sir."

"And what do you do for our firm, Martin?"

"I'm primarily the mail boy, Sir. I also run all sorts of odd errands. You might say I'm sort of a Jack of all Trades. I fetch and carry and cleanup spills."

"Have you ever witnessed the signing of any contracts, Martin?"

"Yes Sir, I have. Quite often when something's been notarized, I am asked to be one of the witnesses to the signing."

"Martin, would you be so kind as to read this contract and tell me if you have ever seen it before?"

"Yes Sir, Mr. Shystwell. This is a contract that I witnessed when it was signed by Sir Hampton."

"Can you testify that is your signature as the second witness to the signing?"

"Yes Sir! I sure can. That was the night I had to stay late to witness the signing."

"Your witness Mr. Fendoff." Mr. Shystwell walked back to his table and a nearly jaunty manner."

Fendoff arose and walked to a point about five feet in front of the witness's chair. "Good morning Martin," he said. "May I thank you for being so kind as to appear here as a witness? I know it must've been a terrible inconvenience to travel so far."

"Oh, that's nothing. Mr. Shystwell is paying my salary while I'm over here. This is the first time I've ever been to America."

"Well, I'm very glad to hear that," said Mr. Fendoff. "It's nice to know you're enjoying yourself. I wonder if you could help me out on a little matter. I'd like to know if you are certain that is your signature on the contract there in the line for the second witness."

"Oh sure, there is no doubt in my mind. The contract was signed by Sir Hampton. I had always wanted to meet Sir Hampton. He is as nice as everyone says he is; he even gave me a sovereign for having to stay so late to witness a signature."

"Am I to gather, from what you said, that this was the first time you've ever seen Sir Hampton with your own two eyes?"

"Oh, no Sir. I'd seen him lots of times before. I just didn't know who he was. I thought he was someone who worked for Mr. Shystwell."

Mr. Shystwell stood up shouting, "Objection Your Honor! He's leading the witness. He's putting words in his mouth."

"Objection sustained," the judge shouted. "Mr. Fendoff, I've warned you about going so far afield. Keep your questions on the subject at hand. Another such deviation and I'll charge you with contempt!"

"But sir," said Fendoff, "my line of question is very pertinent to the case. The reasons will become very obvious later in this hearing."

"Consider yourself warned, Fendoff. Do you have any further questioning for this witness? The judge leaned over and peered angrily at Mr. Fendoff. "Do I make myself clear?"

"Yes, Your Honor. You make yourself abundantly clear." Turning his face from the judge to Martin Wolverton, "I have no more questions for this witness. Martin you may step down."

"Are there any more witnesses for the plaintiff?" asked the judge.

"Judge," Shystwell said, "I have witnesses to prove a conspiracy to kill Sir Hampton and his son Rodney. I will be able to show beyond the shadow of a doubt that because of the way the contract was written with the rights of all of the surviving members of the owners of the Rimrock Land and Cattle Company to inherit the shares of any deceased members of the original owners, the present management conspired to kill both Sir Hampton and his son, Rodney Hampton. May it please the court; I would prefer to divorce that part of this hearing from the part establishing ownership of the Rimrock Land and Cattle Company.

"When I have finished establishing my client's ownership of the Rimrock Land And Cattle Company, giving him access to the Rimrock Bank and Trust and his rightful capital there-in, he will be able to continue the operation of the Rimrock Land and Cattle Company as well of the Vertical X's in a manner to most efficiently utilize the available capital and labor.

"I think by the time this hearing is over I will have given sufficient cause to support the issuing of a warrant for the arrest of the present management of the Rimrock Land and Cattle Company and of holding them for trial for the murder of Sir Hampton and Rodney Hampton; and the attempted theft of all the assets of the Rimrock Land and Cattle Company and the Rimrock Bank and Trust."

A roar of conversation swept across the spectators. The roar held a notable enthusiasm on the side where the employees of the Vertical

X's were seated. A note of consternation was apparent in the sound of the conversation among the spectators from the city of Vacaville.

I exchanged smiles with Mr. Fendoff, but immediately straightened out my face into a sterner appearing demeanor. It was still a little too early for either of us to be smiling while the judge was glaring down at us with a triumphant look in his eyes.

Mr. Fendoff rose to his feet. "Your Honor, I would like you to order the entire statement of Mr. Shystwell stricken from the record and instruct the jurors to disregard it. His tirade has been a blatant attempt to influence the jurors unfairly, unjustly, and illegally. Furthermore, he has gone far afield from anything pertaining to the reason for this hearing."

Judge Pickwick slammed his gavel down on the desk several times in an attempt to restore order to the room. "To the contrary Mr. Fendoff, I find that you, Mr. Seeker, and the rest of the management of the Rimrock Land and Cattle Company and of the Rimrock Bank and Trust, to be a group of rascals, thieves, and confidence men who should not be allowed to walk on the same land as free and honest men."

"Your Honor, I find your behavior extremely prejudicial to our case. How do you expect us to possibly get a fair hearing after what you have just said in the presence of the jury and all the spectators?" asked Mr. Fendoff. "I demand the right to introduce my own witnesses, and to defend my own good name, the name of Mr. Seeker and the rest of the accused parties."

The judge replied, "Mr. Fendoff, I fear you forget yourself. You may be a big-city lawyer but I'm a circuit judge in the territory of Colorado. Justice here is defined by the evidence entered into court and by my rendering of my verdict based upon my analysis of the evidence entered into court. Do I make myself absolutely clear?"

Mr. Fendoff answered, "Yes Judge, I understand exactly what you have said. I also realize that I have a duty to my clients. You may look upon the territory of Colorado as some barren stretch of land beyond the reach of the laws of the United States of America. However the citizens of the territory of Colorado deserve the same benefit of the laws of this great country as do the citizens of the great metropolitan areas.

"I demand my right to present our witnesses and to allow the jurors who are hearing this case to make up their minds without being influenced by any preconceived convictions. Now may I call my witnesses?"

"You have tried my patience beyond the limits that I can or will allow. I will allow you to call your witnesses, but I will serve notice to you now that you will pay for challenging the authority of this court! It is very evident from the evidence that has already been entered in front of this court that Richard Hampton has proven his case. You should all feel lucky that you're not taken out at this moment and hung by the neck until you're dead, dead, dead."

Shouts of agreement with the judge's sentiments arose from the section where the employees of the Vertical X's were seated. Shouts of "Hang 'em," "String 'em up," "Make em dance on air," and other suggestions, laced with profanity and punctuated with vulgarities.

The judge rapped his gavel on the table several times. "Upon further reflection upon the seriousness of the charges being brought against the management of the Rimrock Land and Cattle Company and the way those charges are such an intrinsic part of the apparent plot by that management to steal all the assets of the Rimrock Land and Cattle Company, I have decided to combine the two hearings. Mr. Shystwell, are you in the position so that you feel you can successfully prosecute a case of murder against the management of the Rimrock Land and Cattle Company and at the same time prove your case that they have fraudulently, maliciously, and with malice, plotted, planned, and partially perpetrated their plan to take over the Rimrock Land and Cattle Company and the Rimrock Bank and Trust Company?"

Mr. Shystwell stood up, trying to stifle his satisfaction with the way things were turning out. "I certainly am, Your Honor. I feel it is my duty to do everything in my power to prevent these people from taking advantage of other innocent victims. Beyond the indisputable proof that I have that they were behind the killing of my client's cousin, Rodney Hampton, lies the truth that they were also responsible for the mysterious killing of his uncle, Sir Edward Hampton. I think it is only my duty as one whose client expects to become a new citizen of America, that I do my part to bring civilization to the great territory of Colorado. I want to assure all the citizens who are spectators here at this hearing that my client, Richard Hampton, is taking these steps at great personal sacrifice, anguish, and heartache."

"Then," said the judge, "Please consult with your client and see if he will permit us to consolidate these two important hearings into one. I hope he is as interested in expediting justice, as I am in executing it."

"Your Honor, would you please be so kind as to grant us a five minute recess while I consult with my client?" Mr. Shystwell looked straight into the judge's eyes, allowed himself a quick glance at the jury, who seemed singularly impressed. Could I impose upon the good humor of Your Honor to allow my client and me to converse in privacy for a few moments?"

"You certainly may, Mr. Shystwell." He looked out over the roomful of spectators and added, "You gentlemen just keep your seats. This combined hearing will start five minutes."

The spectators in the court room were astounded. What luck! The ones who were not aligned with Richard Hampton, or who had traveled from Vacaville to see that the Rimrock Land and Cattle Company and their management got a square deal had come here to break the boredom of the endless repetitious days of their lives. Now they were to be the spectators at a trial that would be known throughout the territory of Colorado, the West, and perhaps all of America.

Mr. Shystwell and Richard Hampton had returned back to the courtroom. Mr. Shystwell took a couple of steps toward the judge and said, "Your Honor I beg the court's indulgence, but may Mr. Fendoff and I approach the bench?"

While Mr. Shystwell and Richard Hampton had been outside the courtroom, Mr. Fendoff and I were having a quick conversation. "Can we allow such a combination, Mr. Fendoff?"

"This is more than unusual, it's downright unheard of. However, it appears to me that we should have the proper ammunition here to break up this entire plot in one fell swoop. What is your own opinion, Easy?"

"I reckon this will be the best chance we have to round up everyone at once. Let's give it a shot!"

The judge was answering Mr. Shystwell's request for him and Mr. Fendoff to approach the bench. "Mr. Fendoff please come up here and join Mr. Shystwell."

As Mr. Fendoff approached the bench, he said to the judge, "Your Honor, because of the unusual circumstances of combining these two hearings, I beg your indulgence in allowing Mr. Seeker to join me here. This hearing is of extreme importance, not only to Mr. Seeker, but to the very existence of the Rimrock Land and Cattle Company. I might also add that the charges being leveled against Mr. Seeker and the

Rimrock Land and Cattle Company affect not only the property, but the very lives of Mr. Seeker and others."

Judge Pickwick was feeling very good about the way things were going. He would be able to retire with what he was getting out of this deal. He might as well, he figured, appear magnanimous and allow Seeker to join Mr. Fendoff.

"You do realize," said the judge, "what a serious decision you're making? If you are found guilty of killing either Rodney Hampton, Sir Edward Hampton, or both of these men, it is very likely that you will hang. If you should wish to plead guilty, I would be willing to see to it that you would not be facing the death penalty. Do you understand the hard choices you have in front you?"

"Yes Sir," I answered. "It is highly likely that the guilty party will be uncovered and punished in these proceedings. I have the utmost confidence that justice will prevail."

"Mr. Shystwell, are you willing to proceed with the prosecution of this case to its conclusion?"

Upon hearing Mr. Shystwell's affirmative answer, he said, "Then the three of you can return to your places. I will declare a five minute recess and at the end of those five minutes, I will ask you how you plead, Mr. Seeker." Neither the judge nor Mr. Shystwell could quite mask a satisfaction that bordered on elation.

I walked to the rear of the courtroom and exchanged a few brief words with one of the men who were seated in the last row of chairs where most of the Richard Hampton faction was seated. A couple of minutes later the judge came back out of his chambers, the bailiff had everyone standup, and court was declared back in session.

"I have a special announcement to make," said the judge. "Both the plaintiff and the defendant in this hearing have agreed to broaden the scope of this hearing to include the charge of murder in the first degree. This charge has been lodged against the defendant by the plaintiff, Richard Hampton. It is now the duty of the court to ask the primary defendant against the charge of first-degree murder, Mr. Easy Seeker, how he wishes to plea to the charge of murder.

"Mr. Seeker, please standup and approach the bench." The judge waited a moment while I stood up and walked up in front of the judge's bench. "Mr. Seeker, has your attorney advised you as to the seriousness of the charge you're facing?"

"Yes, Your Honor, I have been so advised."

"Has he also advised you, Mr. Seeker, that it is very likely you will be facing the penalty of death if you're found guilty?"

"Yes, Your Honor, I have been so advised of the penalty."

"Knowing the seriousness of the charges you're facing and knowing the probable sentence if you're found guilty, the court is now obliged to ask you, "How do you plead to this charge?"

"I plead not guilty, Your Honor, since I am not guilty."

"Save your theatrics for when you're in the witness chair," said the judge. "When so much evidence is arrayed against you, you should be more interested in making your peace with God then you are in making flippant remarks to the court. Your best recourse is to throw yourself on the mercy of the court. That's the only way you're going to save yourself from a hanging."

"Your Honor, with all due respect, it appears to me like you've already made up your mind that I'm guilty. I suppose that next you'll be sentencing me to hang and you will be dismissing the jury without the formality of the trial."

The judge looked at me with a mixture of hate, disdain, and a warped pleasure. "Young man, it grieves me to tell you that you're going to serve as an example to all of the crooks and would-be crooks who live in the Bend of the Rimrock. Take your seat while we dispose of the formalities and bring this hearing to a close."

As I turned to go back to my seat, I felt a chill run down my back. I glanced toward the rear of the room and my eyes met those of the man with whom I had spoken earlier during the recess. That brief glance made me feel immeasurably better.

Judge Pickwick suddenly seemed to be all business. He looked down from his podium at Mr. Shystwell and said, "Call your first witness Mr. Shystwell."

Mr. Shystwell stood up and said to the judge, "Your Honor, I would like to make one brief statement. Because of the suddenness of the change in the nature of this hearing, it will be impossible to call the witnesses in the order I would have liked to have called them. I beg the court's indulgence and ask Your Honor to give me the leeway to present my witnesses as best I can."

"Permission granted. Proceed with your witnesses."

Mr. Shystwell said, "I now call Brad Rogers to the stand. I ask the court to classify Brad Rogers as a hostile witness."

"I object, Your Honor," cried Mr. Fendoff. "A witness cannot be forced to testify against himself!"

"Over-ruled!" The judge nearly smiled as he looked at Shystwell.

"I assume, Mr. Shystwell, that you will be able to show the pertinence of this." The judge first rubbed his chin, and then began to twirl his gavel.

Again, a deputy on the back bench walked to the door and said something to a deputy on the outside. The door closed and about three minutes passed before the door reopened and a deputy escorted Brad Rogers to the front of the room.

With a puzzled look on his face Brad was sworn in and took his seat in the witness chair.

Mr. Shystwell approached the witness chair. "Please state your name to the court," he said.

"My name is Brad Rogers."

"And what do you do for a living, Mr. Rogers, asked Shystwell?

"My daughter and I run a ranch called The And Ours." said Brad.

"And what is your relationship, if any, to the Rimrock Land and Cattle Company?"

"I am on the board of directors and at times I function as a senior advisor and operations officer." As Brad answered the questions, he kept his calm eyes fixed on the face of the plaintiff's attorney.

"And in what capacity were you working when you went to London several weeks ago to visit with Sir Hampton?"

"I called upon Sir Edward as a friend, in my capacity as a member of the board of directors, and as an emissary to express our deepest sympathy about the cowardly attack upon his beloved son and our esteemed friend, Rodney Hampton.

"It is natural enough that while I was in London, we discussed our plans for the Rimrock Land and Cattle Company. Although Sir Edward is the majority stockholder in the company, the operations of the company have been handled by his son Rodney Hampton; and Easy Seeker, who is a close friend of the Hampton family and was more like a big brother to his son Rodney Hampton than to a co-owner of the Rimrock Land and Cattle Company. The other two principals of the company are me and my daughter, Earlene. I have already told you what I do for the company. My daughter has been running the bank since the tragic death of our friend Rodney."

Mr. Shystwell clasped his hands behind his back. "So," he said, turning and taking several paces down it to the front of the jury's box, "your daughter has been running the bank, has she?" His tone of voice made it sound as though he was accusing her of some criminal activity.

Again he turned; still clasping his hands behind his back and with his head bowed as though in deep thought, he walked in apparent thoughtfulness back and faced the witness chair.

"Why did you really visit?!" he suddenly thundered. "Do you really expect us to believe that you went there to offer your sympathy over the death of his son, whom you are accused of complicity in murdering, and to discuss your plans for the Rimrock Land and Cattle Company? I submit to this court that you went to London to kill Sir Edward. I submit that not only did you go to London to kill Sir Edward but that you did kill Sir Edward! My private investigator has found that you and Sir Edward went to the docks together on that last fateful night. He also found that Sir Edward, accompanied by you and his secretary, who is also his niece and my client's cousin, boarded a fishing boat and left the dock together. My detective's report also shows that that was the last time any of the three of you were ever seen except for you, Sir! You alone!"

"It is more than strange that while you were in the company of Sir Hampton, everyone else but you has met an untimely death.

The swell of conversation among the spectators made it impossible to hear any of the court's proceedings. Judge Pickwick was pounding the table with his gavel and repeatedly saying "Order! Order! Order in the court room! I'll have order or I'll clear the room!"

The bailiff immediately started back toward the spectators and at the same instant the deputies seated along the back wall started up the aisles to the sides and up the center of the large room. Amidst several shouts for silence, plus the threatening presence of the several deputies, the room quickly quieted.

"Now Rogers! Do you deny the information that I've just imparted to the court? I want to caution you that you are testifying under the penalties of perjury!"

"No Shystwell, I don't deny some of the things you said. However I do deny your implication that there was anything strange or evil about our meeting or about our parting. It would take a person with no humanity to accuse a man who exhibits humanity by offering his sympathy, in person, to a dear friend and business associate."

"Your Honor, would you please direct this witness to answer the questions directed to him without introducing his own little snide comments during this hearing that could adversely affect his future."

The judge glared at Brad. "The witness will please refrain from adding his commentary to his answers to the attorney for the plaintiff."

"Yes, Your Honor." Brad turned his head to look at the judge and repeated, "Yes, Your Honor."

"Do you, Brad Rogers, admit that you were in London on the last day Sir Edward Hampton was seen?"

"I'll admit that I was in London on the day that it is said Sir Edward Hampton sailed for India. There is no way that I can swear, from my own personal knowledge that Sir Edward Hampton was seen or was not seen by others."

"Well then, you will admit that you were in London on the date that Sir Edward Hampton was said to sail for India?"

"Yes, I'll admit that I was in London on the date that Sir Edward Hampton was said to sale for India."

"Will you also admit that his secretary, Cynthia, accompanied you and Sir Edward to the boat where the three of you, accompanied by the boat's coxswain, set sail from the London dock as twilight approached?"

"Yes, I freely admit to the fore-going statement."

"Then," said Mr. Shystwell, "is it your claim that Sir Edward and Cynthia boarded a ship for India?"

"There is no way that I can swear as to where the ship was bound. I have heard that it was bound for India. I read the name, *India Trader,* on the bow of the ship's hull."

"Tell us in your own words what happened next." Mr. Shystwell's voice was becoming exasperated.

Brad paused for a moment before answering. Shystwell cut in by asking, "Are you trying to think up a good answer, Rogers?"

"No, Shystwell. I am trying to remember exactly what we did next, so I can be precise with my answer."

"Ah Ha," said Shystwell. "I note that you just said what *we* did next, not what *I* did next. Are you telling me that you were still accompanied by Sir Edward and Cynthia? Is that what you are telling the court, after first having said that they boarded the India Trader?"

"No, Shystwell, that is not what I am trying to say. If you had been listening to what I say, instead of trying to play Sherlock Holmes, you would have heard me say that Sir Edward, Cynthia and I, accompanied by the boat's Coxswain, cast off from the dock in London. The Coxswain was still in the boat when we left the India Star and headed for the ship that carried us back to America. Since "I" is singular, and "we" is plural, the Coxswain and I, or "we", pushed off from the India Trader and I was carried to the steamship bound for America. Have I adequately explained our actions on my last night in London?"

"Yes Rogers. I think you adequately incriminated yourself enough that you will end up hanging, right along of Easy Seeker."

It was easy to hear the shouts of agreement coming from the spectators seated with the Vertical X's group. It was also easy to see the looks of consternation on our friends from Vacaville and the Bend of the Rimrock. Some of the men among the Vertical X's group could easily be seen trying to instigate some kind of problem; probably a lynching.

"Rogers, you can step down now. I'm through with you."

"Shystwell, you've been involved in enough hearings that you know better than to dismiss the witness without giving the opposing lawyer a chance to cross examine. It seems to me like you're taking an awful lot for granted." Mr. Fendoff walked calmly up in front of the witness stand, smiled at Brad, and said, "How are you, Mr. Rogers?"

"I'm doing very well thank you sir; and how are you on this fine, but interesting day."

"I'm doing fine also, Mr. Rogers, but I just want to make sure that I understand you correctly. I'm going to say what I understood you to say. Please stop me and correct me if I'm wrong. It is my understanding that you went to London shortly after Rodney Hampton was shot and killed. Is that correct?

"Yes Mr. Fendoff, that is entirely correct. I believe I started my trip two days after we buried Rodney."

"Did you have any problems getting from here to London?"

Brad leaned back in his chair, placed his right ankle on his left knee, and held that ankle in his two hands. "No sir, it was an uneventful trip. When I arrived in London, I rented a hansom cab, gave them Sir Edward's address, and soon arrived. I had the cab wait so I would have time to see if Sir Edward was home. I was met at the door by Oscar, his Butler, who left me in the vestibule while he informed Sir Edward of my arrival. A couple of minutes later, he showed me into the den and announced me to Sir Edward.

"Sir Edward stood up, shook hands with me, and asked me if I had taken care of the cab. I told him that the cab was waiting for me out front. Sir Edward sent Oscar out to take care of the cab and bring in my luggage. In the meantime I had informed Sir Edward of the sad nature of my visit. Of course he was greatly shocked to receive such bad news.

"He begged my pardon for a moment, walked over and looked out the window at his garden while he recovered his composure. Then he walked back and took my hand and told me that he knew how much his son had meant to me. He had dismissed the Butler, but he now pulled a sash that hung down from the ceiling and a moment later Oscar returned. He informed Oscar that we were going to his study and for him to bring two glasses and a bottle of Brandy to us.

"He had me sit down in an easy chair, across a low table from where he sat. We sat silently for that brief period of time that it took Oscar to return with the drinks. When Oscar returned, he poured two snifters of Brandy. He dismissed the butler again, we picked up our Brandy and Sir Edward toasted his dead son."

Before Brad could continue, he was interrupted by Shystwell's angry voice. We're not interested in hearing his life's story. Your Honor would you please direct Mr. Roger's counsel to keep his questioning to things pertinent to this hearing."

The judge looked at Mr. Fendoff, with his perpetual scowl, and said, "Mr. Fendoff, I understand how difficult it is when you're trying to defend a guilty man, but try not to wander so far afield."

Mr. Fendoff could not keep his anger from showing. "In all of my years before the bench, I have never before had to stand in front of the court and listen to the judge tell everyone on the jury and all of the spectators that my client is guilty. How do you possibly expect my client to get a fair trial when he has to contend with such breaches of the code of justice?"

"It is only my concern for justice that keeps me from having you jailed for contempt of court. However, even my sense of justice has its limits. You are walking a very fine line, and if you have concerns about a fair trial for your client, it is certainly to your advantage to control your tongue and your temper. Now continue with a more focused approach or your client will find himself on his own. Do I make myself absolutely clear?"

"You certainly do Your Honor, you certainly do," answered Mr. Fendoff. Then he said, "Proceed Mr. Rogers. You had just said that you and Sir Edward had picked up your glasses of brandy and toasted Rodney. What happened after that?"

"Sir Edward told me that he would like to talk about the affairs of the ranch and get his mind off Rodney. I began to talk to him about the seeding of the East Cedar breaks pasture, and our studies concerning goats and sheep."

Again there was a raucous display of profanity and shouts of "*string up the sheep man! Hang the mutton lovers!*"

The deputies had rushed into the aisles, before the judge could even raise his gavel.

Mr. Fendoff continued as though he had never been interrupted. "Now Mr. Rogers, could you please tell us the events leading up to you casting off with Sir Edward and Cynthia on your last night in London."

"Yes Sir, I reckon I can. Sir Edward and I had been called to supper. At about the same time as we arrived at the table, Cynthia came through a door on the other side of the dining room. Sir Edward and I remained standing until she arrived at the table. Sir Edward introduced us and I pulled out her chair for her to be seated. Sir Edward informed her of my purpose in being in London and of the death of Ronald. She and Ronald had been very close and she was very shocked at his death.

The kitchen maid came in with the first dinner course. As we ate our salads, Sir Edward instructed Cynthia to prepare to show me around through London. We continued, course after course, and apparently Sir Edward changed his mind. He informed us that we would have to wait for another visit at another time before Cynthia would have time to show me the sights of London. He informed Cynthia, who is his business secretary and his most important aide, to inform the Captain of the India Trader that they would sail for India that night. He further stated that he had business in India too important to neglect and that it was imperative that he take care of that business. He then had plans to come visit his son's grave in America. It is my understanding that the India Trader sank in a storm with the loss of all passengers and crew."

"As I understand it from what you said earlier, the boat that took the three of you out, dropped Sir Edward and Cynthia off at the India trader and continued on to drop you off at the steamship for America. Am I correct in that?"

"Yes," Brad answered. "That's exactly the way it happened to the best of my memory."

Mr. Fendoff consulted a small notebook and then looked up at Brad. "So then you returned directly to the Rimrock Land and Cattle Company. Is that correct?"

"Yes, that is correct," replied Brad.

"And how long after you returned did you find out about the death of Sir Edward?" Mr. Fendoff was again consulting the little notebook.

"I can't remember the exact time that had elapsed, but he seems to me that it was just a very few days." Brad started to add something to that but then lapsed into silence.

"Did you have something you wanted to add to that last statement?" Mr. Fendoff looked at Brad inquiringly.

"I had just remembered that I was thinking that when the earliest word arrived of Sir Edward's loss at sea, that the letter must have been routed on the stage line that now runs from Kansas to Salt Lake City, Utah. Now, as I think back upon it, it seems to me that the letter arrived at nearly the same time as I returned from the trip to London."

"When you picked up your letter, can you remember anything happening that might make the postmaster more specifically remember giving you the letter?" Mr. Fendoff stood waiting, while Brad pondered his question.

"Now that you mention it, I believe there is something. The proprietor of the Mercantile, Paddy O'Reilly, is also the postmaster at Vacaville. We had a short conversation about when our next shipment of wire would come in. We had ordered a hundred and sixty miles of sheep and goat proof wire and several hundred miles of barbed wire for fencing in our East Cedar Breaks pasture.

"Since the shipment was scheduled to arrive on that very day, it will be very easy to establish the date by having Paddy O'Reilly look at the date on his invoice. I guess that will eliminate all the guesswork from the subject."

Mr. Fendoff was jotting down something in his little notebook. He opened his mouth to speak but before he was able to say anything, the judge interrupted his train of thought.

"Mr. Fendoff," said the judge, "if you have any intention of stalling this hearing by sending people off on a wild goose chase, you can forget it. It is very easy to see after what has transpired thus far in this hearing that you and your client are drowning men who are only grabbing at straws. I applaud your efforts to save your client from hanging. However, the guilty must pay the price.

"I am happy to humor you and I am allowing you a lot of leeway so you can show a good faith effort to mount a good defense for your client. You have to keep the elements of your defense concise, easily available, and easily seen to be pertinent to this case. Now, do you have any other witnesses to call or any other statements to introduce into evidence that have any chance of changing the outcome of this hearing?" The judge leaned back in his chair, pulled out his handkerchief, and began polishing his glasses as he awaited his answer from Mr. Fendoff.

Mr. Fendoff was not long in giving his answer. "I want you to know, Your Honor, and I want to be sure this is entered in the record, that every word I say, that every question I asked, and that every problem I pose is pertinent to this case and will be so recognized in the event of the necessity to appeal your decision."

The judge was furious. He jumped to his feet, his face a mixture of black and red. The blood veins stood out on his forehead. He seemed on the verge of apoplexy. "Fendoff," he shouted, "am I to understand that you are challenging the authority of this court?! I'm going to tell you something and you had better listen and you had better understand what you hear, for if you don't you'll find yourself rotting in jail.

"The territory of Colorado is not run like one of your big cities. Here in our territory, we don't allow murderers to escape justice. We don't allow some smooth tongued city slicker to enter our courts like some cute little girl posturing on the school stage while her friends and parents clap. We take our courts seriously, and we intend to render justice swiftly, surely and honestly."

"Your Honor, the last thing I would want to do is to impugn your authority or your sense of justice. I beg your pardon if I have offended you. I beg your pardon if my methods of uncovering information that I deem necessary to the defense of my client are angering you. I beg you not to let my shortcomings lead to a miscarriage of justice for my client."

"A murderer is a murderer, no matter who defends him," said Judge Pickwick.

"Your Honor, I demand that you quit talking as if my client is guilty. Remember my client is called as a hostile witness for the prosecution. I have every right to cross examine him and to call him again later as my own witness."

"You have what rights I give you Mr. Fendoff," snapped the judge. "Mr. Rogers, please step down from the witness chair. You are excused from further testimony."

"Mr. Shystwell, do you have any more witnesses for the prosecution?" The judge's voice had lost its note of belligerence when speaking to the prosecutor. "I think you have already presented an ironclad case against Mr. Rogers and the rest of the management for the Rimrock Land and Cattle Company. Unless you feel you should proceed with more witnesses, I would suggest you rest the prosecution and we move on to the sentencing stage."

"Judge Pickwick, if you do not allow me to present the defense for my client, I will immediately send riders to the Colorado territorial governor's office, to the commanding general of the Colorado territorial federal detachment of soldiers, and plead our case before the Senate and House of Representatives of the United States legislature. It is beyond my power to override your rulings, but I can certainly see that an investigation is launched into your actions in this hearing."

"I find you in contempt of court, Mr. Fendoff. However, because of my love of justice, before jailing you I will allow you to complete your defense of the Rimrock Land and Cattle Company et al. You will be allowed a maximum of half an hour for each witness you present. I suggest you call your first witness now."

Mr. Fendoff returned to the defendant's table and said to me, "Easy, I have been so preoccupied with my sparring with Judge Pickwick that I have not been able to keep abreast of any of the latest happenings. Who do you think we should call for the first witness?"

"Mr. Fendoff, I think we should call Earlene to the stand. As soon as you get her on the stand, ask her who she saw coming out of the judge's chamber during the last recess. All will become clear to you when you hear her answer."

Mr. Fendoff walked back in front of the judge's podium and said, "As a first witness for the defense, I call Earlene Rogers to the stand."

Mr. Shystwell stood up to object, but the deputy at the back of the court room had already stood up, opened the door, and spoken to a deputy stationed outside the front door. A moment later Earlene was escorted into the room and up in front of the podium to be sworn in.

After she was sworn in, Mr. Fendoff said, "Earlene, I would like for you to have a seat in the witness's chair." He waited for a moment until she had been seated. "Earlene, first I would like to say I appreciate you being here at such a trying time. I would also like to ask you if you saw anything peculiar or unusual during the last recess of the court."

"Yes Sir, Mr. Fendoff. I'm not sure exactly just how peculiar or how unusual this was, but it appeared both peculiar and strange to me, under the circumstances."

"Miss Rogers, just what did you see that struck you as being so strange and unusual?"

"I had expected to be called as a witness some time during the course of this trial. Because of that I have been staying in the room where the witnesses for the defense remained secluded from the court room until they're called to the witness chair. I had to go to the restroom.

"A couple of minutes later, just as I emerged from the restroom, I saw both Mr. Shystwell and Richard Hampton emerging from the judge's chamber. "Because it seemed to me to be very prejudicial to the interests of the Rimrock Land and Cattle Company, I asked the deputy who had escorted me from the witness room to grab the County Clerk, who happened to be passing by, and for the two of them to witness Mr. Shystwell, Richard Hampton, and Judge Pickwick engaged in an animated, but hurried conversation."

"I had the deputy escort me back to the witness room, and continued waiting to be called as a witness," answered Earlene.

"Your witness," said Mr. Fendoff, looking at the prosecution.

Mr. Shystwell walked up in front of Earlene, clenched his fist and extended his index finger and jammed it up in front of her face with the point of his finger only three or 4 inches from the end of her nose. "You know," he thundered, "that there are severe penalties for perjury!

"Yes Sir, Mr. Shystwell, I am very well acquainted with that part of the law. I would like to call your attention to the fact that there are also severe penalties associated with conspiring to prevent a fair trial for the defendants that come before the court. Need I remind you, Sir, that my testimony has been given while the defense holds signed and sworn statements from officials of this county declaring what I have said is the truth."

"Mr. Fendoff," said the judge, in a voice that was beginning to crack, "you may call your next witness."

I thought it was about time for me to confer again with the hard-bitten man seated in the back left corner of the courtroom. He was the same man with whom I had conferred earlier. We exchanged no more than half a dozen words, before I turned and went back to my seat at the defense's table, where I whispered briefly in Mr. Fendoff's ear.

Mr. Fendoff stood up and walked up in front of the judge's podium. "Your Honor, I would like to ask you for a ten minute recess."

"You'll get another recess on the same day that hell freezes over," hissed the judge.

"Judge Pickwick, I advise you in the strongest way possible that you grant this recess. The defense is about to rest its case. I truly believe that you will be much happier if you grant this recess, than if you force us to go on without the recess.

"However, I will leave this up to you Judge! Believe me; this recess will be much more to your advantage that will be ours."

"What, what do you mean? " the judge stammered.

"You'll find out in the next few minutes," said Mr. Fendoff.

"There will be a ten minute recess," the judge said in a halting voice as he rapped three times on the desk with his gavel.

I looked at the back of the room where the man with whom I had conferred had been sitting. He was no longer in the room. Brad and I, along with Earlene and Mr. Fendoff went into a huddle for a hurried conversation. Before we had finished with our conversation, there was a stir inside the courtroom as the hard-bitten man returned, accompanied by ten men, each wearing the star of a deputy US marshal.

Five of the deputies took their place on the left side of the door and the other five took their place on the right side of the door. The hard-bitten man, with whom I had conferred, remained leaning against the door of the courtroom. Each of the men was armed with double barreled shotguns.

While the room was still buzzing, the judge, with the show of bravado rapped his gavel and said, "Mr. Fendoff, please call your next witness."

In a loud and clear voice, Mr. Fendoff stated, "I now call, as my next witness, Mr. Rodney Hampton."

The room fell into a state of shocked silence, followed by questions being asked by men to the man who was his neighbor in the next chair, "Who did he say?", "Did he say Rodney Hampton?", "I must've misunderstood him."

The spectators had very little time to ponder for the deputy at the door swung the door open and Rodney Hampton with an armed a deputy on each side and two more in front and two more in back of him walked to the front of the courtroom and stood in front of the witness's chair to be sworn in.

After taking his oath, Rodney took his seat in the witness chair. He looked as though he had completely recovered his health. Mr. Fendoff picked up a tablet that he had been busily making notes in, stood up and strolled up to the witness chair.

"Would you please state your name for the court," he requested.

"My name is Rodney Hampton," the witness said.

"Would you also state for the record any association that you have with the Rimrock Land and Cattle Company?"

"I am the president of the Rimrock Bank and Trust. I am also a member of the board of directors of the Rimrock Land and Cattle Company. The other members of the board of directors of the Rimrock Land and Cattle Company are Easy Seeker, Brad Rogers, Earlene Rogers Seeker, and the chairman of the board is my father, Sir Edward Hampton."

"And who holds the controlling interest of the Rimrock Land and Cattle Company?" asked Mr. Fendoff.

"The way the charter of the Rimrock Land and Cattle Company is written, there is no controlling interest. All the members of the board of directors are also principals of the company. Each member of the board of directors has one vote. Each vote carries the same weight. Every member, or partner if you prefer to use that word, is an equal partner or is a member of equal standing."

"To clarify what you are saying, am I to understand that each member of the board of directors owns an equal share of the Rimrock Land and Cattle Company?" Mr. Fendoff appeared puzzled.

"No Sir," Rodney answered. "The percentage of our ownership varies from person to person, but the percentage of that ownership has no effect on the voice each person has in the management of the Rimrock Land and Cattle Company."

"Isn't that a rather unusual arrangement for such a large company?"

Mr. Fendoff looked over at the jury as though he were incredulous. That would mean that your father exercises no more power in the company then Earlene, Brad, Easy, or yourself. The fact of the matter is that if you and your father voted as a family block, and Brad Rogers, his daughter Earlene, who is also the wife of Easy Seeker, and Easy Seeker himself, also voting as a family block would be able to control the direction of the Rimrock Land and Cattle Company."

"Yes, that is the truth. However if the directors of the Rimrock Land and Cattle Company voted as a family block, the vote would always be five to nothing. The five of us are a family, as surely as though we were all born from the same mother." The smile on Rodney's face and the conviction in his voice left no doubt in the minds of the jury that what he had said was true."

Mr. Fendoff turned toward Mr. Shystwell and said, "Your witness!"

Mr. Shystwell half rose from his seat. "The prosecution has no questions."

"In that case," said Mr. Fendwell, "the defense will call our next witness."

The deputy at the back of the room stood up, swung open the door, and the same six deputies who had escorted Rodney into the courtroom, entered once more escorting the next witness. It was none other than Sir Edward Hampton.

As Sir Edward paused in front of the witness chair and the bailiff came forward with the Bible to administer the oath, I saw that several people scattered throughout the spectators on the side of the aisle where the supporters of Richard Hampton were seated arose and walked back to the door leading out of the courtroom. They were stopped by two deputies and sent back to their seats.

An ashen faced Judge Pickwick rapped his gavel sharply against the desk. "Order in the courtroom," he shouted. "Order in the courtroom before I clear the courtroom of all spectators." Everyone in the court room fell into a shocked silence.

In all the turmoil and noisy confusion, I had watched in silence as Sheriff Todd Russell, Rod Lasser, and four men whom I recognized as Rimrock Land and Cattle Company cowboys stationed themselves at even intervals along the left wall of the courtroom. The sheriff's chief deputy led the way up the right wall with the other deputies and a man I didn't recognize, and stationed them along that wall. Federal Marshal Hardy was leaning his right shoulder against the front wall of the room. This had him facing the witness box, the judge's podium, and the jury box beyond. Two men stood on each side of the front door leading into the courtroom. All of these men were armed with double barreled shotguns.

Judge Pickwick again rapped on the table with his gavel. "All charges are dismissed! Court is no longer in session. Bailiff, clear the courtroom." He turned to enter his chamber.

"Hold on, Judge! We still have some loose ends to tie up. Come back in and take a seat!" The Marshal's voice cut through the air like a whip.

"How dare you speak to me like that my courtroom? One more display of contempt and you'll spend the next thirty days in jail. I'm the Circuit Judge. Who in the hell do you think you are?" The judge's hand was still on the door knob of the door leading into his chamber. He edged closer to the entrance.

"Judge, I know exactly who I am. I'm a United States Marshal and I have a warrant for your arrest."

"Bailiff, arrest this man! We can't allow the power of the court to be questioned." His voice showed a mixture of trembling fear and thwarted fury. The thwarted fury succumbed to trembling fear as United States Marshal Hardy approached him, handcuffs in hand.

Sheriff Todd Russell stood nearby putting handcuffs on Richard Hampton.

"You don't have jurisdiction to arrest me," cried Richard. This is not part of Vaca County. Release me this instant."

"Well I'll tell you one thing's that's for sure. You may not be in my usual jurisdiction now, but in a very short time you will be. However, for the record, I will tell you that I do have jurisdiction to arrest you because United States Marshal Hardy has made me a temporary deputy United States Marshal. In about two hours from now, we'll be back in Vaca County and you'll be able to tell me if it seems any different to be under arrest by a deputy United States marshal than it does to be under arrest by the duly constituted sheriff of Vaca County.

"I will advise you, that as of now, you are under arrest for complicity in the attempted murder of Rodney Hampton, for conspiracy to defraud the rightful owners of the Rimrock Land and Cattle Company, including the Rimrock Bank and Trust of their ownership of those properties, and of half a dozen more serious charges that will be lodged against you at a later date."

-=-

Sir Edward had fallen in love with the West. Nevertheless it was obvious to everyone that he would soon have to return to London to look after his business interests. Trevor Baker, Cynthia's young attorney friend, stayed for a week before going back to New York. Sir Edward asked her, "Why don't you and Trevor saddle up a couple of horses and explore these valleys?"

"Oh, that would be great, especially if Brad would be able to come with us as a guide."

Sir Edmund was a very discerning man. He noted the shadow that crossed Trevor's face as Cynthia mentioned Brad. "Well," he said jovially, "why don't you ask him? I think he and Easy are down at the corral looking at some horses."

Cynthia's face brightened and she took Trevor by the hand. "Come on, Trevor. Let's go and see if we can pry Brad loose from his work."

Sir Edward saw the conflict of emotions in Trevor's face; a mixture of reluctance to have Brad come with them, but also a reluctance to disappoint Cynthia. He could read the handwriting on the wall; he had no chance with Cynthia, since Cynthia had met Brad. He swallowed his disappointment and determined to enjoy himself on the horseback ride.

Brad and I were discussing the finer points of a young stallion, and whether or not we should keep him for breeding stock.

Brad said to me, "There is no doubt he's a fine looking animal, but I personally feel like we would be better off if we brought in a couple of those Steeldust Stallions and started introducing that bloodline to our horses."

I looked up and saw Cynthia and Trevor hurrying from the house down to the corral. I also saw how Brad's eyes lighted up. I had been noticing the way Brad's actions changed each time he saw Cynthia. Well, she seemed like a great girl to me. I couldn't help but wonder how Brad would feel when she was no longer here, because since she was Sir Edward's most trusted employee and also the person with the most responsibilities, not to mention with the most knowledge of his business and the way he wanted it run, it seemed highly unlikely that he would be able to let her remain.

All of those thoughts flitted through my mind as she was covering the last few yards to the corral.

"Hi, Easy. Have you decided whether you're going to keep that stallion, or sell him to the dog food factory?"

She turned to Brad and took his hands in hers, looked into his face with her eyes shining and said, "Brad I know you and Easy are very busy trying to make up for all the neglect that you've had to give your ranches while caring for cousin Rodney, but I wonder if I could prevail upon you to come along with me so we can show Trevor these valleys."

Brad, still holding her hands, looked over her shoulder at Trevor. "Are you all sure that I won't just be in the way?"

Trevor said, "No Brad, you won't be in the way. I would be very happy if you and Cynthia would allow me to accompany you on this little expedition. I'm going to have to catch the stage back to New York tomorrow, and I just couldn't stand not having seen these valleys.

"Brad I'd like to tell you something. Some years ago, Cynthia and I were both attending the same university. We became very good friends. The university was quite some distance from my home and Cynthia and Sir Edward were kind and gracious enough to invite me to their home.

"I don't normally talk to others about my personal business, but in this case I intend to make an exception. While Cynthia and I were good friends and I would've been very happy to make it more than just friends, Cynthia was quite happy to maintain the status quo."

He turned to Cynthia and said, "Cynthia, I'm very embarrassed to have talked about you as though you were not even here. I hope that I haven't created an awkward moment."

"Brad said, "Why don't we go saddle up the horses? It's too nice a day to waste it here talking. Looking over at me, he said, "Easy, I'll catch you a little later."

I said, "Brad, if I were you I wouldn't take them too close to that camp of the wild Indians. I'll see you all when you get back." I took a last look at the stallion and walked back up to the house, grinning to myself as I walked.

Earlene, Rodney, and Sir Edward were sitting at the table talking. Papers were spread out before them and Earlene was using the papers to bring Rodney and Sir Edward up-to-date. At this particular time they were covering the status of the Rimrock Bank and Trust.

Then they looked up at me as I entered the room and Sir Edward said, "Easy, the more I look at these books, the more I am astounded in the way that you had this all set up initially. By your generosity by dividing so much of the land up in good, viable economic units, you have taken conditions that would have supported a very small country bank at the best and changed those conditions to make The Bend of the Rimrock into an economic region that supports one of the largest and most prosperous banks in the territory.

"When you diverted the mostly underground River so that each of the small ranches you created was amply watered, and with the requirements that each of the small ranchers have their land fenced in with barbed wire in a manner that left roads in between each tract of land and the neighboring tracts, it gave each small rancher a sense of security and pride. The fact that it was necessary for each of the tracts of land to have a good solid house and well, a big barn, and other outbuildings, not to mention corrals, holding pens, and other necessary additions to make the rancher's work faster, easier, and more efficient was a real boon to the rancher and his entire family."

"The upshot of this entire conversation is that I would like to nominate you as president of the Rimrock Land and Cattle Company. Rodney would continue as president of the Rimrock Bank and Trust, and I would try to prevail upon Brad to become chief operating officer of the Rimrock Land and Cattle Company, if you as president, agreed."

"Edward, I surely appreciate your offer. At the moment, without talking it over with Earlene and the other members of the board, I want to ask you for a little time to think it over.

"The primary thing that I would like to ask you at this time, and this will be completely and utterly between the two of us, is do you have any idea of what is going to happen between Cynthia and Brad? Do you know if Cynthia is going to stay in America? I feel sure that Brad would not leave his ranch here. If things are as serious between the two of them as I think they are, it will be a shame if anything keeps them apart. By the same token, Cynthia owes you an awful lot, in addition to the fact that she loves you so much.

"You can't afford to lose her. She can't afford to lose you. She and Brad will each be devastated if they don't remain together. Is this a puzzle with no solution?"

Sir Edward sat with a melancholy look on his face. "That same dilemma is preying on my mind. I wish I knew a good answer. I do know one thing: Her happiness is the most important thing in my life. Listen, Easy. You have had answers to some questions that appeared to be without answers. Give this one some thought. See if you can see some way out of this morass of emotions."

"I'll do that, Edward. I agree with Rodney that the five of us form one family. Whatever else happens, I think our family has to expand to six, with Cynthia being that sixth person. Speaking of us all as a group, one entity, there is no way that we can lose or stifle Cynthia's abilities and value to us as a company. It is even more imperative that we don't lose those abilities and value to us as a family."

We clasped hands and I went outside as Edward went into his room.

Chapter Nine - Page 142
An Accumulation of Events
Shystwell, Shystwell, Upton and Moncrief

The senior partners of Shystwell, Shystwell, Upton and Moncrief had scheduled a meeting with representatives from Shadow Financial. During the meeting, they were shown documents that proved Shadow Financial, a London company, held a lien against Richard Hampton's personal assets, which included the Vertical X's Ranch. They discussed the various options, and gave instructions to be presented to the Rimrock Land and Cattle Company, via the law firm of Fendoff, Pender, Baker and Allen.

Shystwell had also talked to the foreman of the gang of toughs that had made up the crew of the Vertical X's. He also talked to top guns of that organization. He had been able to get the charges dropped that had been filed against them when they were all arrested and jailed at the court hearing where Richard Hampton had tried to take over the Rimrock Land and Cattle Company. Another pact was negotiated.

With Shystwell as the go-between, both the offer from the Shadow Financial Company on the one hand, and the proposition that Shystwell had concocted with his former criminal defendants, were presented to Richard Hampton, who was awaiting execution in the Nugget Creek jail, the contract prison for the Territory of Colorado.

Richard Hampton gave Shystwell the go ahead to make an offer to the Rimrock Land and Cattle Company, through the office of Fendoff, Pender, Baker and Allen.

Fendoff, Pender, Baker and Allen

Mr. Fendoff of the law firm, Fendoff, Pender, Baker and Allen received a proposal from Shadow Financial of London, to sell the Vertical X's ranch and all of its assets to the Rimrock Land and Cattle Company to satisfy debts owed by that entity to Shadow Financial. Mr. Fendoff was to present the offer to the management of the Rimrock Land and Cattle Company without delay, to avoid the necessity of Shadow Financial having to initiate foreclosure procedures against Richard Hampton. In that event, the ranch would have to be sold at auction. It might bring far less at auction than what it might be worth to the Rimrock Land and Cattle Company.

Meeting of the Board of Directors,
Rimrock Land and Cattle Company.

I was in my seldom used office in the RB&T, when I received a surprise visitor. It was Mr. Fendoff, the attorney who had been so instrumental in our success at the court hearing when we had torn down the house of dreams of Richard Hampton. We shook hands and I offered him a chair.

He sat down across the desk from me, placed his briefcase in front of him, and said, "Easy, I have here a proposition from a company called *Shadow Financial.* They are based in London. It turns out that they provided the financing for Richard Hampton to buy the Vertical X's ranch and stock it with cattle.

"Now, in view of what has happened to Hampton, they are trying to recoup their money without going through foreclosure proceedings, which would force an auction of the ranch. They hope to make a deal with the Rimrock Land and Cattle Cattle Company that can result in an easy settlement of their lien. It would also result in the ranch being managed during that interval, which could keep the cattle from disappearing and the assets falling into disrepair.

"Their attorney, our old 'friend', Mr. Shystwell, has been engaged to act for them. After consultations with Richard, they have a proposal they wish for me to present to the Rimrock Land and Cattle Company, through you. I have done a due diligence search and it appears to be a bonafide offer, with the title claims substantiated.

"It seems to be a very good deal. I want you to look at it and let me know what you think. It is probably worth more to your company than to anyone else, because of your proximity to the property, and the fact that you have a working operation that will have a common border along the East Fork for twenty or twenty five miles."

"Just a second, Mr. Fendwell. I think that Sir Edward and Cynthia are in town, along with Brad, making arrangements for their trip back to London. Since Earlene and Rodney are in their offices, let me see if I can get them into the conference room here and let you make us a presentation."

Without waiting for an answer, I quickly left my office and looked up and down the street. I saw Brad's buggy tied in front of the stage office.

Walking quickly, I got to the stage office just as Brad was untying the team.

"Hey Brad! Is Edward and Cynthia inside?"

"They sure are," he responded. "What has you in such a dither?"

"I need all of the board of directors in the conference room right now. I think everyone's here in town. We have someone here with a proposal I want you to all listen to. Get Edward and Cynthia and come on down to the bank. I'll have Rodney and Earlene waiting, along with our guest."

I headed back down to the bank and went into Earlene's office.

"Earlene, I need both you and Rodney to come into the conference room. We have some urgent business to address while Edward is still here."

"What in the world is going on that has to be rushed?" Earlene had stood up and was looking at me with curiosity.

"I'll let someone else tell you all about it. I only have the barest details, myself. Let me grab Rodney. Edward, Brad and Cynthia are on the way down from the stage office."

I walked into Rodney's office, just as I saw Brad tying the team outside the bank windows.

"Hey Rodney, I hate to wake you up, but we are having a full blown meeting of the board in the conference room. It is something that needs to be expedited. I am not fully acquainted with things, myself. We can all find out together."

A couple of minutes later, we were all seated. Everyone was looking at Mr. Fendwell expectantly. Cynthia, with her penchant for efficiency, had her hand poised over a tablet, pen ready.

"Folks, the haste of this meeting is because of the brief time remaining before Richard Hampton is executed. For reasons of his own, he has engaged Mr. Shystwell, whom you will all remember, to work through Mr. Fendwell here, to offer us this proposal. Mr. Fendwell, I would like for you to tell us all, at the same time, just what the proposal entails. Let's hear what you have to say."

While we were talking, Cynthia had arisen and walked to a cabinet in the room. She had distributed tablets and sharp pencils to each of us.

Mr. Fendwell looked up from his papers and said, "Excuse me for not standing up, but I am tired from my hurried trip down here from New York. Here is the crux of the meeting:

"Shyster's firm has been approached by a London firm, *Shadow*

Financial. They have produced papers showing that they have a lien against the Vertical X's. I have done a due diligence check on Shadow Financial and the on the title to the Vertical X's. Both seem to meet the standards one would desire for a business transaction.

"I have in my possession a title signed by Richard Hampton. I have a release of lien and all other claims against the Vertical X's by Shadow Financial. The title signed by Richard is contingent on twenty five thousand dollars being delivered to Shystwell's company in the form of a Cashier's Check made out to Richard Hampton. The release of lien and all other claims by Shadow Financial is contingent on another fifty thousand dollars being delivered to Shystwell's company, made out to Shadow Financial.

"The necessity for speed is that some papers have to be signed between Shadow Financial and Richard Hampton on another matter. If they are not signed before his execution, they will no longer be of importance and the whole deal will collapse. I'll answer any questions you may have. If you have no questions, I will be glad to go out into the waiting room and allow you to have a discussion in private." Mr. Fendwell leaned back and clasped his hands behind his head, awaiting a reply.

"In the interests of time, I am going to make a statement. You all have an equal say, so please stop me on any point that you have questions on or that you object to.

"First, based upon my feelings that we will probably have other business to transact where we will need the services of Mr. Fendwell's firm, I would like for him to remain in the room while we discuss this. Any objections?" I looked around the table. "Remember, we are all family and I am only stating my own opinion. I will not be offended if one or all of you object to what I say. I am just thinking out loud as I go along.

Secondly, the point has already been made that the land under discussion is more valuable to us than to anyone else. I would point out that the house and outbuildings could have a lot of value to us. If the outward appearance of the house reflects its interior, we can certainly put it to good use. Taking it now might prevent transients from destroying some of the value, through carelessness or vandalism.

"Thirdly, judging from the way it appears when looking at it from the west end, it lends itself to being developed in such a way as to provide a much broader base for the bank, and for some other enterprises that come to mind, such as lumber mills, grain mills, grain storage facilities, and other population inducing projects that would have great appeal to a railroad.

"Fourthly, following the same line of reasoning that Mr. Fendwell mentioned in stating the advantages of having a nucleus ready to run a ranch, we also have a nucleus ready to build our bank into a true financial center, our area into a commercial and agricultural center, and a bastion of economic opportunity.

"A fifth thing that we need to take under consideration, is whether we can weather a bad year or two if we take on the responsibilities of pulling $75,000 out of our cash reserves. We need to remember that if times get hard for us, they are also hard for the people from whom we derive our cash flow. If times get hard, we can lose the payments from the ranchers. If we lose the revenue stream from those two sources, it will probably be because the market for cattle falls drastically, which will spill over into the merchants sales.

"When times get bad, there is no profit in foreclosing on our customers, for we can't do any better with their properties than they can. Besides, we are honor bound to carry them, for they bought the land because of their trust in us.

"I am not being pessimistic. I just want us all to be aware of the risks we are taking if we get too far out on a limb. One thing that we have going in our favor is that we don't need to borrow if we take advantage of this opportunity. However, until we build back a large cash reserve, every stray nickel that we get should go into reserves.

"We should even consider spreading our deposits. Edward, what is your assessment of the economic climate in London and the rest of England?

"Easy, I think you have mentioned some very salient points, especially in view of having to speak off the top of your head, with no preparations. I feel my business interests that are carried on from my office in London are very sound. However, I have to remember what happened to Richard's father's fortune when he put all of his money into one venture in the spice business. Then he compounded the error by overloading the ship, trying to get back on safe ground, economically speaking. That contributed to the sinking of the ship, and ultimately to the sinking of his business.

"I run my business as though every year has the potential to be a bad one. That cuts down on my return on my investment and my profits, but it also leaves me able to weather a serious down-turn. I have a reserve that includes gold and silver. I would say we should take the risk and grab this opportunity. We want to remember, we don't owe on any of our assets. Our exposure to loss would be trying to carry our customers through the hard times. It is hard for me to visualize not being able to help out, should the need arise." Edward looked around the table to gauge everyone's feelings.

"I want to go ahead and vote," I said, unless someone else wants to give their opinion from another perspective. I don't feel a secret ballet is necessary, for each of us has the opportunity to give his view. I would feel better about us erring on the side of caution than on the side of too much risk, especially since we already have a very profitable enterprise with plenty of room to expand. However, I am casting my vote that we take this chance and draw up the papers so that Mr. Fendwell can get them back to New York while Richard still has the opportunity to sign his other deal with Shadow Financial.

"Cynthia, please record our votes. Brad, what do you have to say?"

"Easy, it looks to me like a down-turn in the beef market would have to last for several years before we would suffer seriously. I think that if hard times hit, we could limit our loans to subsistence levels only, but put a hold on the payments so that our customer's faith in us would be justified. That would limit our cash requirements a lot, so we could withstand a very long period of hard times. We want to remember, we still have our revenue streams at this time. All of that money should go to build up our reserves before we put more money into expansion. I vote that we buy the Vertical X's."

"What about you?" I asked Edward.

"I say, let's give it a go." I think Easy's reasoning is good on the risks involved. I think they should be rather short term, given that we put our efforts into building the reserves."

"Rodney?"

"I vote yes."

"Earlene, what say you?"

"I vote yes."

"Just for my own edification, I would like to ask another person how they would have voted. Cynthia, please tell us what you would have done?"

Cynthia closed the notebook on her pencil, to hold her place. "Easy, I would vote yes, but only on the condition that we put our immediate efforts into rebuilding our reserves. It happens, that in the course of my work for Uncle Edward, that I also keep my eye on the overall health of the RL&CC. One thing that no one has mentioned is that we still have substantial reserves in the bank in Denver, and enough here in Vacaville to handle all normal transactions.

"I think the risk is fairly minimal, *given that we recognize our position*" she said, speaking slowly and emphasizing the last half of her sentence. "My vote would be yes!"

"Then it would appear to me that we need to get the documentation handled and get back to our normal business. I did note that a figure is given for the number of cattle that go with the ranch. I will have the count done as soon as possible. Now, just in case there are no cattle, I want everyone to know that the real estate alone makes the deal a good one. We have to risk it that the cattle are there. For Richard to take care of his business, we have to act now. It will take time to make a count that is scattered over a couple of hundred square miles.

"If the cattle are there, it is a super bargain. If they are not, we still got a lot for our money. At least, we won't be surprised and feel that we were conned out of our money like some country boys, visiting the city for the first time." I laughed and added, "After all, we are from the big, booming city of Vacaville, located in the Metropolitan area of the Bend of the Rimrock.

"Edward, unless you want to get more closely involved, I will ask Rodney to work with Mr. Fendwell to get the papers prepared. If no one objects, I would like for Cynthia to set in on the preparations."

I turned to Mr. Fendwell. "How long will it take to get things ready?"

"I have everything prepared, just in case your company accepts the offer. Let me go over everything with Rodney and Cynthia."

"Since Earlene has been deeply involved in the banks business lately, I would like to have her set in on it too. Then you can go over it in front of the rest of us. If we can do it in the next half an hour, we will have time to eat lunch before Mr. Fendwell's stagecoach arrives."

"There is one more order of business that I want to advance," said Sir Edward. "This is very short notice, but it is possible that Easy has told you that I hope you will accept him as president of the Rimrock Land and Cattle Company. I have discussed some other recommendations that I have made, but if he is accepted or elected president, he will have the authority to handle those recommendations himself."

By unanimous vote, I ended up with the title of president.

A short time later, the group of us entered Green's cafe, and we had lunch.

"I hate to see you have to leave without some rest time," I sympathized with Mr. Fendwell.

"And you thought that all we lawyers had to do is make flowery speeches and drink good brandy, didn't you?" laughed Fendwell.

"That was a pretty flowery speech you just made. Now, where is the brandy?" I joined Fendwell's laughter.

"If there is time before your stage gets in, I can remedy that little problem over in my office," said Rodney.

"I'll bet you can," said Edward, clapping his hand on his son's shoulder.

-=-

A month had passed since the contract had been signed, transferring the title of the Vertical X's from Richard Hampton to the Rimrock Land and Cattle Company. That would usually be ample time for the deal to have been finalized and notification received. Such word had not been received by the RL&CC or the RB&T. It had been received by Richard Hampton, the law firm of Shystwell, Shystwell, Upton and Moncrief, and Shadow Financial. The cashier's checks had been cashed by a large New York bank, and the debit had been sent to the bank in Vacaville. It just had not yet arrived.

-=-

A cloudburst on the eastern watershed of the mountains had sent a raging torrent of water boiling down every draw and ravine, and every creek and river. All stages roads and trails from the south side of Denver to the New Mexico line had been impassible for the past week. No news had reached Vacaville on either a regional or local level for the past week.

The water had now run off and the mud had dried. Crews of men had repaired the stage roads. Things were coming back to normal.

-=-

An army of forty hard-bitten gunmen staged a jail break for Richard Hampton and Judge Pickwick. There was a heavy loss of life for both the outlaws and the law enforcement officials of Nugget Creek. The renegades fled toward the nearest mountains. Heavy rains made it impossible to track them. No sign had been seen of them. It was believed they had fled into Arizona, enroute to Mexico.

The ranches that had been created, improved, and financed by the Rimrock Land and Cattle Company before being sold to the small ranchers who had once occupied the little shirttail outfits in the South Cedar Hills were enclosed by four strands of barbed wire fence. A broad road ran down each side of each ranch. Since every ranch was enclosed by barbed wire, each of the roads was also enclosed by barbed wire.

At each corner of every ranch, the fence contained a gate. The gate was designed so that it could be opened and fastened to a gate post in the fence on the other side of the road, allowing the cattle to be redirected either to the left or the right.

On this particular night the temperature had been hovering around 5° below zero. For the past week daytime high temperatures had been in the teens with the nighttime lows around zero. A heavy snow had started falling in the midmorning and kept increasing in intensity all day long.

The wind was howling out of the northwest and the cattle in all the ranches were drifting ahead of the wind toward the southeast corners of their pastures. No sound could be heard above the howling wind. Seven groups of six cowboys each had been assigned to this job. One group had been assigned to each of the seven ranches that formed the northern tier of ranches. The ranches were all laid out in perfect rectangles, three miles wide and two miles deep. There were five rows of ranches between the Rimrock and the river.

For several days they had kept a surreptitious watch on the herds. Each group of cowboys knew exactly where the herds were in each of the ranches in the column of ranches that ran to the river from the Rimrock. One man from each group went to the highest point of land in the area and kept watch for anyone not in their group through a pair of binoculars.

The herds of cattle were already moving toward the southeast corner of each ranch, keeping the bitter cold wind to their backs. As the herds approached the corner, one man rode on ahead, opened the gate, and stood by to head the cattle straight down the road south toward the river.

Chapter Ten - Page 151
Brad and Cynthia start for town

"Cynthia, I know it's awfully cold today, but I have a feeling it will be even worse for the next few days. I have some plans that are drawn up that I would surely like to get into town to Rodney. I know you were telling me that you had some things you wanted to go over with Rodney. Otherwise I would ask one of the men to carry this envelope in to Rodney. I'll ask Brad or Easy to ride along with you. You can stay in the offices in the bank or get a room at the hotel until the weather gets better before you return."

"I'll be more than happy to go, Uncle Edward. If it's all the same to you, let me ask Brad if he has the time to go with me."

"It's all the same to me, Cynthia. I've noticed that you and Brad are spending quite a bit of time together. It seems to me like you're getting a little bit fond of him."

"There is no denying we're getting pretty fond of each other, Uncle Edward. I think more of him than any other man I've ever met." Cynthia was looking straight into her uncle's eyes.

"He seems to me to be an awfully nice fellow: smart, capable, good-natured and strong. In other words, he has all the attributes that one could hope for in a man." He walked to Cynthia and took one of her hands. "Cynthia, I've asked more of you than any uncle has the right to ask of his niece. You have been so devoted to me and to our business, that you've really had little time of your own for a personal life.

"I want you to know that as much as you mean to me and as much as I depend on you, I encourage you to take whatever steps you would like to take to fulfill your own personal life. It would require taking several steps to adapt to the circumstances that would arise in the event that you ever did bring someone really close into your personal life, but we can shuffle things around in such a manner that I wouldn't lose the benefit of your wisdom and knowledge of the business."

"Uncle Edward, Brad and I are a haven't completely reached such a point in our relationship, but I would be less than honest if I didn't say there is a strong possibility that we might arrive at that point. You have no idea how much I appreciate you telling me what you just said. You know how much I love you, and there is nothing that could ever possibly happen that would change that. I'm going to go ask Brad to come along with me on my trip to town.

"I want to get started as soon as possible because I agree with you that the weather is probably going to worsen." She stood on tip-toes to give her uncle a kiss on the cheek and a warm hug. Then she turned to leave the room.

She put on her coat and gloves, put on a cap that covered her ears, wrapped a scarf around her neck, and opened the door. She had no more than started toward the barn, when the barn door opened and Brad and Easy came out and started for the house. She met them halfway and walked in between them, turned and took each man by his arm and walked back toward the house.

The combination of her ears being covered by her scarf and the sound of the wind rushing past her head made it impossible to talk. The three of them nearly ran back to the porch, opened the door and entered the warm house.

"Hey Brad, before you get all unwrapped, I have a question to ask you. Uncle Edward has an urgent message that he wants to get into town to Rodney before the weather worsens. I wonder if you'd like to ride along with me." She stood looking expectantly at Brad's face.

"It must be awfully important," Brad said, "for us to go out in this weather. I'd be willing to bet a Yankee dime that it snows before morning. I'd make the same bet that we won't make it back tonight, and also venture a guess that it might be three or four days before we can get back. I'll certainly be happy to ride along with you."

"Easy, you've been in this country long enough to know what one of these blizzards can be like. I'm going to go saddle up Cynthia's horse. I'll appreciate it if you'll go tell Edward not to worry if it takes us several days to get back. I feel it is highly likely that we'll be snowbound for several days and will have to hole up in our offices or the hotel." He turned to Cynthia. "Cynthia this is going to make me sound like an old woman, but out here in the west you always have to be prepared for any eventuality. Anything can happen any time with very little warning. Will you ask Earlene help you put together enough food for four or five days? She knows what we would need in the case of an emergency. Tell her I said we are in quite a hurry and will be leaving in five minutes."

He turned and opened the door, only to see Easy leading his and Cynthia's saddled horses up from the barn.

"We'd better fill both canteens. If you're liable to need food, you're also liable to need water. Have you got some insulating covers for these canteens to keep them from freezing?" I rubbed my hands together and blew on them.

"Yep, I sure do," Brad answered. "I've done some long-distance traveling in the winter time before."

"Well then," I said, "there is no need for me to tell you that you ought to carry winter time bedrolls. That may sound like taking too many precautions, but you can freeze to death five miles from home just as easily as you can 500 miles away."

They hitched the horses at the porch, walked up the stairs and entered the house. Brad went down into the basement and got his winter time bedroll, along with two winterized canteens and went back upstairs taking the steps two at a time.

Earlene and Cynthia came in the front door. "We've been out tying the lunch sacks to the saddles. Just to be on the safe side we split the food and tied one sack to each saddle."

"Hey Cynthia," Brad said, "Darned if you don't look like an Eskimo the way you're all bundled up."

"Oh," said Cynthia, "and I thought I was wearing the latest Parisian styles." She did a pirouette and said, "How do you like it?" She smiled at Brad.

"It looks spiffy enough to be some kind of a fancy style," he said returning her smile. Then he looked over at me and said, "Easy, we've got to get started for town. This trip is bordering on the edge of being foolish. I consider it highly unlikely that we'll be back tonight. If the weather ends up doing like it looks to me like it might do, it may be several days before we can get back."

Earlene came into the room, carrying her overshoes. "Here, Cynthia. Take these. They pull on right over your boots and will sure help you to keep your feet warm."

"No, I can't take your overshoes. You will ruin your boots down in that sloppy barn." Cynthia hugged Earlene and started to go.

"You are not leaving the house without them! You are going on a fool's errand as it is! Here, take them and put them on. There is nothing as cold on the feet as riding a horse in a blizzard. Your feet are surrounded by cold air."

Cynthia started to protest again, but Earlene said, "I am serious. I will not permit you to go out that door without them. Dad, I am surprised at both you and Easy for even allowing such a trip in this weather! I don't want to hear any more about it. Now take these overshoes and put them on. The whole bunch of you, Uncle Edward included, ought to be ashamed of yourselves. One more word out of any of you and I'll shoot the horses and stop you from going at all."

I was feeling pretty foolish myself, for I knew Earlene was right. "I sure wouldn't take any chances if I were you Brad. We can handle anything comes up here." I walked out onto the porch and watched them ride out. The wind howled around the porch like a clan of banshees. I couldn't help but wonder how much stronger it would be outside our sheltered valley on the open ground between the Rimrock and the river. I was secretly very proud of Earlene. I was also happy to see that Cynthia was wearing the overshoes.

-=-

The weather was so cold and the wind was so noisy that conversation was impossible. Cynthia still felt the companionship of the man who rode by her side. He kept casting glances over his right shoulder at the ominous clouds that were riding on the wings of the wind and gaining on them rapidly. The sun was sinking behind the dark bank of clouds as though trying to seek a place to hide from the bitter cold.

Looking across the fence at the Rimrock Land and Cattle Company's pasture that reached from the Oasis River to the west fence of the small ranchers' land, Brad could vaguely make out a large herd of cattle being moved toward the southeast corner of the pasture. Half a dozen cowboys were riding behind them in a somewhat semi-circle formation that pushed the cattle forward and kept them from wandering off to either side.

He had given orders to move the cattle to the feeding area a few days earlier when they had their weekly meeting with the superintendent and the various foremen, and told that that had already been taken care of. No one had mentioned any plans that called for moving a herd. He knew he had to investigate whatever it was that was happening, but he also hated to take Cynthia the several miles to the east, for this would necessitate them riding back into the wind.

He also hated to urge the horses to a faster speed, because the air was too cold for a horse to breathe rapidly without damage to the lungs. He explained his deductions to Cynthia and decided to ride down the road that bordered the Wandering River until it intersected with the road at the southeast corner of the pasture.

They urged their horses to as quick of a pace as they felt the horses could stand, in such frigid weather. When they turned left into the road that paralleled the Wandering River, a few flakes of snow were beginning to fall. Although the sun was about to set, it was lighter in the east than it was in the west and the northwest. An hour later they arrived at the southeast corner of the Rimrock Land and Cattle Company's range. Through the falling snow and the approaching night, they could faintly see the approaching herd of cattle.

It was obvious to Brad that most, if not all, of the entire herd was being rustled. There was no way he could face at least six rustlers. With Cynthia along, it seemed there was nothing he could do to stop them at this time. He called Cynthia's attention to the approaching herd, and explained that that they would have to proceed on down the road.

This was also a very dangerous course because they were getting further and further from Vacaville and the safety of good shelter. Soon they were approaching the gate at the southeast corner of the first of the small ranches. With the poor visibility that existed by now, they had barely passed the corner before they discovered that the herd from that ranch was also being driven out into the road. Brad's feeling of foreboding increased as he continued on down the road east to the corner of the next small ranch. A large herd of cattle was pouring through the gate. It was far too large a herd to come from one ranch and Brad suddenly knew the truth. All of the cattle from each ranch were being herded out the gates on the southeast corner of each. Now here they were, he and Cynthia, trapped between the cattle coming from in back of them and the cattle that were pouring through the gate in front of them.

He was sure that each time they passed one of the columns of ranches; there would be another huge herd of cattle entering the roadway. There would be a herd of thousands of cattle that were being swept from the range tonight. He knew that he and Cynthia would've already been discovered except for the blinding snowstorm that now raged.

There was no way of knowing how closely they were being followed by the first herd of cattle, or how closely they were traveling up on the heels of the herd of cattle ahead of them. All they could do now was to try to keep out of sight of the cowboys who were driving the herds.

Judging by the approximately six cowboys who were driving the first herd that he had seen clearing the Rimrock Land and Cattle Company's herd, multiplied by the approximately twenty small ranches in the block, there could be easily be over a hundred and twenty-five rustlers involved in this grand theft, and for sure at least fifty.

Such a huge herd should be easy to find except for one thing. The snow was falling so heavily now that all traces of the cattle's movement would be covered as fast as the cattle left them. There had to be some place to give cover to the cattle. On the one hand it was nearly impossible to see well enough to keep the cattle together, but on the other hand, the cattle would be trying their best to move toward the southeast to keep the wind at their back.

One thing was for sure: one hundred and twenty-five drovers were more than plenty to handle any size of a herd. At least any herd he had ever seen or heard about, he added to himself. There was no way they could get this herd of cattle across the river. Suddenly he realized something he had not thought of; the river would be frozen over.

He had another matter of more immediate concern. Where would he and Cynthia find cover? It was a cinch they couldn't ride back into the teeth of such a bitterly cold wind. They were fifteen miles from Vacaville by now. The first thing to consider was to get out of the mass of so many riders without being seen and find cover for the night.

His mind was soon made up for him. The herd ahead had reached the end of the road and had stopped, apparently to wait for the herd behind to catch up so they would only have one herd to deal with, albeit a big one. He stopped his horse as he reached out and seized Cynthia's arm to stop her. She was a smart girl and was well aware of their problem. She was trying to uncover her ear to hear what he wanted to say to her, when suddenly the trailing herd was upon them.

They allowed the first of the cattle to walk alongside of them. Brad signaled to Cynthia to follow him and they galloped their horses forward until they came to the herd that was bunched up ahead inside the narrow road. Several of the rustlers were behind of the cattle. They were hunched up inside their coats trying to stay warm. As Brad and Cynthia rode up to them Brad shouted, "Open the gate! Open the gate! Let them on through! Don't let them bunch up!

Two of the men begin working their way through the cattle toward the gate, yelling "Open the gate! Open the gate! Let's move them along! Move them along! Let them through! A few minutes later, Brad could sense the beginning movement in the herd as the leaders began to accept the gate. By this time, riders from the trailing herd had moved up to tell him to open the gates. Brad waved his arm at them, signaling them to come on. Each group probably thought Brad and Cynthia were with one of the other groups. It was impossible to identify anyone, the way they were all bundled up from the cold.

Several men were grouped together just outside the gate, watching the cattle come through. They were looking at Brad and Cynthia curiously, when one of them said, "Hey there! Wait a minute!"

"I have to give this message to Harry!" He urged his horse to a gallop, Cynthia close by his side. He looked back over his shoulder and saw half a dozen of the rustlers galloping after them. He leaned over his horse's neck and the horse leaped into a dead run. Cynthia's horse had his belly to the ground, running as though the hounds of hell were in hot pursuit. Brad wondered if that wasn't exactly what was happening.

They vanished into the snow, but they both knew it was only temporary. They angled sharply to the left, running to the northeast. After about fifty yards they turned straight north. After another hundred and fifty yards, Brad turned straight west and pulled the horse down to a walk, fearful they would run headlong into the east fence that ran north and south along the east edge of the north – south road along the block of land contained in the small operators ranches. They reached the fence a few minutes later and Brad turned north along the fence. They rode along the fence, keeping a close eye out for a gate. When they finally came to a gate, Brad knew he had reached the north side of the first row of the ranches nearest to the Wandering River.

They took the road that led west on the cleanly laid out grid of roads that neatly separated all the small rancher's spreads. It was an hour until they reached the next south bound road to head back toward the river. They were still two hours from the river, and three additional hours from Vacaville. That was considering if the snow did not get deep enough to slow the horses even more. Three inches of snow had fallen already, and it seemed as though the snow was falling faster, although it was hard to tell because so much ground snow was also blowing in the vicious wind. It was also necessary to take into account the fact that they would be quartering into the wind for the last three hours of the trip.

Enough time had passed that Brad was quite sure they must be reaching the River Road. Although it was very hard to do because of fatigue, Brad was trying to maintain a high state of readiness. All in a single instant, one of the rustlers became visible, hunkered down by the corner post on each side of the road.

They saw him and Cynthia at the same instant that he saw them. He sent a quick shot of each of them, sending them scrambling as he leapt his horse forward into the cover of the smothering snow. He had quartered their horses to the left, as a hail of bullets was fired blindly into the snow where the two rustlers hoped they had gone.

Brad reached over and caught the bridle of Cynthia's horse and pulled both horses to a stop. He tore the muffling material up from Cynthia's left ear and bent over to yell to her, "ride straight to the river crossing and wait for me on the far side."

Cynthia yelled something unintelligible and her horse leaped forward and out of sight. Brad walked into the wind leading his horse. He kept the wind on his left front in an attempt to walk straight north. In a moment he came to the fence, tied his horse to the top strand of barbed wire, and grabbed his rifle. He shuffled up the fence in a crouching run and arrived at the corner just as the two rustlers were mounting their horses.

He drove a bullet into the nearest rustler, but slipped and fell as he turned to shoot at the second, who was disappearing into the snow. Brad knew he had only a short time to get to Cynthia and find a place to hide before half a hundred rustlers were spread out through the snow looking for them.

He circled back to the right 100 yards to be sure he was upriver further than Cynthia. Arriving at the river, he cautiously but quickly crossed the ice, and started riding down river. A minute later he came to a river of water flowing sluggishly into the Wandering River and knew he was at its junction with the East Fork. Much of the water from the East Fork was fed by springs and had not frozen.

Brad immediately realized, since he had not found Cynthia since he had crossed the river and ridden down to the East fork, she must've crossed further downstream. This also meant that she had attempted to cross the river where the ice might be very thin, because of the warmer water from the East Fork making the water of the Wandering River too warm to freeze solid.

These thoughts had no more than flashed through his mind, when he caught a glimpse through the swirling snow of Cynthia's horse. He galloped a few yards upstream on the East Fork to keep from being swept into the Wandering River, and rode his plunging horse across the East Fork. He rode downstream along the Wandering River until a solid sheet of ice covered surface. Trying his best to scan across the river and yelling at the top of his lungs, he continued riding downstream.

His heart was filled with cold terror that Cynthia had fallen through the thin ice. There was no other explanation for her horse being on this side of the river, unless she had been crossing the river and the ice had broken through. He knew he had to go down river far enough for the ice to appear to be a solid sheet, or Cynthia would not have attempted to cross. There was a brief lull in the gusty winds and he caught a brief glimpse of her. She had broken through the ice and was feebly clinging to its edge.

Brad swung off his horse, dropped his reins to ground hitch the horse, and took a quick hitch on the saddle horn with his lariat. He backed up a few feet, ran and leaped as far out into the river as he could and worked his way towards Cynthia, paying out his rope as he went. He got to her just as her last strength gave out. The only thing that had been holding her was her half frozen hands, formed into the shape of hooks, too cold and stiff to turn loose of the edge of the ice. Gasping and numb with cold, barely able to move, he slung her over his shoulder. This allowed him to use both hands to pull himself along his lariat to where his horse stood holding against the pressure of the lariat, like any good cow horse would.

Cynthia's horse disappeared in the storm. Brad knew that he had only moments to get Cynthia warmer or she would die. He slung her over his horse's saddle, put his back to the wind and begin frantically looking for shelter of any kind. He saw the silhouette of the dark empty branches of an oak tree. He pushed toward it, leading his horse with the inert girl across the saddle. Nearby another tree had fallen, with its roots extending across a deep empty hole.

Brad grabbed his bed roll off the saddle, along with the food sack. Moving as rapidly as possible, he leapt into the hole and scraped all the snow he could reach out of it. He unwrapped the ground tarp from the bed roll and pulled it over several large roots. The surplus tarp was large enough to spread across the ground beneath the roots, forming a small tent. He quickly spread his heavy blankets on the tarp forming the floor of the small tent. Taking Cynthia into his arms, he jumped into the hole and laid her down and began to strip her wet clothes from her shivering body. He rapidly dried her off with a shirt from his saddle bag. Dragging her to the edge of the tarp, he unrolled his bedroll and covered her. He stripped the saddle from his horse and threw it into a corner of the hole where it was also covered by the tarp. He pulled the bridle from his horse and released it. Throwing all his gear underneath the small tent, he removed his sodden clothing and threw them onto his saddle and crawled under the cover and took Cynthia's frigid body in his arms.

They both lay there; shivering so hard it was nearly convulsions. Their teeth chattered like castanets. It took thirty minutes before they began to warm up a little. Brad stuck his head out from under the cover and looked up toward the tarp. Beneath the tarp it was darker than a cave; so dark that he was unable to see. He reached his hand up and could feel the snow laden tarp. The howling wind was muffled by the snow-covered tarp, and the hole was rapidly drifting full of snow. Very faintly he heard voices, and realized the rustlers had parties out searching for them.

A small group of the outlaws apparently had stopped by the tree. "There is no way in hell that we can find them. If you ask me, they are under the ice drowned." The man cursed loudly and added, "Let's head on back and try to catch up with the herd. I'd bet a month's pay that they're dead."

"I'm all for that," another voice agreed.

The snow muffled sound of hoof beats disappeared back toward the Wandering River.

Brad lay there with his body curled around Cynthia's. Although they had warmed up a lot, they would still have spasms of shivering. He lay there wondering what to do next. Their horses were gone; their clothing was frozen as stiff as a board. There was no telling whether or not the rustlers would come back and search for them more when the storm stopped. There was no way they could move until their shoes and clothing had dried. There was a chance they could break enough dead branches off the fallen tree, beneath which they sought refuge, to build a fire; but even if they did, it would be too dangerous to because the smoke could be seen if the sky cleared. If they tried to get out from under their improvised tent, it would be easy for any passing person to see the disturbed snow when they crawled out from under the tarp.

It appeared to him like the only thing they could do now was to wait until the storm had blown itself completely out. They might have to wait longer so that if any rustlers were still in the area searching for them, they would have a chance to see that there were no new tracks in the area. They would then have the give up the search and continue to try to get the herd out of the country. The snow was certainly too heavy to move the herd now. This job had been so well planned, and there were so many rustlers involved, that it would be foolhardy to go looking for the cattle right now.

It appeared like it would be necessary to remain where they were for at least several days, before they could risk trying to build a fire and dry their clothing. It was certain that it would be near a week before anyone thought to search for them. In all probability someone would have to go to town for supplies and find out the message had never been delivered to Rodney before anyone thought to search. He fell asleep while pondering all of the possibilities.

During the night, Brad was assailed by a complete menagerie of dreams. Some of the dreams were nightmares with some very preposterous circumstances. Part of the time he and Cynthia were running naked through the snow, pursued by dozens of shouting rustlers. They were firing bullets that were narrowly missing their marks, but had him filled with great concern and fear that he would be unable to save Cynthia. They were both freezing and were unable to find a place to hide.

Others were very erotic. He awoke during one of these, afraid to move for fear of waking Cynthia. He was no longer cold and the way he and Cynthia were curled together, it was impossible that she would not know of his physical arousal. Brad was an honorable man and there was no way that he wished to take advantage of the situation in which they found themselves. By the same token, there was no way that he could hide the reality of the situation and the physical effect it was having upon him. The way she was moving restlessly in her sleep was serving to make the situation worse. He lay as quietly as possible, trying to not even breathe. Suddenly the worst thing happened. His body released that potent potion, and he could not stop the pulsing of his flesh. He remained as immobile as he could, pretending that he was still asleep. He could feel a change in Cynthia's body and knew she was lying there awake.

His flesh was softening and shrinking; he could feel it retracting across the soft flesh of her inner thighs. He had never been so embarrassed in his life. He had no idea what he should do or say now.

"Brad, my right arm is very painful from lying on the hard ground on my right shoulder. I wonder if we could both roll over so we're lying on our other sides."

Brad rose up onto his hands and knees, gathered himself and lay down on his left side. A moment later he felt Cynthia do the same thing. He was trying to lay straight on his side, but Cynthia bent her knees up against his knees and said, "Curl up a little bit so I can keep warm." She wriggled up against him, threw her arm over his body, and pressed herself against him, shivering momentarily.

"Cynthia listen," he began...

"Shhh," she murmured sleepily. "Everything is all right. Don't worry about it. Let's go back to sleep." She snuggled up against him and that's just what she did.

If Brad had suspected he was in love before, there was not the smallest doubt in his mind now. His wife had died when Earlene was born. In all the years since then, he had never entertained the slightest notion that he may have found a woman whom he wanted for a wife. His interest had first been piqued when he met her the first time in Sir Edward's London office. She was lovely and smart and had a great personality. The rides they had taken together since she and Sir Edward had made their visit to the United States had opened a whole new world for Brad. He knew how much she loved and respected her Uncle Edward and how successful she was in her career as an executive in his company. If she felt the same way about him as he felt about her, it would be a very difficult decision she would be faced with. Sleep finally came and relieved him of any further agonizing over things that might be.

-=-

I got up early the next morning after Brad and Cynthia had started for Vacaville. For some reason I had a strange feeling of foreboding. I knew that Brad had been born in the West. I also knew that he always thought things out very carefully and was not the type of person to be stampeded into making unwise moves. It was a fact that the storm that was still raging outside was very severe, even for this part of the country where it was usual to have severe weather.

Earlene had got up as soon as I had the fire going, eggs cooked and bacon fried. I could hear Sir Edward stirring around in his room. Ordinarily, I would have gone out and tended to the animals before eating, but because of the extra time it might take during the storm, I decided to have my breakfast first. I washed up for breakfast and before I could sit down, Sir Edward entered the kitchen.

He walked over and kissed Earlene on the cheek and received the same from her. "I'll swear, Earlene," he said. "How in the world did a rough old country boy like Easy ever manage to rope such a pretty girl as you are?"

Earlene had taken up the habit of calling Sir Edward "Uncle Edward" since she had become such close friends with Cynthia. "Oh, I guess he's just a good roping cowboy," she laughed. "Girls always have a soft spot in their heart for a tall, dark and handsome cowboy with a shiny six shooter."

"Hmmm, I wonder if it's too late for an old English businessman to learn how to be a cowboy. The last time I was in Vacaville, I saw several likely young fillies."

"Easy," he said, "how long do you think it'll take you to teach me to be a bronc buster?"

I laughed and answered him, "It depends a lot on how much dedication you have in learning. Would you like to take a lesson today or had you rather wait till it warms up a little? You see, there are some pros and cons about it. On the one hand, you've got those big soft snow banks to land in if a bronc jumps out from under you and leaves you momentarily setting in the air. On the other hand, as cold as it is today, when your ears freeze it's easy to crack one off and lose it in a snow drift. When the snow thaws out in the spring, some hungry coyote is liable to find it and eat it before you can have it sewed back on. You want to look at all the pros and cons before you decide whether you want to be a bronc buster or not."

Sir Edward laughed and said, "Is it all right to wait for spring weather before I have to make up my mind?"

"You two can stop being comedians, and eat before your breakfast gets cold. Your milk would already be clabbered if it weren't so cold. Just remember, it doesn't hurt me a bit to be cold, but the same doesn't hold true about biscuits. If I were a trail cook, I would've already thrown it out."

"Well I sure don't want you throwing it out," I said running for my chair.

Sir Edward made a big leap and sat down in his chair. "Ha, Ha," he said. "Easy, I'll bet you didn't know I could move like that! But then again, who wouldn't hurry to get some of Earlene's biscuits?"

"We have some hens that are starving, a milk cow whose udder is about to burst with milk, and more hungry horses than you can shake a stick at. Are you all out tending to them? No!" Earlene shook her dark hair in mock anger. "There the two of you set after your morning tea, trying to be funny, and letting the poor animals starve. If I weren't busy cooking, I'd get the broom and sweep you out into the snow."

Cold weather has a way of making one feel extra hungry. A few minutes later, I had finished eating, bundled up in my warmest clothing, picked up the milk bucket and headed for the barn. It didn't take long to slop the hogs, milk the cow, feed the horses and fork plenty of hay into the mangers. Before leaving the barn, I gathered up a basket of eggs and walked back to the house.

The snow had turned into sleet and a glaze of ice covered the surface of the snow. This storm was turning into a real humdinger. It seemed to me that some kind of an ominous threat hung in the cold air. Furthermore, it also seemed to be something other than the weather that was bothering me. It's sort of like when you have an itch, and don't know exactly where to scratch.

I clomped up the steps of the porch and stomped the snow off my feet. I took off my scarf, coat, gloves, cap, and overshoes. Then I walked over and gave Earlene a big kiss and a pat on the rear and walked over and looked out the window.

Earlene walked over and stood by my side and said, "Easy, you're about as restless as a lobo wolf. What's bothering you? Are you worrying about Brad and Cynthia?"

Earlene was always able to read my mind. "Oh, I'm not actually worried, but I just have a funny feeling about this. I know they said they weren't going to be back until after the storm cleared. I'm getting to be just like some old woman, worrying about everything. That sleet has already put a crust of ice an inch-thick on top of the snow. If the storm doesn't stop by the end of the day, we're going to have a big problem hauling hay out to the cattle."

"I couldn't help but overhear your conversation," Sir Edward said. "I feel like I made a real mistake in sending Cynthia in to talk to Rodney. I had what I considered a pretty urgent communication for him, but I failed to take into account the differences between the American West and the streets of London. When I look outside at the storm, it begins to dawn on me how different the logistics are out here.

"I didn't realize that business comes to a complete standstill when such a storm hits. Had I known that the storm would be this severe, there is no way I would've asked for such a difficult task to be initiated." Sir Edward walked over and looked out the window over my shoulder; then turned and walked over and looked out the side window. "It surprises me to find that I'm pacing around like a tiger. By Jove Easy, I believe I'm about as worried as you are."

"I'm going to make a hole in the ice, here at the head of the bed. I want to be able to poke my head out and see what would be entailed in getting some wood together and building a fire here in our igloo. I want to be sure we are in a position where we won't be seen. We might even do it at night, so the smoke can't be seen. I think that very little light would be able to shine out through a small hole. There are very few roots for the fire light to shine on, anyway. We need to see about drying out our clothing and seeing if we can make it to safety."

"What can I do to help? I'm ready, willing and able to do whatever is necessary." Cynthia sounded ready to face anything.

"Just wait until I get my folding spade. I want to take a peek out, first thing." Brad crawled back and she heard him moving his saddle and other unseen objects around while he searched. A few minutes later he came back, teeth chattering, and crawled into the covers. "Whew, it sure is cold," he exclaimed.

They lay there together, huddled for warmth, and suddenly Brad sat straight up, bumping his head on one of the roots.

"Cynthia, do you hear that crackling noise?" He waited to hear Cynthia's word of assent before he continued. "That is the sound of sleet falling. It is forming a sheet of ice. This has an upside and a downside. The upside is that no one who wishes to harm us can hunt for us without the icy crust cutting their horse's feet and legs up. The downside is that no one who is hoping to help us can come looking for us. We also sure don't want to cut a hole in the snow while it is sleeting."

"Another downside is that we're being sealed inside this little man-made cave like we were in a cocoon. We're hidden away as remotely and hard to find as if we were shipwrecked on a desert island. However there is also an upside to that downside. I'm here with an extremely attractive and personable young woman."

Cynthia laughed throatily. "That's easy for you to say now since we're in the pitch black and you can't see me. When we're lying here in the pitch black darkness, afraid to talk for fear the rustlers will get us; unable to see one another because it's so dark; and the necessity to entwine our bodies like pretzels or an old tangle of barbed wire to keep from freezing, it's a lot easier to forget reality. Since we are trapped here under about as intimate conditions as can be imagined, perhaps we can use some of the time for you to tell me about your life. How and when did you lose your wife? Where were you born? What did you do when you were a boy? What circumstances brought you to the Bend of the Rimrock? Finally, and perhaps the most important: what are your hopes, dreams, and aspirations at this point in your life?"

"Okay." Brad snuggled a little closer to her and said, "I'll go ahead and start with the first chapter of my life. But don't think you're going to get off all that easy! You're certainly going to have to intersperse among the chapters of my life, corresponding chapters of your life. Better yet, why don't we both start at the beginning and have a more or less interactive conversation as we move through time to the present?"

"Okay but there is one thing I'd like to ask you. Were you by any chance able to salvage some of the sandwiches and other food that Earlene fixed for us?"

"I should be kicked for not thinking of it sooner, but with it being so dark in here, there is no way to judge the time. I have a watch in my pants; that is if it will still run after getting soaked with water. I probably have some matches in a waterproof container in my pants, but my pants are probably frozen so solid that it would ruin them if I tried to straighten them out enough to get my hand in the pocket."

"Well, we don't need a watch when it comes to eating." She rolled away from him enough to turn her stomach slightly up and he could hear her slapping her hand against it. "This," she said, "is clock enough for me to know when it is time for the dinner bell to ring." She laughed for a moment, and then said, "I can easily hear that dinner bell ringing right now."

"Well," Brad answered, "let me see if I can find where I threw that saddle. I want to warn you though, after I've poked around looking for the saddle in some corner of this 'igloo', when I come back half frozen, it's going to be up to you to help me get warm again."

Cynthia could hear Brad rustling around somewhere a little beyond her feet. She could sense, as much as hear him, as he moved the saddle around, unbuckled the flap of one of the saddle bags, and the scuffing sound of the bag of food being removed. He turned around and hitched himself back to the other end of the bed roll, half crawling on all fours, and half walking on his knees. For a moment he braced himself with one hand on her upper thigh. A moment later he was under the cover, shivering with cold and with his teeth chattering. She drew him against her and began vigorously rubbing his back.

"Is this helping?" she inquired, slowing her rubbing, but pulling him tightly against her, rolling her body half above his, and throwing one leg over his.

"I should hope to say so!" His shivering was beginning to abate.

She started to roll back to her side of the bed roll.

"Whoa there!" He pulled her back and added, "I said it was helping, but I didn't say it had already worked! While you're warming me up we had also better be thinking about what you're going to do about this food, which judging by my feet, is probably as frozen as a block of ice."

"Well," she said, "I can think of several remedies, but before I even think of using one of them, just make sure just how frozen the food is! There's not anything better than a cold sandwich, in my estimation. That is, if we're still talking about food, and I guess we are. Hand me that bag! Let me take a look, or perhaps I should say a feel, of what we have available."

Brad handed her the sack of food. She took it but then lay back down at the head of the bed-roll and moved around so she could roll up onto her hands and knees. Scooting down toward the foot of the bed a little, she raised up on her knees, taking care to keep the cover pulled over her shoulders. She rustled around in the bag for a moment and said, "it's hard for me to believe, but this food doesn't feel frozen to me! I can't believe it!"

"Hmmm," said Brad. (Cynthia could just imagine him scratching his chin in concentration) "I guess our body heat must have our little igloo heating up to above freezing temperatures. It sure seems colder than that, but it is obvious that with the top sealed off by snow and ice, and no way for air to enter except for the airways kept open by our breath, the natural reservoir of heat in the surrounding earth is going to tend to raise the temperature in our shelter here."

"Yes, I understand what you're saying. Put out your hand where I can find it and I'll put a sandwich in it. Wait a minute! First, see if you can find your canteen so we'll have something to drink as we eat."

"I already have it here. I haven't taken the lid off because the last thing we want to do is spill our water. There's no telling how long it has to last, not to mention how bad it would be to get our bed wet.

Give me the sandwich now. You've talked about food so much you've got me as hungry as a bear now."

Cynthia laughed. "Speaking of bears, this is about as close to being in hibernation as anything I can think of. Maybe we should just cuddle up and wait for the spring thaw."

"As warm as your body is, that would sure work for me!" Brad chuckled and took a bite of his sandwich. "Hmmm," he said. "I don't know if it's actually because I'm hungry or not, but this sandwich is really good. I suppose that now we won't have to try your various methods for thawing out a frozen sandwich."

"I suppose not," Cynthia answered. "I'm not sure if that makes me happy or sad."

"Well I know how it makes me feel, but I'm not going to get into that at this point. We'd better go ahead and eat these sandwiches. The way we're holding these covers up, it's letting too much cold air underneath them. By the way, while I'm thinking of it, try not to get any crumbs on my side of the bed."

"Picky, picky, picky! What in the world does it take to keep you happy? Here we are in our nice, snug little cave with a great sandwich in our hands, and all you can do is worry about crumbs?"

"Well to tell you the truth about it, I guess I'm not really that worried about the crumbs. Actually, I was fibbing when I said that. I'm no fan of crumbs in the bed. However, now since I'm finished with my sandwich, I am ready to get warm again. How about you?"

"I have a kind of a delicate subject to bring up. I was unconscious or very nearly unconscious when you improvised our little home away from home. I have no idea how this little igloo, as you called it, is laid out. Since Mother Nature is whispering in my ear, you might give me some guidance as to what part of our home we can retreat to, to take care of those types of things."

"Being as how our clothing, wet and soggy though they may be, are laying beyond the foot of the bed near my saddle, I imagine the best thing to do would be to crawl straight down past the foot of the bed until you come to the saddle and move to the right until you feel where the end of the tarp that forms the wall drapes down and meets the part of the tarp forming the floor. Lift up what part of the tarp you find necessary. If you can, keep your feet on the tarp and dispose of the waste on the bare ground outside our little igloo. That's as far from the saddle and our clothing as we can get, without being up at this end of the bed, where our heads are. If you'll wait just a moment, let me grab an old newspaper from my saddle bags." He scurried off and returned a minute later. Cynthia heard the rustle of paper as he handed her a sheet of newspaper. "Here, let me guide you back to the place I was talking about." He helped her crawl back toward the corner of which he spoke, guided her hands to the canvas edges of the tarp, and scurried back and crawled under the cover.

A couple of minutes later she returned and joined him under the cover. She huddled up against him, shivering and teeth chattering. "Boy, it sure is cold," she said between her chattering teeth. "I think when you go below ground level, you must also be able to go below just plain cold. I think when I laid down under the cover, I could hear my body clatter against the frozen earth. Brrr! I've never been so cold in all my life. Every time I drew a breath while I was outside the covers, my breath froze and fell down on my poor frozen toes and chipped pieces off of them. If you think I'm joking, just roll over and let me put my feet up against your back. You'll be able to feel the jagged edges."

She laughed at her own joke as though she were at a party in some fancy drawing room, instead of being held prisoner in a dark icy cave by weather, rustlers, and fate. "You know what the worst thing is about all this? To me, it is the complete and utter disorientation. I have no idea whatsoever of any direction, except for up and down. It is one of the strangest feelings I have ever had. Have you ever slept in a strange bed in a strange place and woke up where you had no idea of where anything was in the room? In such a case, I have always found amusement in keeping my eyes closed while I concentrated on where the door was that I came into the room by, where the bed was in relation to the door, and which way I was facing. I would gradually orient myself by doing these things."

"Yes!" exclaimed Brad. "I find myself doing exactly the same thing. I have done that several times, here in our own little igloo."

"The bad thing about this case, for me, is that I have absolutely no idea of how anything is, because I wasn't cognizant of my surroundings when you put me in here. It causes me to have just the strangest feeling. While I enjoy any adventure, I do think I would enjoy things more, in fact a lot more, if I had my bearings." Cynthia straightened her legs out a little.

"Are you warmer now? asked Brad.

"Just as warm as toast, straight out of the oven. I feel like I'm lying on a feather bed, covered by my own best comforter." Cynthia laughed and wriggled around as though she were snuggling down into a warm and feathery nest.

"Okay then," said Brad. "I want you to straighten your legs out and roll over on your stomach. I want to see if I can't get you properly oriented."

"Hmmm," said Cynthia. "I'm not sure about how you're going to do that. However it is, it sounds interesting. In all seriousness, if it works, it will be worth it. Get to orienting!"

Then it was Brad's turn to laugh. "You sure are going out on a limb, being as how you don't have the foggiest notion of what I'm going to do. I can think of all sorts of ways I could turn a statement like that to my advantage." Before he could continue, Cynthia interrupted to say:

"I see several fallacies in your train of thought. First, what makes you think I don't have the foggiest notion of what you're going to do? Secondly, what makes you think it would be to your advantage and not to mine? Let's see how you answer those questions."

"Hmmm, before you get to feeling too cocky, you'd better remember you're not talking to some character in a book. I'm flesh, blood, and heat. If you press a little closer to me, you might feel my pulses beating and if you were to lay your head on my chest, you would undoubtedly hear my heart beating. Be careful or you might dig yourself a hole that's harder to get out of than this icy little igloo we're in."

"Ha, Ha, Ha," she laughed. You're the one who had better be careful. It takes a pretty dire threat to scare me!"

"Okay, okay! So you've made me back down." He hesitated for a second and said, "For the moment." However, we'd better get back to the task at hand, which is to get you oriented. If we go any further on that other fork of the trail, we run the risk of never even wanting to leave our little igloo, but having it melt from over our heads and drown us in the boiling runoff from the snow and ice. Now, now, now! Just leave the rest of what I've said unanswered, and roll that hot little body over on your stomach. Let's get this little lesson in orientation underway."

"Alright," she answered meekly. She rolled over on her stomach and cradled her head on her arms. "Now get on with your orientation."

"Okay, right now you are lying with your head pointing nearly directly west. I hope the blankets on your back don't interfere with the feel of my fingers, because by necessity the blankets are going to move as I move my hand up and down your back. I want you to try to visualize your back as a map I am drawing. Here," he said, as he drew one finger lightly down her backbone from her neck to its end, "is the Wandering River. I am sure that you remember that the Wandering River is the river that runs between my Ranch and Vacaville. It is the same river that we cross over each time we go into town for supplies."

Again Brad laid his hand on her warm back and placed his finger on her spine between her shoulder blades at the base of her neck. "Here is where the desert begins. It rapidly changes to good grass land as it comes along here," he said, as he trailed his finger down her spine halfway to the small of her back.

"The spot where my finger is right now is approximately where the bend of the Rimrock turns back north to the entrance of my ranch. As you know, since your head is pointed toward the west, this side," he said as he gave her a light spat on her right buttock, "is the north side of the river. This," he added as he spatted the other side, is the south side of the river.

"Now let me repeat. The river, running from the desert, which would begin about at your neck and runs along here," he said, as his voice followed his finger. "Now right here," his hand stopped and he pressed his finger a little harder and wiggled it against her skin, "represents where the Rimrock Land and Cattle Company begins." Again his finger moved along her back and stopped once more. "This spot," and once again he pressed his finger harder against her skin, "is about straight down from where my ranch's entrance is."

It was impossible for Cynthia to keep from squirming as his finger trailed along her back, or pressed down to denote a landmark.

His finger continued down her back, leaving a delicious trail of tingling sensations. Once again he moved his hand further down as he said, "About here is Vacaville and about right here," he said as again his finger made a little circles on her back, "is the junction of the East Fork with the Wandering River.

"Here is what happened to cause you to fall into the river. The East Fork is fed by some large springs. Although the water from the springs is cool, it is quite warm in comparison with the frigid temperatures that had frozen a thick enough surface on the Wandering River to cross a large herd of cattle on it, if the rustlers did what I suspect they did. Of course, they may have continued straight east, and not have crossed the river at all. Anyway, when you came to the Wandering River, you arrived at a point so close to the warmer water of the East Fork that the ice was too thin to cross on.

"Anyway, let me get back to the map on your back." His finger once again began its journey down her back. "Here," he said, moving his finger to her tail bone, the very last vertebra, "is where you tried to cross the Wandering River."

He lightly dragged his finger back and forth near her tail bone, his palm smoothing along on the adjacent areas of her skin. She gave an involuntary, shuddering shiver. "Remember, this is where you tried to cross the river." He lightly pressed the spot, moving his finger in little circles again.

His finger felt its way back up toward her head for the length of two vertebras. "This is where I crossed the river, making certain that I was upstream from you, so I couldn't miss you on the way back downstream." His finger drew an extremely delicious path back toward her feet for the length of one vertebra. "Here is where I came to the East Fork and discovered that its waters weren't frozen. It was at that instant that I saw your horse come out of the river."

"I wheeled my horse and galloped a few yards up the East Fork to be sure I could cross without being swept into the Wandering River and perhaps under the ice downstream. I crossed the East Fork and galloped back to the main river, with a feeling of terrible dread that I couldn't find you."

His finger went back to a spot an inch to her left from her tail bone, climbing the steep, firm, smooth slope of that curve. "Here is where I found you. I took a hitch over my saddle horn with my lariat and took a running jump into the water when I saw you clinging to the ice. My horse was a little upstream of you, so I could try to keep us from being swept under the ice. I was unsure that I could reach you in time, and also filled with fear that if I did reach you, I would be unable to get you back to shore, for I could scarcely breathe, I was so shocked with cold.

"I got you just as your hands slipped loose from the edge of the ice. I had to grab your hair with one hand while I used the hand that was holding the lariat to try to hold us from going under the ice together. I managed to work you over my right shoulder, to keep you on the upstream side of me, so you would be washed against me, not away from me."

He trailed his finger up the swell of her body and said, "Here is where we came out of the river. I threw you over my horse's saddle and let the wind blow us along. It was snowing so hard that I couldn't see. I knew you were freezing to death. I was not far behind you, for my clothes were so stiff with ice that I couldn't bend my knees. You were freezing to the saddle.

"I grabbed my ground tarp and was spreading it on the ground to try to get us out of the wind and into my bedroll right there on the spot, when through a swirl in the snow, I saw the big oak tree. It was only about fifteen feet away. I wanted to get in the lee of the tree to try to break the wind a little.

"I moved my tarp and bedroll into the lee of the tree, when the snow parted a little and I saw this fallen tree. I leaped into the hole left by its roots and scraped the snow aside as fast as I could. I threaded the end of the tarp through some of the lower big roots. I pulled the rest of the tarp back along the ground and back up to the roots to form a little tent. The tarp was large enough to pull the sides down to make it where we had four walls for our tent.

"I had to more or less pry you loose from the saddle and I carried you down and laid you on the edge of the tarp. I began undressing you as rapidly as I could. Some of your clothing, I was able to pull off of you. Some of it I had to break off of you. I got you undressed and rubbed you dry with a spare shirt from a saddlebag. I spread out my bed roll enough to lay you down and cover you up.

"With your body on the very edge of the tarp, I was able to finish rolling out the bed roll. I was barely able to climb out of the hole and strip the saddle and bridle from my horse. I threw them into the hole where they are now laying, and tore off my clothing. My hands were so cold that my fingers wouldn't work. I climbed into the bed roll and pulled you tightly up against me. I wrapped my arms around you and began to lightly rub my hands up and down your back. That was so awkward to do that it was well-nigh impossible.

"I rolled over with you on top of me and placed your hands between our bodies and again began to rub your back, your face, your arms, and as much of you as I possibly could. I would sometimes rub the length of your legs with first one of my legs and then with the other. When I felt sure your hands were no longer in danger of frostbite, I rolled us over on our sides.

"This put your back toward me. I pulled your knees up against your chest and curled my body around yours. Then I alternated putting first one of your feet between my legs and then after a minute, changing over to the other foot.

"Although you were more or less in a coma, your teeth were chattering so hard that I was afraid they would break. You were also shivering so hard that periodically, you would be in a spasm of convulsions. I was afraid you would never recover. I was also shivering and my teeth were chattering so hard it sounded like one of those dancing girls that use castanets.

"That was right here." He again pressed his finger against her skin. He sat up momentarily and bent forward and placed a light kiss where he had marked as the spot they now were. "That opening in the snow may have been all that saved us. I may come back when we get out of this mess, and build a little monument to luck and providence." The break in his voice testified to the earnestness of his statement.

His arm relaxed and dropped its weight across her back. He slowly drew his arm back up her back, his entire arm brushing her back as lightly as a thistle.

She lay there without moving, without speaking and probably without the power to do either. Brad continued his story.

"It was probably only about ten minutes later that we had both fallen asleep. I have no way of telling or even guessing how long we slept, but for however long we did sleep, my sleep was filled with dreams, or what might more aptly be described as nightmares. I dreamt that we were drowning in icy water. We were swept under the ice and I was clawing at the ice trying to make a hole, so that I could get you out of the water before you drowned.

"Nearly the entire time that I was asleep was spent in frustrating attempts to escape, sometimes from the rustlers and sometimes from the weather. I imagine that it was later on after we had warmed up and got a little rest that I finally had a different kind of dream."

"Yes," said Cynthia. "I think that was about the time that both of us awakened. It is easy to believe that the proximity of our bodies, one to the other, had the same effect on both of us. I see nothing unnatural in such a reaction. It's just that the physical manifestations of such a reaction are more obvious in a male than a female.

"One thing is for sure. I'm not used to waking up with a pretty girl under such embarrassing circumstances."

"Oh?" If the igloo had had even a trace of light, Brad could have seen the delighted smile on Cynthia's face.

"Under just what kind of circumstances are you used to waking up, when you are with a pretty girl?"

"It's my belief that the only way to keep a secret, is to keep it secret. The only way I know how to keep a secret secret is to not tell the secret. What is your answer to that, Miss Smarty-Pants?"

"I think it's rather strange that you would call me Miss Smarty-Pants, when I'm wearing my present attire. Just exactly what do you mean by that?"

Brad shook his head in the darkness and grinned. "Cynthia, we have an old saying here in America. It goes something like this: "Quit while you're ahead." I think I'll just fall back on that axiom that is carried forward from the past. Why don't we cozy up and see if we can get a little warmer?"

"I would like to, but for one thing. I want to take an exam to see if I understand. Now I have a certain point that I want to lead up to. I think it is an important one. Please don't interrupt me until I am completely through. Okay?

Cynthia could not see the puzzled look on Brad's face as he started to roll over on his stomach.

"No, we don't have time for that. Stay on your back. Follow what I am doing and saying. My map will not be to the same scale yours is. Here," she said, "is where the Bend in the Rimrock is." She trailed her fingers from the top of his head around the right side of his face. "Right here, if I understand you correctly, is where your ranch is." She placed a finger where his throat joined his left shoulder. She reached over and took his left arm. "Lay your arm along your body just so." She placed his arm so that it lay along the edge of his body. "No," she said, "as she ran her hand down along his arm to his hand. "Open your hand and lay it flat, like this." She placed his hand so that it was flat against his leg, palm down, with the inside of the hand lower than the outside.

"Now the Wandering River flows along here." She trailed her index finger from the center of his right shoulder up across his right nipple to the center of his chest, and from there straight down until it reached a brushy area. Moving her hand a couple of inches to the left, and also a couple of inches back toward his head, she said, "Here is where the East Fork joins the Wandering River." She then went back down to the left side of the brushy area and said, "Here is where I tried to cross the river. It is at this point that you found me and rescued me.

"You got me on your horse, put the wind at your back, and had to go toward the southeast. At this point, you saw this big oak tree." Her fingers brushed against the obstruction, standing like an oak. "You went right around the oak tree and saw the fallen tree. You spread your tarp over its roots, like this." The palm of her hand lay over a soft, tarp-like part of his body. "You and I are now here, below this tarp, covered with snow. You can verify that by noting that this is you," she said, "and this one is me."

Brad had tried his best to ignore the feel of her hands, and he tried his best to ignore her suggestive remarks about their igloo. The oak still remained an oak, however.

"Now listen closely," she continued. "We are coming to the point that I want to make." She reached over until she felt the arm that she had laid along his side. Her hand started at about his elbow and trailed along down his quivering side until she reached the hand that she had spread, palm down, on his body.

"Your hand represents the Old Buffalo Trail down from the Rimrock." She moved her finger up hill across his hand to his smallest finger. "Here is Post. Here is the trail the Vertical X's crew follow when going to and from Post." She trailed her finger back across his hand and across his legs, just below their igloo, and laid her hand flat on his right leg. Her thumb was touching the part of his body she had called their igloo, the spot where they now found themselves.

"Now, Brad, here is my question. Are we or are we not, right in the front yard of the Vertical X's ranch house?"

"Oh, how in the hell could I have overlooked such an obvious thing?! We might be in a spot where it would be suicide to try to dry our clothing! That sure points out a big complication." Brad drew a deep breathe, and said, "Well, so we have a whole new set of problems, or I should say, we are now aware of a whole new set of problems. This is going to require some thought."

Cynthia noted that the oak tree no longer towered above the igloo. She patted that area in sympathy, and they curled up to find a little more warmth.

They lay together, each of them thinking of the new viewpoint of their problem. Fifteen minutes later, Brad said, "We can't risk starting a fire and drying our clothes, since we are so close to the Vertical X's ranch house. We will have to make clothing out of the blankets and tarp and walk out, leaving everything here to recover later, except necessities. It appears that the sleet has stopped.

"I'm going to make a hole and look out to see just where we are, as far as being in plain sight of the ranch house. He hardly made the remark before he had grabbed his little spade and made a hole in the snow to look out.

He stuck his head out into a dense ground fog.

"Quick, Cynthia. There's a heavy fog. This changes the whole picture. We have to get ready to make a run for it right now, while we can still stay hidden. Cut this tarp along here," he said, holding the tarp up between his two hands. She began slitting the tough material, cutting along the path he was making. As they finished cutting the strip off, he said, "Roll this up into as tight a roll as you can." As he said the words, he had grabbed the spade and cut another hole in the other end of the igloo.

He climbed up, saying, "Hand me the tarp, Cynthia."

She did so and he said, "Get me the hatchet while I spread out this tarp."

Again, she reacted quickly, handing him the hatchet. She stood up and watched him as he walked along the tarp, which he had spread along the trunk of the tree. She knew he was freezing, but couldn't help but marvel at how well nature had formed the human male.

Seconds later he approached with an armload of dry limbs and twigs. She jumped out of his way and he dropped the load through the hole and followed the wood down with his own body.

Cynthia had anticipated his actions and had a wad of newspaper under the other hole. She had enlarged the hole to where it wouldn't cave in and smother the fire, as it began to melt. In moments, the fire was blazing. Their small ice covered den was blazing hot a moment later. As soon as Brad's feet had thawed a little, he jumped back up out of the hole, grabbed the hatchet and began to cut more limbs.

This time, he stayed out long enough to get plenty of wood to keep the fire going for a couple of hours. He dumped the wood through the opening and came down, scraping his ribs so badly he was bleeding like a stuck hog. He lay down on the remaining tarp, feet to the fire.

This time it was Cynthia who was chafing his hands, his arms, his shoulders and upper body, in a reversal of their roles. He lay there for several long minutes, rubbing his feet together and trying to get feeling back into them.

He knew he should rub them with his hands, but the feelings

generated by Cynthia's hands as she briskly rubbed the circulation back into his skin was so far beyond pleasant that he couldn't bring himself to move. As the part of his body that had been exposed to direct contact with the snow begin to warm beneath her hands, she expanded the area of her ministrations. In a brisk and businesslike manner, she covered every square inch of his body. She ignored his body's response to her hands, and did not allow this to stop her until she was certain he was warm. They then lay, clasped tightly together, for what must've been a quarter of an hour. Just before he began to disentangle their limbs, their lips met in a passionate kiss. It lasted only a moment before Brad tore himself away and crawled back to a corner on the opposite to the hole they had just made. Retrieving his hunting knife from near the fire, where where it had been placed after cutting the tarp the first time, he handed it to Cynthia.

"Cynthia, I truly can't believe that a city girl like you can be so versatile, tough, and adaptable to rough conditions. You have no idea how proud I am of you! I know you've heard about how tough the mountain men were. What a great mountain woman you would have made. I can imagine how happy a mountain man would have been to have a mountain woman like you."

"Hmmm," she answered in a very, very low voice. "I wonder what a valley rancher would think of one."

"Excuse me Cynthia, but I'm not sure I caught what you said. Would you please repeat it?"

"Oh, I was just mumbling to myself." She carefully placed several more branches onto the fire and crawled around next to Brad. "Scoot over a little, you fire hog!" She lay down next to him and crowded him over by hunching her hips and shoulders against him. The heat from the fire radiated throughout the igloo.

Cynthia was lying on her back with her left arm thrown across her eyes. This was the first time that Brad had really had a chance to see her body. It glistened with sweat that reflected the colors from the wood fed flame. Her body was so well proportioned that his breath caught in his throat. Her curves on the side away from the flames lay in dark shadow.

Her left leg was stretched straight out and her right leg was drawn up to a point where her knee was brushed by the edge of the canvas.

Brad thought that he had never, not even in the most vivid images that his imagination could concoct, seen such a perfectly formed work of art. Her lightly muscled lower abdomen, blending with the sides of the hips, made a perfect lead-in to her waist. Her chest and breasts rose and fell with each breath she drew. The lower rib on each side curved outward and downward in a perfect line of demarcation between her chest and her upper abdomen.

The soft glow of the firelight shifted and changed the colors reflected from the moist sheen of perspiration on her skin as her stomach rose and fell with each breath.

He reached for her body and very gently slid his open palm across first her left breast and then the right, until it lay between her arm and her body. His outstretched thumb lay along the upper edge of her chest with the curve of his hand from the thumb to the tip end of his index finger following the curve of her rib cage. As gently as a butterfly landing on a flower, he moved his hand down, caressing her right side from her armpit to her raised right leg and then onto her lower abdomen. He let his palm feel the warmth of her skin for a moment and then rolled over with his mouth above her and gave her a long and tender kiss; untwined himself from her arms and legs and started to get up on all fours.

"Wait! Brad, I want to ask you a question and I want you to please answer it honestly. Exactly what were you searching for just now? What were you, what are you trying to find?"

"Cynthia, there are such a wide variety of small connections of which I have dreamed. Some of them may exist in real life; others are probably nothing but fabrications from my mind, imagination, and the fantasies created by my loneliness. Because of all the complexities involved, and under the pressure of time that we are facing now, we would not be able to even mention a small fraction of them. There is one thing that I would like to mention right now, though. I have a hunger that will never die until I memorize the appearance of your body with my eyes and with my hands, along with all of my other senses, so that if fate decreed that we would never again meet, I would have that one image that I could call upon at those times when there is that certain emptiness that may never be filled, that haunts my mind.

"I know that I have a tendency to sometimes be very circumspect when I am speaking from the depths of my heart and soul, so I can only hope that you understand what I'm saying. I was trying to absorb you with my eyes, to soak you into my body, to memorize you with my soul, so that I will have a part of you that I can never lose as long as the heart beats in my body and the blood flows through my veins.

Chapter Twelve - Page 182
An Empty Saddle

The storm raged through the night and the next day it began to sleet. Soon a heavy coat of ice lay on top of the powdery snow. This created the most dangerous kind of travel, because if one were to break through the heavy crust, they would sink deeply into the powdery snow below. The sleet stopped late in the afternoon and a very faint glow from the sun could be seen just before darkness fell.

The way the wind was channeled through the &RR, it had kept the eastern-most side swept clear of snow, but on the western-most side where the wall of the canyon broke the force of the wind, the snow had fallen out into very deep drifts. We wintered our cattle in the upper end of the valley, which was the most northern end. At that point, the valley had narrowed into a canyon.

We had a large barn, filled with hay. The front of the barn, which faced to the southeast, had rails installed along the front in a manner so that the cattle could eat through the rails without being able to soil the hay.

By five o'clock the next morning, Earlene and I had moved a fresh supply of hay along the rails, making sure the cattle had plenty to eat. An hour later we were back at the house eating breakfast.

Earlene, Sir Edward, and I had finished with breakfast, but were sitting around the breakfast table drinking an extra cup of coffee. We were having a desultory conversation, talking about everything except what was uppermost in our minds. I had a strong premonition that things were not well. Ordinarily my premonitions were well-founded.

The morning had dawned crisp, cold and clear, with a light blue sky. A soft breeze blew out of the south. Ordinarily, we would've already taken care of the chores. This morning, we were running late because of riding to the upper canyon to feed and check on the cattle there.

I took a last sip of coffee and stood up and begin putting on my coat, gloves, and a warm cap. I pulled on my overshoes, noting that Earlene was all bundled up and ready to go. An hour later we had completed our morning chores and had returned to the house.

The day crept by, occupied by playing cards. We mostly were playing poker for matches, but our hearts were not really in it. As it began to get dark, we again took care of the evening chores and returned to the house. We played three handed moon with dominoes for a little while.

Sir Edward excused himself, saying that he was going to read for a while. He went to his room and closed the door.

I got up and pulled Earlene to her feet. We stood in the front of the fireplace, basking in the heat for a few minutes and sat down on the sofa and began kissing. After a few minutes we went to our bedroom, snuggled up, and fell asleep after a tranquility inducing session of lovemaking.

In the wee hours of the morning, I was awakened by the sound of a horse in the front yard. I got up and looked out the window and there was the horse Cynthia had ridden. It was under full saddle and had one rein dragging and the other had been broken off. I quickly started dressing and called out to Earlene, telling her what had happened.

We went into the living room and I pulled on my coat, cap and gloves. I went outside to take care of the horse. I took it down to the barn, unsaddled it, and gave it a good rub down. I looked him over carefully and could see no sign of injury.

When I pulled the saddle from his back, I noted that it was heavy with ice; so was the saddle blanket. It made me believe that the horse had been in water, which had frozen too quickly for the water to even drip off. To me, this could only mean trouble. I gave the horse a double ration of grain, and hurried back to the house.

Sir Edward had been awakened by the noise we made getting dressed. He and Earlene were sitting at the table, waiting for me to return from the barn. A platter of bacon and eggs was sitting on the table and a fresh pot of coffee was steaming on the stove.

I washed up for breakfast and sat down and took a drink of the hot coffee, and began bringing Earlene and Sir Edward up-to-date on what I had seen and what my conclusions were.

"So what are we going to do now?" Sir Edward's eyes reflected his worry and concern.

I sat for just a moment warming my hands on the cup of hot coffee and trying to think of a plan.

"Okay! This is what we're going to do. Earlene, put together enough food for a week for two men. Add enough food for a couple of days for another two people, so when we find Cynthia and Brad, we have some food for them. They'll be really cold and hungry.

"While you're doing that I'm going to the bunkhouse and get Rod Lasser. There's no telling what we're liable to run into. Earlene, we can't afford for both of us to be gone. By the time we get back, the cow's udder would be ruined. We're going to hitch up that old sleigh before we come back by the house. Rod and I'll take our bedrolls, but I'd also like to take several warm quilts and blankets, along with a tarp, just in the case Cynthia and Brad are in position where they need to have them. We will be leaving in just a few minutes."

I turned toward the door but then stopped and looked back. "I think we'd better have some warm winter clothing for Brad and Cynthia just in case. The fact that Cynthia's horse has been in the river may mean that Brad has too. They may be suffering from exposure to some pretty bad weather." I hurried out the door and rushed to the bunkhouse.

I entered the bunkhouse and walked quickly to Rod's bunk and touched his shoulder.

He quickly set up and asked, "What's up, Easy?"

"I think we may have an emergency, Rod. Get up and put on your warmest clothing, including overshoes if you have some. While you're getting dressed I'm heading for the barn to hitch up the sleigh.

"It wouldn't be a bad idea to bring your rifle and make sure you have plenty of shells. I'll fill you in as quickly as I can." I hurried out the door to the barn.

I harnessed up the team, and led them outside the barn and over to the large equipment shed. The sleigh set at the far corner of the shed. I backed the team up to the sleigh and hooked them up. I walked beside the sleigh as I drove the team back up toward the house. The horses snorted clouds of white vapor as they chomped on the cold bits.

Rod had started for the barn, but he veered off toward the house when he saw the sleigh tied at the front porch. He ran up the steps and rapped on the door. Earlene immediately opened the door and came out with a load of bedding in her arms. My bedroll was already in the back of the sleigh. As I walked out the door with a few more items, I saw that Rod had tossed his bedroll in the back, before coming into the house.

I walked over to Sir Edward and placed one hand on the older man's shoulder. "Try not to worry, Edward" I said. "We'll do everything humanly possible to find Cynthia. There's no way we can know what happened until they tell us, but I can tell you this: Brad is a seasoned westerner. He is a very cool, and reacts quickly, but thoughtfully. They left here with emergency rations. The fact that his horse hasn't come home tells me that it's very probable that he was able to acquire the necessary things to survive, even in a storm such as this one. We don't have time to tarry, because the sooner we find them the better off we all are and especially the better off they are. We'll see you as soon as we can. I kissed Earlene goodbye, and Rod and I went outside and started the sleigh toward Vacaville. Wisps of fog curled along between the snow drifts. Rod had not eaten, and was munching a sandwich that Earlene had handed him just as we were leaving.

I put the team in a rapid walk, trying to weave around the drifts and keep them walking where the snow had nearly blown off the grass. I allowed the team to trot when I was able to see the top of the grass protruding from the snow. When I knew we were in deeper snow, I was afraid to trot the team for fear it would make them break through the crust of the snow.

I brought Rod up to date with the latest information, as I knew it. I also told him what deductions I had derived from that information.

"From what you've told me," said Rod, "I think you've arrived at as good an idea of what happened as anyone could, with the information available."

"We'll just have to proceed by our intuition, our deductions from what we know has happened, and just hope we get real lucky. I guess the first thing to do is to head straight in to Vacaville and see if they're safely there. There is the possibility that Cynthia's horse fell through the ice right there on the edge of Vacaville and ran off in the storm so that Brad didn't catch it. The horse could've found a place to get out of the wind and stayed there until the storm was over, and then found its way home. Brad and Cynthia may be safely and comfortably waiting until it is easier to travel. I hope that's true but I don't believe that it is. Still we have to make sure before we do anything else."

"I buy that," said Rod. "There is something that I find surprising. Have you noticed that there is not a sign of any of the X-Pan-D cattle? I would have figured we would have run into some of them by now, we are so near the southeast corner of the big pasture. There is no doubt the cattle will have bunched up there."

I grunted my assent, and we kept a close eye out, not only on the right where the X-Pan-D cattle would be, but on the left where one of the small ranches was located.

Rod stood up on the seat, scanning the prairie on both sides. The sky was clean and a bright sun was reflecting so brightly off of the snow that it was hard to see, but the wisps of errant fog were thickening as we got closer to the river. Rod took his binoculars and carefully checked everything in range. There was no sign of a cow.

"If we don't see any cattle as we near the southeast corner, we should turn back to the east to the next road, and see if any cattle have drifted to the southeast corner of that pasture."

"I have to agree with you. If it wasn't that we have to go into Vacaville anyway to see if they're there or not, I would opt for going on searching for them and worry about the cows later. In fact, I don't think we can afford to lose the time to make that detour. When we get to town, while I'm checking with Rodney at the bank to see if they are there, or have been there recently, I want you to go to the sheriff's office and tell him that we suspect that outlaws may have swept the entire north side of the river completely clean of cattle. Tell him that Brad and Cynthia are missing and Cynthia's saddled horse came back to the house. Tell him we're going on to hunt for Brad and Cynthia and that he needs to send some deputies to verify our suspicions about the cattle. Tell them we'll be back just as soon as we can. I'll pick you up at the sheriff's office, or somewhere between the sheriff's office and the bank.

When we came to the crossing over the Wandering River, the river had a heavy sheet of ice over the surface. Glancing down stream, one could see a thickening river of fog, following the course of the river. We crossed on the ice, and a couple of minutes later I pulled up in front of the bank.

"Here, Rod," I said, take the sleigh and go on and give your message to the sheriff. You can pick me up here, on your way back."

Rod nodded, took the reins, and headed for the sheriff's office. I walked quickly inside the bank to Rodney's office. Rodney looked up in surprise. "What brings you into the big city on a cold day like this?" He laid down his pen, stood up and shook hands with me.

"Rod, from the way you greeted me, I can tell that Brad and Cynthia haven't been in to see you."

"No, they sure haven't. From the look on your face I'd say that they should have been in. Since they haven't, we must have some kind of a problem."

"Yes! Rod and I checked to see if they were here. We're on our way to hunt for them. Cynthia's horse came back to the house fully saddled. We have seen nothing of Brad's horse. We also suspect that rustlers might have swept all the cattle off the north side of the river. That includes those of the Rimrock Land and Cattle Company and of all the small ranchers. Well, I don't have time to tarry any longer. We're as worried as the dickens about Brad and Cynthia. Since they haven't been here, they have been somewhere out in the elements for over three days; either that or they have had a run-in with the outlaws. I'll try to keep you posted."

I turned and walked out of the bank. Rod was waiting for me with the sleigh. I could see two of the sheriff's deputies turning right along the far bank of the Wandering River.

"Rod, there is a good chance that they have run into the outlaws. If they have, it is hard to believe that they could have escaped. It's for sure that the rustlers wouldn't let them escape to spread the word. There would be too much as stake for them to take any chances.

"In any event, we have to start our search as though we think they escaped the outlaws. I think I have a good clue as to where to start searching. Ice was frozen over Cynthia saddle and the saddle blanket was frozen stiff. This indicates to me that the horse has fallen through the ice. When we crossed the Wandering River, it appeared to me to be frozen solid or nearly solid. The water of the East Fork would have to still be pretty warm when it runs into the Wandering River. There are too many large springs feeding it near the junction with the Wandering River for it to be otherwise.

"I don't know how far down river it would take before the river is frozen solid again. I think it would be a good bet that they crossed the river at a point where it had iced over, but not strong enough to support the horses.

"That would account for Cynthia's horse having so much ice frozen to the saddle. If the horse was able to make it out of the cold water, it might have finally made it home. One rein was dragging and the other was broken off. I believe Brad would have been too wise to cross the river at a point like that. That tells me that Cynthia was alone when she crossed the river.

"That sure doesn't bode well for Cynthia and it doesn't bode well for Brad, when one considers the reasons he might not have been with her. If rustlers have swept all or part of the cattle from the range between the Wandering River and the Rimrock, there is a very good chance they could have run into the rustlers. Brad might have told Cynthia to run across the river. They may have made some kind of plans for Brad to catch up with her later. He may have been fighting a sort of rear-guard action, to protect Cynthia.

"Why don't we go down the north side of the Wandering River to its junction with the East Fork and see if it is frozen. If it isn't, let's ride on down the Wandering River until we come to the point where we can cross where it is solid. Then we will ride back down the other side to where there is enough ice to look solid, but not thick enough to support a horse.

"We will begin our search there. We can try to leave a trail they will recognize, in case they have survived the storm and are trying to get back to safety. We might periodically fire rifle shots so that they can hear it if they're within range. Can you think of a better plan, Rod?"

"I think that plan is as good as any we can come up with, and will make a good starting point." Rod was still using the glasses to scan the river banks.

We waved to the two deputies who had turned north up one of the roads that ran between the small ranches.

As I had predicted, the water was flowing freely from the East Fork. The water in the Wandering River was flowing for fifteen or twenty yards. An ice sheet began along the banks on both sides of the river. The ice sheet thickened quickly along the banks and grew rapidly until the ice joined in the center. Twenty yards down the river, it once again appeared thick enough to easily cross with the team and sleigh. It looked to me as though one would want to go a quarter of a mile further downstream before crossing with a herd of cattle.

We crossed the river without going further downstream. As soon as we had crossed the stream, I pulled up the team. Standing up on the seat, I began to inspect the nearby landscape.

"Rod, do you see any place that looks like someone could find cover?"

"Easy, I don't see a good hiding place. If they had come out of the river, all wet and freezing, they would've had only a few minutes to find such a place. As cold as it was the other day, their clothing would have frozen nearly instantaneously."

I had sat back down and shook the reins of the horses. They started off, stepping gingerly to keep from breaking through the ice.

"Rod, I'm going to swing back close to the East Fork and go upstream for a quarter of a mile and swing back east for a couple of hundred yards. Then I'll come pretty straight back to the Wandering River, go east for another hundred yards or so and head back south parallel to the East Fork."

Rod had not stopped using the binoculars, even when answering me. We passed over the crest of a hill and I swung the team east. A minute later, I heard shots. I pulled up the team and said "did you hear that?"

"I'm pretty sure I heard rifle shots. I imagine we had better answer them. I also figure we had better keep our rifles ready, in case it's someone else hunting for the same reason." He tilted his rifle up and fired three shots, in quick succession.

I swung the team back toward the sound, and scanned the area ahead. If there was someone over the hill, I wanted to see them before they saw us. I saw the top of two heads come into view as we came over the crest of the hill.

"It looks like we've found them," I said.

"It sure looks like it," Rod answered.

Chapter Thirteen - Page 190
Leaving the little Igloo Homestead

"I wonder how long we've been here. What would be your guess?" They both figured that their estimation of time would be completely warped by the constant darkness, the close proximity of one to the other, and of their vanishing food supply. Brad asked the question, knowing that there was no good answer, only guesses.

"Your guess is as good as mine," said Cynthia. "It does seem like circumstances are forcing us into doing something as soon as we can. That fog won't last forever. What do you propose to do as our first step?

"Cynthia, I'm going to hold the tarp while you cut it with a knife. We'll cut it as nearly as possible as I described earlier. I'm going to try to leave enough for us to rest on and be comfortable while we cut our new clothing..." As he had spoken, he had crawled around and taken hold of the tarp. It was very awkward get into a good position to work, for the space was very cramped.

"Cynthia, I'm sorry to put you in such an awkward position, but you are going to have to get in front of me and cut while I hold the tarp."

"Where are you going to start, Brad?"

"I guess right here is as good a place as any," he answered.

She moved in front of him walking on her knees, and when Brad took hold of the tarp, she begin cutting rapidly straight down along the side. She would stop momentarily, each time Brad needed to move his hands down and get a new grip on the tarp.

They were both very conscious of how her body, moving with the motion of her arm as she sawed on the canvas with her knife, moved her back against his front. Motivated as much by a feeling of awkwardness as from the cold, they had soon cut the piece of canvas tarp to the dimensions they had selected.

She thought back to the comments that Brad had made about how lucky a mountain man would be to have a mountain woman like her. She knew a valley rancher who could have a mountain woman like her any time he wanted her.

"The fog is liable to go away at any time. We can stay fairly warm while we make some clothes from the blankets and tarp. We have to leave before that happens."

"I think that what we are going to have to do now to wrap our feet with strips of blanket until we can only barely get our overshoes on. We will have to cut holes in some blankets and our tarp and figure out how to split the part that hangs down to our feet and bind it around our legs to keep them warm and still give us freedom of movement. We will leave everything else but the guns and our canteen and start walking.

"We can't take a chance on someone seeing or smelling our smoke, so I will put it out with snow when we get out. I will bring the saddle bags with what paper we have left, in case we have to build a fire. We will cross the river on the ice and walk down the bank until we pass the East Fork, so we will have solid ice to walk on. Then we will walk on the river if it is blown clear of snow. Otherwise, we will walk in the road.

"We'll play it by ear as to where we will go. If we see a ranch house nearby, we'll go to it. Otherwise, we will head straight for Vacaville. Do you think of another way you believe to be better?"

"No, that sounds good to me. I do think that we should conserve all of the tarp we can, just in case we should have to hole up again. We sure can't afford to get wet, or even damp. I do think we should make a hole or two in the roof of our igloo, so we can see what we're doing, without exposing ourselves to unfriendly eyes." Brad noted that Cynthia was not overly perturbed by their plight.

"I have already cut some strips of blanket for our feet. Stand over here on the tarp while I bind up your feet and lower legs. That will help a lot while we make the rest of our clothes." She very adeptly began to wind the blanket around his left foot. "Now, while I hold this end before wrapping some pigging string around it, let's see if you can get your foot into the over-shoe. How does that feel? Is it going to be comfortable enough to walk from here to town?"

She cut a piece of pigging string and when Brad answered in the affirmative, she pulled his shoe off and began binding the blanket strip, so it couldn't slip down and become uncomfortable.

When they had finished, Brad bound her feet up in the same way. "We sure are lucky that Earlene made such a fuss to get us to take her overshoes for you. I would have hated to have to drag you on the blanket, all the way from here to Vacaville." He finished with her shoes and grabbed a blanket and wrapped around himself.

Cynthia picked up a blanket and folded it in half. "Here, let me see it if will wrap around you well enough to keep you warm and keep from shocking whoever finds us," she laughed.

"Yeah, we don't want to shock anyone." Brad grinned back at her and added, "I need to have the opening in the front, just in case I need to use the rifle. I don't want to be bound up like a cocoon, so tightly that I can't protect us!"

"Yes, and judging from my experience when I was taking my map examination, you might have another reason that you have to be able to open the blanket."

Brad couldn't remember the last time he had blushed, but he felt the flood of blood to his face. "Okay, okay! So you win this round. Just remember, your fancy frock has to have an opening somewhere too. Just be careful that you have it in the right place, or it might be me who has the last laugh. After all, I'm not made of stone."

"You couldn't prove that by me or by another oak tree either!" Cynthia fought to keep a straight face.

"Listen, you little mountain woman, you! You had better not use your party room jokes on me; at least out here in the wilderness. You might just find out a whole lot more about oaks and stone too!"

"Hahaha! You've already found out that you don't scare me! I've never seen a bluff work when you are just holding a pair, pun intended, when your hand gets called!"

"Yeah, you had better be glad I'm not calling your own bluff, because if I wasn't afraid I would end up having to carry you all of the way back to Vacaville, you wouldn't be wondering if you had put your blanket on the right way or the wrong way. Come to think of it, there might not be a wrong way!"

They had been working while they were talking. They had cut the blankets from the top of their legs on down. They needed only to fold them around each leg and bind them there. Then they would pull their canvas ponchos on over them and start walking.

Brad rolled over to Cynthia and put his hands inside her blankets. "This may be the last time I will ever get to do this," he said, and allowed his blanket to open up so they were skin to skin. They hugged each other closely and had a long kiss that shook each of them to the ends of their toes.

"If it is," said Cynthia, "I will definitely find someone who wants a mountain woman badly enough to make sure those kisses aren't just one of a kind."

"You don't even have to leave our igloo to find him," answered Brad. "That is an iron clad promise. Let's get out and start walking now, while my resolve holds out."

"Hmmm, I always wanted to see how a resolve looked, when it is held out." Brad's "resolve" was pushed to the side as Cynthia began to bind the blanket leggings into place. Minutes later, she had finished with him.

She was soon as well bound up as he.

Brad eased his head up enough to allow him to take a real good look around. The fog was thinning. "The coast is clear. Give me your hand and let's get going."

"Well, like Uncle Edward always says, "the only way to get it done is to do it," so I guess we might as well get to it.

Brad felt Cynthia's hands seeking him out in the semi-darkness. She took his whisker stubbed face between her hands and momentarily warmed his lips with hers. "That was for luck," she said.

"We may have hours of walking ahead of us, Cynthia. If things were different – Well, just if things were different –"

The unfinished sentence hung suspended in the air, although carrying the weight of a stone.

"Brad, believe me I do understand. I do understand you perfectly. I understand you only as someone can understand another when they experience the same feelings themselves; and believe me I do share those same feelings."

"Okay, Sweet Baby. I know that if we get any deeper into this conversation, we might as well just hibernate here for the rest of the winter and feed on love. By now the theft of the herds, as well as our absence will have been discovered. We have friends and loved ones who are probably frantic with worry about us. I suppose it's necessary that we try to get back to them. Let's get started."

Shortly after Cynthia had built the fire, she had taken the canteen and packed it as full of snow as she could. She had set it near the fire and checked it periodically. Each time that she found most of the snow had melted; she had added more snow until the canteen was full of water. One doesn't drink much water when the weather causes little evaporation from the body, but it never hurts to have water, she mused to herself.

Brad set the saddle, the hatchet, and all the other things that he didn't intend to carry with them in the center of the remaining tarp, and wrapped the tarp around them to protect them from rain or whatever other weather might come along. The fact was not lost on Cynthia that he was bringing his rifle. They clambered out of the hole and begin to walk northwest, drawing close to both the East Fork and the Wandering River. Brad knew that they had to cross the big river before getting too close to the East Fork, where the ice would be thin. A hard frozen crust covered the snow and most of the time they could walk on the crust without falling through.

"Well, at least we got to start off with our feet and good warm," said Cynthia. "You've got to admit it is a splendid day for a walk!"

Brad grinned at her. "You've got that right," he laughed. "At least we get to walk without a breeze this morning, balmy though it might be. The only downside to not having a breeze blowing that cold refreshing air in our face, is that we have to walk along in the smell of our own body odor, from about three days cooped up in that little hole without a bath."

The two of them walked along, chatting and joking. They found that they were enjoying themselves immensely, despite the fact of having a long, cold walk in front of them. There was also the specter of having to recover the herd of cattle from a veritable army of rustlers.

They had only been walking about twenty minutes, when Brad exclaimed, "wait a minute, Cynthia!"

Nearly whispering, Cynthia asked: "What in the world is it, Brad? Do you see some rustlers?"

"No, Cynthia. Look there, though!" He pointed ahead to where two sets of horse tracks cut across the path they were taking, heading west.

"Oh no," exclaimed Cynthia! "Surely it's not some of the rustlers, still hunting for us. You would think they would be trying to escape with the herd." She looked over at Brad, and saw a broad grin on his face. "What do you find so humorous about these tracks?"

"What I find so humorous about it, is that I think I know who it was who made those tracks."

"I don't understand what makes you think that you know what men were riding the horses that made those tracks. You've got me just a little bit baffled. You don't think those are the tracks of our horses, do you?"

"No." Brad grinned at her again. "Since I called you a Mountain Woman, you've got to live up to the reputation. A Mountain Woman has to be able to read sign. I want you to look at these tracks real well and then I want you to tell me what makes me think that I know who made the tracks." He grinned and looked at her expectantly.

Cynthia studied the tracks for a moment. "I have to assume," she said, "the curious tracks in the snow might have something to do with it. Now, since you've made me put on my thinking cap, I feel ashamed of myself. As many times as I've been on sleigh rides, I can't believe I didn't recognize the sign of a sleigh. I guess I was used to seeing them on snow, instead of ice. I'll bet my face is red with embarrassment."

"Yes, your face is red, but it shouldn't be with embarrassment. It should be just what it is, the exertion of walking across the snow, in the face of what could be danger. Of course it may be red because you know it makes you look so appetizing that I'm liable to kiss it. Despite the temptation, I'm still not going to let you get out of answering the question that I asked you. In fact I'm going to ask you to tell me who was driving the sleigh."

Cynthia didn't even hesitate. "I'd have to pick Easy, I suppose. Is that who you think it is?"

"You hit the nail right on the head," Brad laughed, "and you didn't even hit your thumb."

Brad aimed his rifle straight up in the air and shot three times. "It's hard to say how far he may have gone, but it would be my guess that he's going to drive the zigzag trail up the river for a mile or two and then cross over to the other side and make the same zigzag pattern all the way back."

"And I suppose that's to leave the type of trail that we would be most apt to stumble across in case we had lost our horses, which we have, and that we're afoot, which we are."

"Right you are, but we better listen and see if we get an answer."

They listened intently and a moment later the sound of three shots echoed across the frozen countryside. Again Brad lifted his rifle and fired three shots.

"The reason I fired again," he explained, "is to give him a better chance to pin point our location." He began to replace the six shells he had used. "It's always best to be prepared," he said as he slid the last bullet into his rifle.

"From the sound of his shots, I would say he's not over a mile away. The sound of the shots has had to travel over the hills, and that weakens the sound. He is liable to be here before I can finish giving you a good kiss."

"Let's test out your theory, starting right now." She turned her face up to his and placed her hands on his shoulders.

Brad wrapped his free arm around her waist and pulled her tightly against him. "Ahhh," he said. "That sure does feel good, but I have to confess that it's not like it was when we were marooned in our igloo. There is a vast difference in kissing you with our coats between us, than it was when we were skin to skin."

They broke apart as they heard a yell drift down the snowy hill.

There was a very gradual slope to the hill, but Easy had to brake the sleigh to keep it from running up on the heels of the team. It stopped alongside them a moment later. The faces of Easy and Rod Lasser grinned down at them.

Easy and Rod both dismounted from the sleigh. Easy quickly stepped forward and embraced Brad and Cynthia, both at the same time.

"I had sort of hated to let you two tender-feet go off by yourselves on horseback. I figured you might fall off your horses and have to walk back. I suppose that's exactly what happened."

"You made a pretty good guess, alright. We fell off our horses a little ways south of here. The weather was so nice that we've been strolling along picking bouquets of daisies. It was so pleasant that we just sort of lost track of the time. It surprises me that you ever missed us. What happened? Did some kind of job come along where you would have to get your hands dirty? I knew if something like that happened, you'd start looking around for me. It is sort of strange that you didn't miss Cynthia though. After all, she is about the prettiest girl in two counties, two towns, and fourteen villages. It looks like you would have missed her, the very first thing."

"Well, something did feel a little bit funny, but I couldn't put my finger on what it was. Anyhow, with things as they are, we'd better get on back home. There is an awful lot of stuff we've got to get done, and we've got to start doing it pretty quickly."

Brad and Cynthia climbed up to the backseat of the sleigh and pulled a blanket up over their laps. Before Easy snapped the reins over the horses, Brad said:

"Easy, we've got to swing on down south a little ways and pickup my saddle and a few other things. Did either of our two horses show up back at the ranch? Cynthia's would've still been wearing the saddle and bridle. My horse wouldn't have been wearing anything."

"Cynthia's horse came in some time during the night. I discovered it early this morning. I thought I heard her horse in the yard and got up to look. It was about 3:30 this morning. I woke Earlene and she put together some food, while I went to wake up Rod. Earlene took over doing all the chores, so I could get Rod and start looking for you. She sure wanted to come along, but knew that we couldn't neglect the animals. That old milk cow had to have attention.

"We were pretty worried when your horse came in all saddled up, Cynthia," I added.

Rod got a sack of sandwiches out from under the front seat, and handed it back to Cynthia. Then he handed back a small parcel that was wrapped in a blanket. "Earlene said she hoped that blanket would keep the jar of milk that she put in there from freezing. If it did freeze, it still frozen or that blanket would be a mess."

"Make sure I don't forget to tell her thanks when we get back to the house. I don't believe I've ever been this hungry before in my life." Cynthia had dug a couple of sandwiches out of the bag and handed one of them to Brad. They begin to wolf down the sandwiches, passing the jar of milk back and forth between them.

We pulled into the &RR ranch house around 1:00 PM. Earlene had stayed home from her office, just in case her father or Cynthia needed care. We ate a quick lunch and I told Earlene that Rod and I would be headed back to town to see if there were any leads on the cattle rustlers. Earlene said that she would ride in with us, for she wanted to get the information to Rodney that Cynthia and Brad had started in to deliver, before running into the rustlers.

We crossed the river, which was still iced over. A shallow layer of water was flowing on top of the ice. If the weather stayed like it was today, the ice on the river would have to breakup soon.

"Earlene, are you going to be here long enough for me to put your horse in the stable for you? Do you want to leave it tied here in front of the bank?"

"I think I'll just leave it tied here in front of the bank. I want to get back out to the ranch and have a long talk with Cynthia and Dad." She leaned over and gave me a kiss. "I'll see you guys later. I imagine you don't have any idea what you're going to be doing until after you talk to the sheriff." Her last sentence was half in the form of a question and half in the form of a statement.

"You've got that right," I said. "I have no idea whether they have gotten any leads or not. As much snow as has fallen, I don't expect there to be any physical clues left. It is just going to take a systematic search."

Rod touched the brim of his hat to Earlene and said, "be careful. There's no telling who may be roaming around out there in the snow."

Earlene slapped the stock of her Winchester. "They won't be roaming for long if they come into rifle range." She smiled at Rod and winked at me as she stepped out of the saddle. She was hitching her horse as Rod and I started up the street toward the sheriff's office.

We dismounted and hitched our horses to the rail in front of the jail. Climbing the steps to the porch, we stomped the snow off of our boots and used the scraper.

We walked inside and saw the sheriff taking a hot pot of coffee off the potbellied stove.

"Hey Todd. How's it going? We're about to freeze from standing out there on your porch in the cold air, peeping through your window to see when your pot of coffee was going to be ready. We knew the only way we could get in on it was to come in just as you are taking it off the stove."

Todd turned toward us with a big grin on his face, but then turned his face back to the coffee pot, cursing, as his inattention caused him to let the coffee pot touch one of his knuckles. "Danged if you don't go to a lot of trouble, trying to mooch a cup of coffee. This coffee is made out of day before yesterday's coffee grounds. You all need to raise my expenses." He looked over at Rod. "Hey Rod, I never thought you'd be running around with a moocher like Easy. What happened? Did all the rest of the crew out there freeze during the big storm?"

"No, they had already died of poison from the cook's poor grub. They've been having to live on skinny old jackrabbits. Easy has been afraid to jar loose from any money for good grub, since the rustlers have cleaned everyone out of cattle."

Sheriff Todd had set three cups on his desk. He poured them full of coffee and set a can of evaporated milk and a bowl of sugar on the desk.

"How's this for all the comforts of home?" he asked, settling himself in his chair. You fellows bring me up to date."

"Actually, there's not much we have to tell you, Sheriff. After finding Brad and Cynthia and getting them home, we only had time to grab a bite of lunch and head back into town to see what you have going. Did your men find any clues as to where the rustlers are? Do you know who all lost cattle?"

"First, we haven't found a single physical clue. The storm has wiped out everything. Secondly, as to who all lost cattle; it was everyone on the north side of the river. Well, that's not exactly right. They didn't send men into the valleys of the &RR and the EEZ. They cleaned out every ranch on the north side from the Rimrock Land and Cattle Company to the last of the small ranchers."

"Well," I said, "there are no options open except to recover the cattle. If we don't, it'll bankrupt this entire region and put the entire state into bankruptcy or near bankruptcy. That includes every business, including the bank."

"Here's the way it looks to me," said the sheriff. "First, there is no way in hell they can move that big of a herd without leaving an easy trail to follow. They can't have moved the cattle after the storm got well underway, so they have to be holed up near here.

"Second, there are only so many places to hide a herd. Now there is bound to be some of the small ranchers who became familiar with the area east of the East Fork. We can canvass the men who used to live in the South Cedar Hills.

"Third, whoever staged this job has to be aware there is no way to get away. It is my thought that they know that and have something else up their sleeve. Before I give my idea of what they are planning, I want to hear what you guys think, to see how it tallies out with what I suspect."

"Rod, do you want to go next?" I asked. "I have a pretty good idea of what I think they are planning."

"I'll bet we all have a similar idea," said Rod. I'm going to say that if they don't think they can run away from us, they must be thinking of stopping us from chasing them."

"You have exactly the same idea that I have. With the amount of men they had to have to make such a big gather so rapidly, they are going to let us follow them into some place where we can never get out of again." I rubbed my chin for a moment. "That nearly leads one to believe that someone sure has a grudge against us all."

Todd broke in. "You guys are on exactly the same path that I am. I just wanted to see if I was seeing something that doesn't exist. They took such a big bite out this country that we have no choice but to come after them. They expect us to be so furious that we will charge right into their trap with scarcely a look.

"Since we all seem to have the same idea as to what they want to accomplish, now we have to figure out how they expect to accomplish it, and in what manner. Do either of you have any ideas". The sheriff took a drink of his coffee and grimaced. It was nearly as cold as one of the snow banks outside the door.

"I'm not sure of what to expect when it comes to their plans. I think that it is enough to know that they are going to do something along that line. Since we don't know what they're going to do, I think the thing that we ought to do right now is to plan for a long campaign. I think that we ought to get wagons together with enough food, ammunition and supplies to last us for a month. I think we ought to come prepared with everything we need to have a comfortable time on the trail.

"I think we should swear in forty or fifty men as deputies. I think we should bring along several cases of dynamite, a couple of rolls of rope, a chuck wagon, axes and shovels, and plenty of extra water. I would even go so far as to say that we ought to bring along some extra horses. I think when we leave on our expedition; we should be prepared not to come home empty handed."

Mike Thomas, Todd's young deputy came in the door. "Hello everyone, I'm glad you're all here. Sheriff, I have a message here that looks to me like it might be pretty important." He tossed an envelope onto the desk in front of the sheriff.

The Sheriff opened the envelope, withdrew the letter, glanced at it, and handed it to me. I looked at it and turned it so that Rod could see it. The note was from the sheriff of Golden County, where Richard Hampton was jailed in the township of Nugget Creek, pending his appeal of his sentence to be hanged. It said, "A large group of armed men broke Richard Hampton and Judge Pickwick out of jail. There is the possibility they may be headed your way.

The brief letter was signed by the sheriff. It was written on his official stationery.

"Hmmm," I said. "Everything is beginning to come together now. I'm beginning to see where the financing came from to put together such a large rustling operation. I don't recall whether I've mentioned this before to anyone else, but the Rimrock Land and Cattle Company purchased the Vertical X's ranch several days ago. I'd bet anything that the money we paid Hampton, via his attorney's office, made this whole raid possible.

"I'll bet there's not a head of cattle left on that ranch either. I think I've mentioned a little bit earlier that it seemed to me like there was more involved than just money in this big raid. You know Todd, we were talking over the various actions that we anticipated the rustlers would take when we chase them down. I think this news makes it nearly certain that our guesses were right. If there were ever a time to be cautious, this is it."

I sat there pondering for a minute.

"Todd, I'm just making a suggestion. I'd feel a lot better about this whole operation if it were all under the official auspices of your office.

I don't know how you're going to want to organize this, but I think we should put the plans that we outlined earlier into effect. How long do you think it'll take us, about three or four days, to get all the supplies and equipment together that we're going to need? I'll send someone out to the X-Pan-D and have the superintendent pick out ten good men from there. I sure don't want to leave anyone so shorthanded that they're unable to defend in their home place. When I say home place, I'm not only talking of our places and the X-Pan-D ranch, I'm including the independent ranchers.

"Easy, it all sounds good to me so far. Besides that we have to have a starting point. I think we should advance all of the ideas that we can think of, and try to put together the best campaign we can come up with. With that goal in mind," he said looking over at Rod, "I think you should jump in any time you want to with your comments." He looked over at Mike Thomas, his young deputy, and said, "Mike, why don't you go round up the other deputies and bring them back into the office. I want all of you deputies to have an input, but I want to get the preliminaries over with and start putting the plan into action right away."

By unspoken common consent, the three of us left in the office talked of inconsequential things, awaiting the sheriff's deputies. "I think we should keep several men who are based on the independent ranches out of the posse. We should organize them into a defensive unit. If all of this suits you, I think we should have one of your deputies head that group." Before I could continue, Mike returned with the rest of the duties; Tex Lonigan, chief deputy; Faron Stern, second deputy; and of course the returning deputy, Mike Thomas.

"Easy, since you are the most intimately involved in this whole affair, why don't you outline your preliminary plan, and how you think our department can help you? I know there will be some fine tuning to do as we go along."

"First," I said, "we have to remember that we are dealing with a pretty smart hombre. Keeping that in mind, we want take special precautions to have a strong guard here in Vacaville. It would be just like the master mind of these criminals to draw us out of town and come in while the town is largely unprotected and rob the bank and the businesses. He might even have taken the entire herd of cattle, just to use it for a reason to get us out of town. The herd is worth a lot more than the money available here in town, but with money, one doesn't have to worry about keeping a huge herd of cattle undercover while moving it from where ever it is hidden to a market. It won't be easy to find a market for such a big herd.

"Excuse me, Todd, for seeming ambivalent, but now that I mention it, that idea seems as plausible to me as the one we initially were discussing here. For those of you just getting in on this discussion, let me recap what Mike, Rod, the sheriff and I have covered thus far."

I went back over what had been mulled over earlier, and then added, "I hope that you all noted the element of revenge that was mentioned. I am going to mention it again to stress it. Because of the difficulty of moving, hiding, marketing and all the rest of the logistics of such a huge robbery, we came to the conclusion that the rustlers were going to lure us into a trap and wipe us all out. This would have satisfied Richard Hampton's desire for revenge. I suppose that Mike has already told you that the news came in on today's stage that a large group of men broke both Richard and that crooked judge, Pickwick, out of jail the other day.

"Rod and I have had a run-in with Hampton and his vertical X's ranch crew. There is no love lost between Hampton, his pet gunfighter, foreman, and key men on the one hand and Rod and me on the other.

"For those of you who don't know it, the Rimrock Land and Cattle company bought the Vertical X's a couple of weeks ago. We bought it from Richard Hampton. I imagine the money he got for the ranch was used to hire the outlaws who made the cattle sweep.

"Here is what I propose. We begin outfitting three expeditions. Our first step in that direction is to locate the wagons necessary to operate as I have already outlined to Todd. However, before we will be able to proceed very far on that project, in view of the latest possibility to cross my mind, I would like to see Rod and one or two of your deputies come with me on a scouting trip to ride out the Vertical X's. I will not be greatly surprised if we find all of the cattle hidden in some canyon back on that ranch. There are several hundred square miles or so in that block.

"I would venture to say that if my latest hunch is right, Hampton will bring a crew in to rob and strip the town when we ride out to hunt him down. He will take the money from the bank and flee the United States. He will turn the stolen cattle over to his hired outlaws for their pay. His outlaws will be all that we catch and punish.

"While we recover the cattle in a battle with forty or fifty hardened outlaws, Hampton will find sanctuary in some foreign country with enough money to set him and the judge up for life. He may even kill the judge, and keep all of the money for himself. He'll do all of this with little or no personal risk. That is to say, if that is what he does.

"However, while Rod and I, along with one or two of your deputies, if you can spare them, check out this theory, it is necessary that we prepare for a long road trip. Todd, if you need him, my cook out at the &RR would be a great person to prepare the lists of provisions.

"Since we have covered some of the things that we need, you have a good idea of what armaments we would need. Along with the ample supplies of dynamite, see if you can locate a couple of good bows and a lot of arrows. If no one has them, someone should make them. You might also add a ball of good, heavy twine.

We will have to prepare to recover the cattle from the outlaws, even if we capture Richard Hampton here. We need to take special precautions to protect Sir Edward and Rodney. Anyone who would go to all of the trouble that Richard Hampton went to in order to steal their belongings, even to having them charged with a murder that they actually planned, even though it failed by a hair width, is probably vindictive and will go out of their way to get even for their foiled plans."

"That all makes sense to me," the sheriff said. "Mike, why don't you go with Easy and Rod? This will be an official county operation. However, Mike, I would like you to let your actions be guided by what Easy says. I'm not going to deputize Easy or Rod, on the premise that they might have a little more leeway when going as injured parties, than if they were going as officers of the law." He turned his face toward me and Rod. "I know that I can expect you guys to conduct yourselves in at least a close imitation of what Mike will be conducting himself."

"You can depend on it," I answered for both Rod and me. Rod nodded his head in agreement.

"We're heading out right now. I hope to be back by tonight with information as to whether the cattle are hidden on the Vertical X's. It wouldn't surprise me at all if the rustlers don't even know that we now own that spread." I turned toward Mike and Rod. "Mike, Rod and I came prepared for the possibility of having to camp out. Why don't you pick up your warmest clothing, just in case, along with a winter bedroll? Rod and I will meet you at the cafe and we'll grab something to eat before we start.

"Todd, we have to go where the trail leads, so don't be too worried if we don't get back tomorrow. It will take something pretty unusual to keep us away past the day after tomorrow night, however."

"We'll start a crash program preparing to get started. I will have a picked crew of about ten or fifteen men and have them hidden here in Vacaville. They'll keep out of sight and be prepared for a raid on the bank and merchants here in town."

The three of us stepped out into the street. Rod and I headed for the cafe, and Mike for the boarding house where he lived. "Rod, why don't you go on over to the cafe and get us a table. I'm going to stop off at the bank for a moment."

I went into the bank and walked on past the teller's cages and rapped on Rodney's open office door before walking on in. Rodney had looked up from his books when I rapped on the door jam. He jumped up and walked around the desk and shook my hand.

"Hey Easy, how's it going? Since the storm came, I haven't had a chance to talk to anyone. What brings you into the big city?"

"I had no idea you hadn't been included in the loop, since we located Cynthia and Brad. There is a lot of news you haven't heard.

"I haven't talked to anyone since we had our meeting where we decided to buy the Vertical X's. Other than finding out that the cattle on the north side have been stolen and that cousin Cynthia and Brad had a close call with the rustlers, the only thing that I have heard lately is that you and Rod found Cynthia and Brad and got them safely home this morning."

"Yes," I said, "all that did happen, but that's not the end of it. Rod, Deputy Thomas, and I are planning to make a scouting trip this afternoon. Rodney, before I give you a real brief rundown on what we figure to do, I need to fill you in on some news that arrived just a few minutes ago on the afternoon stage. Your cousin Richard and that crooked Judge Pickwick have been broken out of jail by huge gang of outlaws.

"We, and by we, I mean all of the Sheriff's Department, plus Rod and I believe that there's a good chance of this transpiring:

"First, it is a given that we'll get together a large posse to go after the cattle.

"Secondly, we think they know there's no way of getting away with the theft of so many cattle. The logistics are too difficult to carry out.

Certainly, we think the only way they can possibly pull it off, would be if they set a trap and exterminated the entire posse.

"Thirdly, knowing what little I do know about your cousin Richard, he is going to try to keep his shirttails clean from anything as brazen as the massacre they are planning for the posse.

"Fourthly, here is what I think your cousin will be doing. I think he will either have spies or will be hidden somewhere where he can watch the town through his binoculars and see when the posse rides out. When they ride out I expect him and eight or ten outlaws to ride into town, rob the bank, and sack the town. I also expect him to kill you and Earlene if you are available here in the bank.

"To offset that, we need to have several men hidden somewhere in the bank, armed with double barreled shotguns. We need to have several more hidden in one of the stores across the street, with the same armament. We should try to take them captive, but we should do anything to make sure that none of them escape.

"No one should know about this, except the ones that have to know about it. I guess that will be up to Todd to tell anyone who needs to be told. However I wanted it to be your responsibility to make sure that neither you nor Earlene are hurt.

"I expect your cousin Richard to take the money from the merchants and the bank, along with whatever he has left from selling the Vertical X's and escape for some foreign country.

"I don't have time to talk any longer. Rodney, I'm depending on you. Rod is waiting for me over in the café. I don't expect this to happen until the posse rides out. Try to make things look as average you can. If I were you I'd have a double barreled shotgun within easy reach, just in case.

"Take care, and in case I get sidetracked and can't get back to town for a couple of days, bring Earlene up to date, and put this note on her desk. I tore a note off his pad, folded it in half, and handed it to Rodney."

A couple of minutes later, I sat down across the table from Rod. He had ordered us a special, and it had just been delivered to the table as I entered.

We cantered out of town and turned east, riding along the river. Although the Vertical X's was now part of the Rimrock Land and Cattle Company, there was no telling who might be holed up there. Fording the East Fork, we turned right and rode south, taking care to stay out of sight by riding along through the trees that bordered the river.

Mike called my attention to a dim light, shining through one of the back windows of the large house. We rode south along the river for a couple of miles and made camp in a thick copse of trees, partly up the side of the hill, and well above the river. None of us were hungry enough to eat a sandwich. We spread our bedrolls for an early start on a night's sleep. We intended to get an early start in the morning. During the night I thought I could hear the distant lowing of a cow.

The next morning dawned cold and clear. We found enough dry brush to build a smokeless little fire. A few minutes later, we had hot coffee to go with our sandwiches.

"Did anyone besides me hear anything last night," asked Rod?"

"I thought I heard a cow bawling for her calf. It sounded to me like it was off to the southeast, toward the far corner of the pasture." I looked over at Mike.

"I suppose we all must have heard it. What do we do now?" asked Mike.

"Since we're here so close to the East Fork, we'll just stay in the cover along the trees and go south, hoping that maybe we can find cover going back east somewhere along the way. There'll surely be some creeks running down to the East Fork. Maybe one of them will have some cover. We're gaining altitude pretty rapidly. We can't see the range of hills from here. They're blocked off by this long rise of land that's in front of us.

"If you listen closely, you can hear the rush of the water in the East Fork. It flows pretty rapidly for several miles along here. Look how much higher we are than the river. There may be a canyon running into it on up ahead. That might even be where the cattle are hidden." I started to say more, but Rod held up a warning hand.

"Watch it! he whispered. "Some one's coming from up ahead. Let's get up the slope to those trees and see if we can see them go by."

We quickly rode the twenty yards to another thick grove of small pine and dismounted. Three men rode by, keeping well back in the brush along the river. We could vaguely hear their conversation. I made out a few words. One of the men said something about cutoff and Post. A hundred yards further on and they cut to their right, away from the river and on what I estimated to be on a course for the town of Post. The direction they were taking should intercept the wagon road from the Vertical X's ranch house to the old Buffalo Crossing on the Rimrock.

When they had crossed the swell of land that put them out of sight, I commented, "It looks like we guessed right. No one would be riding in this out-of-the-way place unless they had a specific reason for being here. We had better keep a really close eye on things now." The land flattened for a ways when we crested the rise in the ground. Ahead one could see the edge of a canyon.

A small arroyo crossed our path. We rode our horses down into it and out of sight of anyone who might be passing by. We rode east toward the head of the canyon for a mile and began to hear the unmistakable sound of a large herd of cattle being held in strange surroundings.

"I'm going to take a look. Why don't you two stay here where you can cover me, if someone should see me." I ran from bush to bush until I neared the canyon edge. Dropping to my knees, I went on all fours for two or three yards and dropped down and bellied up to the edge by the side of a dense clump of brush.

There, spread out across the grassy canyon was a huge herd of cattle. It had to be the stolen one. The walls of the canyon were very steep and surprisingly deep. I turned and waved the other two men toward me. They inched up to the canyon edge.

Chapter Fifteen - Page 209
Richard Hampton Dies Laughing

"This doesn't really look like a likely place to wipe out a big posse," said Mike.

"No, but it fits part of the pattern we were talking about in the sheriff's office. It is easily found and looks nearly impossible to defend. That has all of the reasons to make a posse think they would have a cinch, killing or capturing all of the robbers." Rod gave all of the apparent reasons a posse would attack such a layout with little fear.

"If some men were stationed on the rim on the other side of the canyon, from what I see, there would be no way for them to escape. If it's a trap for an ambush, the bait is there, alright, but how are they going to spring it?" Mike was cautious by nature, and was trying to figure the rustlers' angle.

"Hmm," I said. "I just wonder if they are trying to make it look too easy. Maybe they are trying to make us let our guard down. Let me set up a hypothetical situation. See that fork in the arroyo up ahead? What if a heavy force of the outlaws were hidden up that fork? What if our people came up the arroyo to this point, left the arroyo and then spread out up and down the rim of the canyon? Then what if the outlaws came down that fork in the arroyo where they were hiding and lined up along here, directly behind where the posse was lined up along the edge of the canyon? What if each of them were assigned a number that correlated to the number of the man on the rim, counting from the left? What if then, when the first man shot, every man shot the man he was assigned to shoot? In ten seconds the battle would be over. All of the men along the rim who thought they had such an easy task of killing the outlaws would then be dead.

"I know that that is a lot of what-ifs, but if Richard Hampton has his heart set on revenge, he'll make some plans as to how to get it.

"Anyway, we have found out what we came to find out. Let's make sure we aren't seen, on the way back to Vacaville."

We had no more than got started when Rod said, "you know, Easy, I'm no tactician, but after listening to all of your 'what-ifs', it makes me wonder what would happen if we made sure that they did see us, but that they thought that we didn't know that they saw us. Wouldn't that fit right into the plan? They would be sure that we would be right back with a big posse, leaving Vacaville unguarded. Whatever plan they have for receiving us when we come back, it would be thrown plumb out of kilter if we just pretended to leave, but had our forces strategically located to make sure none of them could escape from Vacaville."

"I think you have a good idea, Rod. If we go back to the East Fork and continue on to the mouth of the canyon and start up it, as though we are still searching for the cattle, we might put a little more bait in the trap. We can ride in as though we are investigating. You know that they will have some look-outs. Maybe we can spot one of them to be sure we are seen. Even if we see one, we can be assured they won't give themselves away by attacking just the three of us. We'll ride right on past a lookout until we see the cattle. When we do see the cattle, we'll pretend to have an animated conversation, with a lot of pointing at different cattle. Then we can turn our horses and act as though we're in a great hurry to get back to Vacaville, to report in. For sure that'll limit the amount of men that can cut loose to help raid Vacaville. That will make it easier for the ones in Vacaville. Great idea, Rod!"

Mike shook his head in admiration. "You might not think so, on account of my age, but I've already been involved in a lot of law business. I've seen my share of gunfights and shootouts between outlaws and the law. I have to tell you two guys, I feel like I'm back in school. I think I'll approach my deputy duties in a whole different way, from now on."

"We all learn as we go along, Mike. Speaking for myself, I'm sure you know a lot that I could learn. I saw the way you handled yourself, back when Baby Boy Burly was ruling the roost in these parts. I've been around a lot of law men in my day, and I'm sure Rod's been around even more in his day, but I personally have never seen anyone with a cooler head than you and the other deputies working for Todd. I don't think you have to take a backseat to anybody."

We had come to a sizable creek flowing down from the left. It was flowing out of the canyon that we needed to go up as though we were still looking for our cattle.

"Okay fellas," I said. "We want to bear in mind that everything we're doing is based only on conjecture. The outlaws may have a completely different plan, than anything we've considered. We want to remember we're in a life or death situation, and if we have guessed wrong, we may have to try to shoot our way out of this. I don't want us to just be pretending that we're very watchful. I want us to be very watchful."

We rode carefully into the canyon, each of us carrying our Winchester across the swell of our saddle.

"I see one on that ledge just to the left, screened by the top of that tall pine tree, said Mike.

"Yeah I saw him," said Rod. "There is another one in that jumble of big rocks partway up the talus slope."

"Ride on as though you are still looking. Don't avoid looking right at the place where they are hiding. It wouldn't do for them to think we are avoiding looking at them. It might seem too obvious." I couldn't stop a chill from running down my spine. It was impossible not to be braced against the feel of a bullet slamming into my back.

We rounded a slight bend to the left in the canyon, and there were the thousands of cattle, spread from wall to wall and continuing up the canyon as far as we could see from our vantage point.

We pulled up quickly with a show of surprise.

"Look at all the cattle," I said animatedly, flinging my hand in an arc that took in the whole canyon.

"Yep, that is cattle alright," said Mike, "if my eyes aren't failing me or my jitters making some of the bushes look like cows."

Rod stood up in his stirrups and turned his head from side to side as though he couldn't believe his eyes at the magnitude of the herd. "Mike, I have looked three or four times and I'm pretty sure that it isn't your mind playing tricks. They are too big to be jackrabbits, and their back doesn't have the hump that buffalo have, so I'll have to go along with you that they are cattle, alright."

"Okay men," let's light a chunk out of here. Let's all stay in a group. Let's keep looking back behind us as though we are afraid someone is after us." I put Calliope into a full gallop, looking back over my shoulder. Rod and Mike rode abreast of me.

As we came back near the place where we had seen the three outlaws cut off on the trail to Post, I saw what I guessed would be the same three men returning. I saw them see us about the same time we saw them, for I saw one of them point at us. We bent lower over our horses' necks as though we were urging our horses to a greater effort. We passed over a little rise that hid us from view. Just before dropping out of sight, I glanced over my shoulder. The three had broken into a gallop back to the mouth of the canyon.

"I think we've been pretty convincing," I said as I pulled Calliope down to a foxtrot. The others grunted an affirmative, and three hours later we rode into Vacaville.

We rode straight to the sheriff's office to report on what we had discovered.

We walked in to see the sheriff and his other three deputies mapping out the campaign on a sheet of paper. They looked up as we entered and stopping working to see what we had discovered. Then the sheriff filled us in on his progress in putting together the posse.

"Todd, here's what I think we should do. Tell me what you think of this plan. Let's keep the contingent of men that are going to stay here to guard Vacaville out of sight. Let's go out and rush around as though we're just now trying to get a force put together.

"We'll call a big meeting right out in front of the City Hall, at the entrance to the Sheriff's office. We'll be all excited about finding the herd, and I'll suggest that we split the posse in half. I'll tell the crowd that we're sending half of the posse out the trail to the X-Pan D ranch. That half will circle around behind Promontory Point until they are well past the canyon, turn east until they are south of the canyon and come at the rustlers from the south. We'll send the rest east along the Wandering River to the junction with the East Fork. We'll travel up the East Fork to an arroyo. We'll travel up the arroyo and remain hidden in the arroyo until we see the rest of the posse deployed along the south side of the canyon. We'll then move our force out of the arroyo and place them along the north edge of the canyon until the signal to open fire.

"Let's get on out and spread the word of the meeting. We'll be sure to tell everyone to get a good rest tonight, because we'll be setting out early in the morning. I feel sure there'll be a couple of spies that'll come to the meeting. The bank and most of the businesses are already closed. I feel sure they won't attack the town until the bank and the business owners are open and they have seen that each posse has departed on its respective route.

"As soon as the posse that is headed for the X-Pan D gets a couple of miles out of Vacaville, they'll cut over west to the old dry creek bed and follow it back north until they come to the Wandering River. They can remain under cover there until they hear gunshots. That's only one mile west of Vacaville, so they can be back in just a few minutes.

"As soon as the posse that is headed for the East Fork gets a couple of miles out of town, they'll circle south for a couple of hundred yards and ride back to the edge of town under the cover of the mesquite trees. Their job will be to cut off all retreat to the south and east,

"Those in the posse that headed out for the X-Pand-D will have the duty of cutting off all retreat to the west and the south. It will also be the duty of those of you leading each posse to make sure each member of the posse knows what he has to do."

We went outside and begin to spread the word of the meeting. Since we had the posse already standing by, it didn't take long to have a sufficient crowd. Sheriff Russell, his deputies, and I stood on the steps and I addressed the crowd. The only information I gave them was that we had located the herd and that our posse would be leaving first thing in the morning to go and recover it. I suggested that everyone in the posse should have a good night's rest, because there might be a long hard day of fighting tomorrow.

We had six well-armed men hidden in the loft of Arnold's livery stable. Six more were in the mercantile, and another six were spending the night in the court room at City Hall. The last six, including both Rod and I, were hidden in the bank. Each of these groups spent the night in the location where they were expected to be the next day. We didn't want to take a chance on the word getting to any of the rustlers. I had noticed two men whom I had never seen before in the crowd that I was addressing when I laid out our plans for the next today.

The town came to life early the next morning, with Green's Café doing a bustling business. Saddled horses were being led from the livery stable and tied to hitch rails along the street. After a few minutes two groups of men began to assemble. One was in front of the livery stable, the other in front of the jail. Sheriff Todd Russell was leading the group that was assembling in front of the jail. The one in front of the livery stable was being led by Tex Lonigan, Sheriff Russell's chief deputy.

Tex led his group of men out of town at a trot, moving down the trail toward the X-Pan-D. A minute later, Sheriff Russell's group trotted out of town north to the outskirts, and turned east down the Wandering River. Both groups looked alert and ready for business.

The town suddenly seemed nearly deserted. Most of the able-bodied men in the town had become members of the posse. Two old men were down at the mercantile loading several spools of barbed wire into a wagon. Up the street at Greens Café, Harlan was washing the windows while Ellie was sweeping off the sidewalk.

The sound of Arnold's hammer, hitting the anvil, made a little double bounce after each blow that echoed down the street. It was a warm day for winter, and especially welcome after the snowstorm they had had the previous week. An old hound dog found a place in the rising sun's rays in a dusty patch of ground in front of the sidewalk. He lazily turned around twice, before lying down and stretching his legs out, enjoying the meager warmth.

A cavalcade of hard-bitten men rode into town from the north end of the street. They trotted their horses slowly down the street. Two men pulled out of the group and tied their horses in front of the gunsmith's shop, which was located in the building just north of the bank and on the same side of the street. Two more of the men rode on past the bank, and pulled up at the barbershop and tied their horses. The barbershop was in the building just south of the bank. The other six continued straight down the street. When they came to Donahue's saloon, they stopped and talked for a moment, looking at the empty hitching rail. As though they had made up their mind about something, they slowly rode back and tied their horses in front of the bank, dismounted and walked inside.

A teller was placing bills into his register. Rodney's office door was open. One of the men, who appeared to be the leader, walked halfway to the door of Rodney's office and said, "I wonder if you'd mind stepping out here for a moment. I have a question I'd like to ask you.

Rodney stood up and walked around his desk and came to the door and leaned against the right doorjamb.

"How can I be of service?" He smiled at the man and said, "I don't believe I've seen you men before. If you're looking for a place to settle, I don't believe you can find a better place than Vacaville."

"Well now," the man replied. "That makes me wish I were able to settle here." Two or three of the men behind him chuckled. "The truth of the matter is, we came in here to make a withdrawal."

"I don't understand what you mean," said Rodney. "I'm sure I'd remember you if you had an account here."

"I certainly understand why you don't remember us," the man said, grinning. "It's not our accounts we want to make the withdrawal from. We want the money in everyone else's account, including all of the money in your safe. This is what you might call a bank robbery."

"Mercy! Surely you jest." He took a step outside his office door, and said to the men, "Now I want every one of you to look me right straight in the eye. I want to make sure that you fellows are joking. It's nearly sure that a fine looking group of men like you aren't actually planning on robbing my bank."

The leader laughed again and said, "I'm sorry Mr. President, but that's exactly what we're going to do."

Rodney took another step to the left, placing the men's backs more nearly square with the teller's cages. "I'm so sorry to hear that, fellows. It seems to me you picked a mighty risky vocation. Are you sure you don't want to change your mind?"

"Look, Mister Bank President! You have to admit that I'm trying to be very pleasant. However, I have no more time for this little ceremony. Get on over and open the vault. We've all had our little laugh for the day. Open that vault or it will not be a laughing matter anymore! Understand? He patted his holstered gun.

"Oh, I don't think it's a laughing matter. That is the reason I would advise you to look at the teller's counter. I would certainly advise you to leave your guns holstered, so you can have a chance to laugh again, although it may be a long time before that happens."

The six men turned and saw four double barreled shot guns looking at them over the counter. Before they had time to digest that, I stepped out of the area where the vault was located and showed them my shotgun, and Rodney reached down inside his door and picked up his shotgun.

"You had better get those hands high and straight. Those of you who have your gun in your hand had better drop it, now! If any of you so much as sneeze, I'm afraid that it will get all of you killed. You, Funny Boy! Unbuckle that belt and let your gun drop! Now, kick it over against the counter. Now you," I said to the next man, you do the same!" Each time a man dropped his gun and kicked it over to the counter, I waved him back a step.

Rod had come around the counter and was standing, holding his shotgun pointed into the middle of the group.

"Rod, put these cuffs on all of them and cuff them all to each other, back to back.

"Hey, Joker! There is one way to keep those four men outside from being killed. We've got six men across the street in the livery, six more at the mercantile, and another six are in the city hall. What's more, the two groups that you saw ride out to recover the herd have come back and are positioned all around and through the town. The only way out for your outside men is either in a coffin or if you call them in here and let us disarm them. You will be doing them a big favor."

I handed my shotgun and pistol to Rodney and went over to the men. I turned them around so that the joker could look out the door. Pulling the door open, I pulled the group over close enough that the funny fella could lean out and see his outside cohorts.

"Men," he said. "I have some bad news. The two groups of men that we saw ride out are back in town, with men hiding in all of the buildings, the alleys and roofs. In addition there are six men with shotguns aimed at you from the stable, the mercantile and the courthouse. We have been disarmed and are all handcuffed together, back to back, by six men with double barreled shotguns."

"You are all good men, and I hate to see you die. Come in and be disarmed, or in one minute you will all be dead."

The men were facing toward the bank door. Two men with shotguns stepped out from the corner of the gun-shop. Two more stepped out from in back of the barbershop, flanking the other two. They signaled across the street and men began to converge on the four men.

"Fellows," one of the men called out to his companions, "I think we drew a mighty poor hand. I'm for chucking our weapons and living. If you feel differently, I'll go ahead and die with you. If you agree with me that we have no choice if we want to live, I'll be the first to drop my pistol."

There was no answer for a minute. Then some young man who couldn't have been more than twenty years old said, "My wife is carrying a baby. I don't have the right to leave it without a father." He threw his .44 into the dusty street.

Three others followed in one long thud, and the four men walked out into the street in front of the bank.

"Rod, help me cuff them. Don't give any of them a chance to grab a weapon." A moment later they were all inside the jail. That was far more men than had ever been inside the new jail at one time.

When the men were searched and locked up, I asked them, "Have you men had your breakfasts?"

"No, we were told that everyone would be gone and we could just leisurely ride in, rob everyone, and ride back out and eat later." It was the young fellow whose wife was going to have a baby.

"Mike, would you send over to the cafe and tell them to send over ten breakfasts?"

"Men, I want to know where you were going to deliver the money. We are going to make a clean sweep and get everyone, including the ringleader."

The man whom I had called the joker, answered. "I'm the ringleader."

"Look Fella, I already know who the ringleader is. What I want to know is where you were going to meet him and give him the money?"

"We were going to escape with the money and divide it up and go to Mexico," the joker replied. "There is no other ringleader."

"I want you guys to listen to me. I don't know if you are aware of everything that he has done. He hired two men to kill Rodney. Rodney is his own cousin, and he had no compunctions about killing him. He thought he had succeeded. That is why he was so surprised when he got caught and arrested. Rodney nearly died. We told everyone that he had died. We had a fake funeral to convince everyone that he was dead. We knew Richard was trying to steal Rodney's inheritance.

"For Rodney to have an inheritance, they had to kill his father, Sir Edward Hampton. They sent a man to London to arrange his death. We forecast what he was up to and staged Sir Hampton's death in a ship wreck, so we had him to refute the false testimony that your ringleader, Richard Hampton, gave.

"Do you think for one minute that he will protect you? He would have killed you when you delivered the money to him. You can all collectively get together and decide to tell me. You have not killed anyone. You didn't threaten to kill the people in the bank. You are only wanted for attempted bank robbery, although we know that one or all of you had orders to kill Rodney and Earlene.

"You can make it a lot easier on yourselves if you tell me what I want to know. Otherwise, I will take you one at a time and talk to you. One of you will tell me, and none of the others will know who, until he either gets off or gets a light sentence for turning territory's witness.

"If I don't find out in the next fifteen or twenty minutes, you won't have this chance, because, as I said, we know the people involved. We just don't know where they are.

"They will know something is up if you don't show up in the next little while and they will be gone. Then the last chance you have for helping yourselves in court, by your cooperation will be gone. You know that if he will treat his own kinfolk in such a manner, if I were to turn you loose, it would be signing your death warrant. I'm leaving you to talk it over between yourselves. I'll be back in ten minutes. It will be too late if you don't tell me as soon as I get back. I won't even consider putting in a good word for any of you then, except the one who tells me in secret."

"Mike," I said, "Rod and I are going to grab a cup of coffee. You'd better stay here and keep the door latched. Someone may try to kill them before they can tell anything. We'll see you in a few minutes."

Rod and I walked down to Green's Cafe. We walked in and were greeted by Ellie and Harlan. We asked for a quick cup of coffee and a couple of donuts each, eating them without talking. We knew that each minute made the chance of catching Richard Hampton before he disappeared beyond our reach was decreasing. Ten minutes later we returned to the jail and rapped for Mike to let us in.

"Okay," I said. "Do you as a group have anything to say? If you do, you'd better say it quickly. I'm going to take each one of you out and talk to you separately. No one will know if it was the first or the last of you who spilled the beans. I'll throw in another little warning. I am not going to let Richard get away. There is an easy way for you to tell me and there is a hard way. If I have to get the information the hard way, I'll do the same deal as I offered you now, to the extent that if I have to beat the information out of you, I'll beat each of you the same, no matter if the first person has told me. You have ten seconds to tell me. Eleven seconds and it will be too late. Well?"

"The Joker said, "I don't believe in taking a beating if it's not going to change anything. We were supposed to take the money to Richard at Post. They never go to any saloon but the Cowboy's Lament. If you hurry, maybe you can catch the son of a bitch. You'd better watch out for Amos. He is faster than a rattle snake and a whole lot colder blooded. If he baits you into drawing against him, you are signing your own death warrant."

"Okay, fellas. I understand why you didn't want to talk. I'll see what I can do to keep your actions from ruining your entire life. You'd better hope we get there in time, though."

We walked outside and saw the sheriff approaching. "Hey, Todd! Rod and I are headed for Post. We'll try to be back by tomorrow night. We have to leave Deputy Thomas with you to tell you what we had in mind for the main gang of rustlers. If you wait until morning to go after them, maybe Rod and I can meet you near the mouth of the arroyo. We'd better hit the trail."

"Good bye and good luck. Watch out for whatever Richard has planned for you. He's gonna have a plan B for everything." The sheriff was plainly concerned.

"We'll watch our step. Don't let that bunch ambush you. That Richard should have been a general." I nudged my horse into motion. Rod fell in alongside of me.

When we were nearing the north town limits, I said to Rod, "You know, as carefully as Richard arranges his little expeditions, I think we ought to prepare for this one. It would be just like him to have a trap set for us at the Old Buffalo Crossing. There is a way up over the Rimrock in the back of the EEZ. Let's use it and circle around and come into Post from the north east. This might give us just the element of surprise we need."

We each still had our shotguns stuck down into the boots we had on the left side of our saddles. We were carrying them loaded with double-ought buckshot.

"I didn't know there was a way up any closer than the Old Buffalo Crossing. That is a handy thing to know. That is going to take us a couple of extra hours to get to Post, though."

"Yeah, but it may save us a life-time getting back," I replied.

"I'd say that is a good investment, wouldn't you?" Rod laughed softly.

"Rod, I know that I am taking a hell of an advantage of you by having you side me into Post. They may have half a regiment of outlaws with them."

"Listen Easy. With there being just the two of us, I think it is no time for me to stop and spank you for even mentioning such a thing. Just the fact that you said it is enough to make me happy that I'm with you. I'd like to mention one thing; with the numbers nearly certainly skewed in their favor, I think we should have a tendency to shoot first and listen to their crap later. If they even look like they are moving to box us in, I say we should kill a half dozen of them before they know we are going to draw."

I laughed. "Your mind is running in the same channel as mine. When somebody like that makes war on me, I think that is all the warning he needs. I don't remember signing a truce with them. I sure as hell don't intend getting killed and leaving my pretty young widow for some slick son of a bitch to court. A rabid skunk will appear merciful compared to how I'll be."

"Then let's make an agreement. If the chips are down, each of us will be prepared for the other to do something. We won't have time to signal one another. Agreed?"

"You can believe it! We won't let them crowd us to where they know we have to do something. We'll just start it and finish it as soon as we have looked around to see where everyone is."

We alternated trotting and loping our horses until we had circled around and were approaching Post from the northeast. We rode down a backstreet until we were behind the Cowboy's Lament.

Rod said, "Let me check the back door and see if I can get in." He took his shotgun and walked to the back door. The knob turned when he twisted.

"I'll take both horses and tie them in front. They'll be easier to keep our eye on them there. I don't want to run back here and find the horses gone," I said. "As soon as I get them tied, I'm going to go straight inside and let my eyes get used to the dark before I start anything. That'll give you plenty of time to get set. I'll see you inside." I started Calliope around the building and tied him to the hitch rack. Pulling the shotgun from the boot, I walked inside and stepped to the left to accustom my eyes to the dim light."

I was holding the shotgun across my chest. I glanced quickly around the room, then again, more slowly. My entrance had not gone unnoticed. There was not a sound in the room. Richard and some fella dressed somewhat as a dandy were setting at a table with two other men.

I had let the barrel of the shotgun drop until it was directly on the group setting around the table.

"Well fancy that," I said, looking at Richard. "I thought you were in the territorial prison. Was your smell so bad they kicked you out?

Richard must have had steel nerves, because he never changed expression. "While I was waiting for my sentence to be appealed, it was either my sweet smell or the sweet smell of money that enticed some men to come and rescue me. Let's just say that maybe it was the sweet smell of the money that will make me half as rich as the King of England. The sweetest smell of all will be from knowing that it is from the money provided by the cattle that you and the others in the Bend of the Rimrock have been so kind as to have given me."

"I see that you haven't received the news yet. All of your bets were called and raised. When the hands were shown, all of your men were in jail, the cattle are on their way back to the ranches they came from, and you are on your way back to territorial prison."

"That is sure big talk from someone who won't live out the next fifteen minutes." Richard looked at the men at the table. "Do any of you see anything to give Seeker such an air of insufferable confidence? I personally don't." He looked back up from his friends at the table, and turned his malevolent gaze to me. "Just what make you feel so cocky?" he asked.

"Well, since you want me to get specific, I might mention that if and when I drop the hammers on this shotgun, the four of you at that table will be hamburger meat."

"If you live to pull the trigger," Richard said. "You see, I have a man behind you that has a cocked gun nearly against your head."

"Richard, it is a fact that the shotgun will turn you to hamburger meat. However, if you get blasted from the side also, you will change from hamburger meat to mince-meat. Also, your man who may or may not be aiming a gun at my head will be pretty reluctant to pull the trigger, for I have a man with a double barreled shotgun aimed right at his gut. It might interest you to know that I have pulled both triggers on this shotgun and only my thumb holding the hammers is keeping you from the devil's alternative to the pearly gates."

That's a nice ploy, Seeker. It won't work on me. You are a country hick. You have never studied tactics. Tell me, how do you want to die; from a quick gunshot or a slower death from a knife? You see, I know better than to have all of my forces concentrated in one place. If you will look to your left a little, you will see the face of my body guard. His job is to see that I don't get molested, and he is very good at his job." His mouth widened in a big grin.

I grinned back at him in a friendly manner. "Excuse me if I don't look, but if you will look at him, you will see that your gunfighter is right in the line of fire from my man's double barreled twelve gauge. I think that one barrel will be enough to stop your gunfighter. The other barrel will sweep your remains from the wall where they have been splattered, right on out the door for the dogs to eat."

Richard shook his head and began laughing. "You just don't know..."
I was still grinning when I let my thumb slip off both hammers. Pieces of blood and guts, but no glory flew right against the wall where I had

predicted they would go.

The first roar of Rod's shotgun flew by me and hit the man behind me a split second after my own shotgun discharged. My .44 had swung toward the gunfighter, but there was no reason to shoot. What had been a gunfighter a moment earlier was now more fit for a mince-meat pie for a cannibal than a body guard.

"Does anyone in here feel the desire to take up the fight where these guys left off? Those of you who went to the trial where he tried to steal the Rimrock Land and Cattle Company know that he is a killer and a sneak thief. What you don't know is that the Rimrock Land and Cattle Company bought the Vertical X's. If you ever want to get a dime from us, you had better make sure that you are in our good graces."

I looked over at Rod. "We have to meet some people, Rod. Are you ready to go? I know these folk are itching to clean up this mess."

Rod nodded to me and I walked to the door and looked out carefully before stepping outside. Rod backed out behind me, the black snout of the shotgun peering hungrily back into the room, looking for the faintest sign of a threat.

Rod looked back into the bar room. "Hey, you! Come here!"

"Mmme?" came a stammering voice.

"Yeah, you!" snapped Rod.

A man sidled through the door and said, "What do you want of me?"

"Where is the trail that the Vertical X's use to go back and forth to the headquarters?" Rod's voice didn't invite any friendly banter.

"You have to go back to the Old Buffalo Trail. When you get to the bottom, there is only one trail that heads off toward the west. It leads straight to the Vertical X's. You can't miss it. About seven miles out, the trail forks. The left hand fork was made when there were some small ranchers in the South Cedar Breaks. It hasn't been used since all of those ranchers moved to the north side of the Wandering River."

"I thought it was worth a shot to see if there was a horse trail to the bottom that we don't know about." Rod grinned at me. "You never can tell what you can find out some times, especially when you have just blown away half the people in a saloon."

"I reckon I've noticed that my own self." I grinned back. "Old Richard was a smart hombre, but his weakness was that he thought he was the only one who thought ahead."

Chapter Sixteen - Page 223
Ambushing the Bushwhackers

We had both figured there was only the one way, but sometimes a fellow can be fooled. When we got to the place where we had seen the two rustlers leave the trail along the East Fork to the arroyo near the mouth of the canyon that held the cattle, we turned off and angled toward it. It was the trail the South Cedar Breaks ranchers used to use. It looked well used for the last few days. There was still one chore to complete.

Upon reaching the mouth of the arroyo, it was obvious that our expedition hadn't arrived yet. After waiting for about fifteen minutes I said to Rod, "Rod, why don't you wait here to meet the posse as they come up the river. Ask them to wait here with you until I get back from a little scouting expedition. As you know, we've been expecting the outlaws to have a major portion of their men, perhaps all of them, hidden up this arroyo past the bend.

"I think there is a good chance that we will be correct. However, it would be rather stupid of us to follow our tentative plan, just on the strength of our projections. I noticed there is a grove of tall trees on the ridge beyond the arroyo. What I'm going to do is circle back the way we came in from until I'm far enough down the slope to be hidden from anyone who may be stationed in the bend of the ridge.

"What I'm hoping to do is to remain unseen while I get into the grove of trees. I wish to leave my horse tied back in the brush and advance through the grove of trees, until I am lined up with the arroyo, after it has made its bend. Then it is my hope that I can climb one of the trees high enough so that I can see down and into the arroyo, where we expect the outlaws to be hiding. If they are going to hide there, it is obvious that they would have to be there now, because our men should arrive at any time.

"If you will recall, I asked the sheriff to try to get a couple of bows and some arrows. I'm sure you also remember that I told him to get plenty of dynamite."

Rod interrupted me by beginning to laugh. "Say no more," he said. "I'm sure I have the picture now. However, I suggest that maybe I should work my way back down the stream and try to meet the posse a little further from the field of action. Do you go along with that?"

"I only have one thing against it. I would like to have you and your rifle in range, just in case I get spotted and need a little help trying to get away."

"Your point is well taken," Rod replied. "In fact, you see that big fork in the tree?" Rod jerked his thumb toward a huge pecan tree, and continued, "I think that would make a real good point of vantage for a sniper. I also think it would provide an easy way to also make a quick getaway if circumstances should warrant it."

I rode back downstream until I was far enough over the ridge to be out of sight of the arroyo. "I sure hope there's no lookout in one of those trees," I thought to myself. Then I shrugged my shoulders philosophically. A fella can get so hung up on all the ifs, ands, and buts, that his mind freezes, and he doesn't get anything done.

I bent over my horse's neck to leave as low of a silhouette as possible. Keeping back in the trees, I rode back up the slope until I could just barely see where the arroyo started. I threw my horse's reins across a bush, and worked my way further up the slope until I was lined up with the arroyo. I chose a pine tree that had enough brush around it to screen me from anyone who might be in the arroyo, as I climbed the tree.

I worked my way up the tree, keeping the trunk between me and the arroyo. When I was high enough to see over the other trees, I cautiously peered around the trunk, my movements slow, and deliberate. Between the beginning of the arroyo and the bend, beyond which the outlaws expected our posse to be deployed, was nothing but an empty arroyo. Using the utmost caution, I worked my way back down to my horse, mounted up and retraced the route I had followed when coming. The rustlers might be anywhere else except in the arroyo.

Just before emerging from the trees, I saw a large group of men approaching. I looked quickly around, trying to choose an escape route. It would not be easy to cross the East Fork at this point. I would have to ride to the southeast. That way I would be quartering away from the approaching group. In case we had guessed wrong, the ambushers might be hiding elsewhere. I prepared to burst from cover, when I thought I recognized one of the horses. I was pretty sure it was the sheriff's dun horse. A moment later, there was no doubt left in my mind. Holding my reins in both hands, raised high enough above my saddle horn so that the posse could see that I had no hostile intentions, I rode out of the brush and toward the posse.

Calliope had distinct enough markings that there was no mistaking who I was. The sheriff held up his hand in a gesture to stop the posse, continuing on up the slope until he arrived at me. I had stopped, waiting for him to approach. I wanted to give him my information in private.

"It seems like I find you wandering around in the strangest places! I've heard tell that they have some good beer in Post. I figured you would be taking advantage of that, along about now."

"I'll tell you one thing for sure, Todd. It's not from the lack of temptation. However, one of the damnations of my soul is my wanderlust. I just had to see what lurked on this side of the hill. It just so happens, I found some pretty green grass growing. The place where I told you the arroyo bends and that I thought might be a very good possibility for the outlaws to group and ambush us when we deployed along the edge of the canyon? Well that is not what I found. The outlaws must have somehow heard of what happened in Vacaville. It appears to me that they have abandoned the herd and headed for parts unknown.

"It is possible that someone has outrun us from Post and given them the news that Richard met an untimely death about an hour or two ago. In any event, I think we should scout out the area to be sure they are gone. We may leave our RL&CC herd here to winter. That will depend on the condition of the fences, etc. The canyon will be good shelter, and there is plenty of hay put up at the Vertical X's.

"We do need to start cutting out the small rancher's herds and get them moved back. We can send them out, one herd at a time, about fifteen minutes apart. It'll be an easy job, since they have the roads between all of the ranches. Half a dozen men can handle each herd." I waited to see what the sheriff thought of the news that Richard was dead and the outlaws were gone.

"Well, that is sort of anti-climactic. I can't say that I'm sorry we don't have to fight such an army of outlaws. I had better get the word out, because I imagine there will be a flock of robberies as they leave out of the Bend of the Rimrock country and find others places to work their mischief. I guess that all-in-all, we would have been better off to take them out of circulation in one big battle."

The sheriff started down the arroyo to spread the word among the other half of the posse.

Brad and Cynthia were riding toward the back of the &RR. She had always noticed how enthusiastic he was when speaking of his plans for his ranch. The two of them had been very close before they were marooned in what they referred to as, "Our Igloo." Now they had feelings that created nearly as much sadness as happiness. The sadness was caused by the fact that Sir Edward was planning on returning to England on Thursday of this week. Today was Tuesday.

Brad knew that her decision to stay in America didn't come easy, for he was very conscious of Sir Edward's business needs for her, and also his love for her, his only niece. She was saddened because of having to leave the interesting position she had, and because of her great affection for Sir Edward. She felt she owed her Uncle more than she could ever repay. Women holding down jobs that had so many responsibilities and carried so much authority were very rare. She had to admit to herself that she could never be totally happy if she were relegated to being a housewife and mother. Her cheeks colored as she thought of being a mother.

One thing was certain in her own mind; she would never consider having another man than Brad father a child with her. There was no duty that could ever make her leave Brad and go back to England. She just wished there was a way that she could have her cake and eat it too.

They came to the end of the valley, where it pinched into a canyon and then abruptly stopped at a sheer wall.

"Brad, have you ever been to Earlene's secret hideout, her refuge from the world?"

"No, Cynthia. I never knew it existed until it was necessary for her and Easy to use it to go to a spot on Easy's ranch, when we were so much under siege by Burley Dobbin's men. I was made aware of it then, but I have always respected Earlene's right to privacy."

"Earlene took me there a couple of days ago. She and I have grown very close. She wanted me to know about how she met up with Easy, and to certain parallels between them and you and me. I'd like for us to go there now."

"Alright, if you don't think we would be violating Earlene's right to have her own secret place."

"Actually, she told me that she would like for the two of us to visit it. She said that she found so much happiness there that she wanted us to go there too. She wants us to find that same happiness."

"Cynthia, there are only two things that stand between us and total happiness. I feel like a thief, taking you from Edward, knowing how he loves you. I know that you love me, as I love you, but I fear that you would find things dull here, after your position in an exciting place like London. I never want to clip your wings."

"I understand. However, a mountain woman is sort of out of place in London. She would feel stifled after living wild in an igloo, especially with such an accomplished map-maker."

-=-

"Easy, would you like to take a walk with me?"

"Sure, Edward." It was an unseasonably warm day for this early in the year. We walked outside and Sir Edward led the way back toward the front entrance to the &RR ranch.

"What are some of the plans you have for the immediate future for the RL&CC? I have heard you mention several different things, but I don't recall you putting them into a time related framework."

"I had planned on making each new venture sort of pay for itself as I initiated them. However, it we could come up with the cash and still maintain sufficient reserves, here are some of the things. We have a surplus of water from two sources. One of them is from the stream that heads in the &RR. The other is from the stream that heads on my ranch and that I turned through the land that we dedicated to the small ranches. Now that I have harnessed the additional water that was going back underground, I was thinking of perhaps taking the cattle land that lies on the north side of the Wandering River and is between the river and the Rimrock, and turning it into farm land. I thought that would open the door to putting in a big grain mill, either along the Wandering River or one of the two streams that are actually under the control of Brad and Earlene or me.

"I think that we might want to put in a packing house for beef, and depending on how well the irrigated land responds to corn or other grains, we might also add pork to the beef for the packing house. I have an idea for an ice house that I believe could give us capacity for a year around operation for delivering our dressed out beef and pork.

"This could open the way for a freight line, carrying meat to this section of the territory. There is also the possibility that we might obtain the land adjacent to the east side of the small ranches and think about using it for future development as either farms or ranches.

"We might even break the irrigated land into farms. I believe that the banking business might turn out to be the most stable part of our business. We could probably make more money if we farmed it ourselves, but it would bring a big labor factor into the equation that could give us more problems than the additional profit we would make. We might have a wool buying operation, for if our sheep pan out, others who have marginal land will want to follow our example.

"We are near some mineral deposits, such as iron and copper that could make it worthwhile to start a foundry. I believe that by picking our projects carefully, we could do like we did with the small ranchers, and make it so that each thing we started could both feed upon the others, and allow the others to feed upon them.

"What is your objective in asking the question, Edward?"

"Easy, I think that if we could build an organization that needed the benefit of a great amount of additional experience, intelligence and dedication, we might be able to kill two birds with one stone. The one bird could be someone to help such a plan as you mention to succeed. The other is to give Cynthia a position that would remove some of her feelings that she is betraying me by staying here with Brad.

"It is easy for me to see that Brad has those same feelings about asking Cynthia to stay here with him. I also know that he is afraid that Cynthia would regret leaving her exciting job in London. I would like to see her have a job that is equally exciting for her, right here in the Bend of the Rimrock. If we were to carry through on your plans, you would need another key person to help.

"All told, there isn't a more capable executive than Cynthia. She is the kind of person that one can build a business around, not have a business and fit her into it. In other words, I would hope to see us start out on your plans with a deliberate haste, and we will do what we have to for financing. I think that she could be instrumental in getting a railroad in here. I could work behind the scenes to that same effect."

"Edward, are you giving me the green light to place our plans into operation? If you are, I think I will call a meeting of all of us and tell of my recommendations for expansion. At that time, I will ask Cynthia if she would accept a key position in achieving our goals. I will not tell her that she will be to me here, what she has been to you there in

London, but allow that fact to just happen as our expansion got under way."

"Okay, Easy. Consider that you have my vote to follow through. Of course, that is subject to your being able to convince the majority of the other owners."

-=-

I passed the word to the rest of the owners that we were having a meeting the next day in the conference room of the Bank. At the meeting, I outlined my plans, stressing that many things were not yet solidified. I also emphasized that although I wanted to start at once, that we would proceed with caution, and would have a plan drawn up to outline our goals and track our progress. I put it to a vote and it carried unanimously.

I then said that I had another order of business. "I want to offer Cynthia an executive position here in the Bend of the Rimrock," I began. I want her to be in charge of our expansion plans, and to be the chief liaison with the London office. This, of course, will depend upon two things. The first is that you approve of me hiring her in the stated capacity. The second is, of course, if she will accept the job.

"First off, Cynthia, I want you to go into Earlene's office and wait until your hiring is discussed. I hope that you will be considering whether or not to accept the offer."

Cynthia left the room. Earlene said, "I vote yes, without discussion."

Brad said, "Out of my respect for the rest of you, I want to abstain from voting. I don't want to be placed in the position of voting for her, when I want her to work with us for reasons that would be completely and utterly selfish, even if she were not so highly qualified. Hell, I am doing what I said that I wouldn't do. Pass the vote on around the table."

Rodney voted yes. Sir Edward voted yes. Earlene went to tell Cynthia to come back into the conference room.

"Cynthia, you are okayed by the board. Will you accept a job with us?" Somehow, I had a fear that she might not.

"Oh yes, I will happily accept your generous offer. Now Brad and I have something else to say. We are being married tomorrow, before Uncle Edward leaves. I couldn't bear it if he weren't here to give me to Brad."

-=-

The wedding was held at the &RR. Because Edward was leaving for

England that afternoon, Brad and Cynthia requested that only our closest friends attend.

I was best man for Brad and Earlene was bride's maid for Cynthia. When the wedding was over, I offered a toast to the bride and groom.

"I have heard it said in the past that *You Can't Win Them All*. This event shows that old saying to be untrue. There is no one better suited for Brad than Cynthia. There is no man more suited to Cynthia than Brad. There is no better addition to the RL&CC than Cynthia. There is no better group of people than this group of people who are fortunate enough to have one another here in America, and to have Sir Edward for our everlasting friend in London.

"The group of friends who came to see this wedding is as close to us as blood kin. I raise this glass to the everlasting love of this couple. Here is to Brad and Cynthia! May they love forever!"

Everyone joined in the toast and started giving their well wishes to the bride and groom.

"One minute, everyone. I want your attention! Let's all now make a toast to our friend and companion from England. Here is to Sir Edward Hampton. I don't mean to take attention from the bride and groom, but to say farewell to Sir Edward, who is leaving here to catch his stage!"

Every one drank the toast, and Sir Edward was carried in to catch the stage. His son, Rodney Hampton rode beside him, and Arnold Smith drove the wagon. The entire Sheriff's Department of Vacaville escorted them out of sight.

Brad and Cynthia ate their wedding meal with Earlene and me. Then they rode off for the Oasis where Earlene and I had spent our honeymoon.

A soft breeze heralded the approach of spring to the Bend of the Rimrock and Seeker's Valley.